Pat Chapman's

# TASTE
# OF
# THE RAJ

# Pat Chapman's
# TASTE
# OF
# THE RAJ

Hodder & Stoughton

10 9 8 7 6 5 4 3 2 1

First published in Great Britain by Hodder and Stoughton. A division of Hodder Headline PLC

A CIP catalogue record for this book is available from the British Library

ISBN 0 340 68035 0

Typeset by Hewer Text Composition Services, Edinburgh
Printed and bound in Great Britain by
Clays Ltd, St Ives plc, Bungay, Suffolk

Hodder and Stoughton
A Division of Hodder Headline PLC
338 Euston Road
London
NW1 3BH

# ACKNOWLEDGEMENTS

RESEARCHING THIS book necessitated taking a journey to Lucknow, Calcutta, Agra and elsewhere in India to verify facts and to review the few fragments of the Raj which remain.

I am immensely grateful to Satya Rao, European Regional Director of Air India, for his assistance in making Dominique's and my flights to and from India so comfortable.

I would also like to thank Ajit Kerkar, Chairman and Chief Executive, and Lenny Menezes, International President, of the Taj Group of Hotels for their courtesy and generosity, also our Indian travel agents, IndTravels, and one guide in particular, Dinesh Kapoor, whose skills speeded us to our various ports of call.

Thanks also to Tessa Forbes, British Film Institute Library Information department, for verifying facts on page 88, to Eileen Davis for the loan of period and Victorian props for photographs, and to Major Rising, Secretary of the Royal Yacht Squadron Cowes, for the loan of their burgee.

Photography by Colin Poole.

Photographs styled and food prepared by Dominique and Pat Chapman.

# CONTENTS

# DEDICATION

This book is dedicated
especially to my mother,
Lena Gertrude,
and to my
uncles and aunts,
Bill, Alice, Jim, Frank, Alec, Edwin, Edith and Arthur,
grandparents,
Alexina Hope and William Henry Hawley,
great grandparents,
Alice Henrietta and Alexander Lemmon,
and their parents,
Sarah and Abraham Beatson and Caroline and John Lemmon,
indeed to all my ancestors,
the Lawrences, Wheatleys, Petries, Highberts,
and those whose names I do not know
who served
in the India of the Raj
and without whom
I would not
have been able
to write this book.
I hope they like it.

# FOREWORD

*TASTE OF THE RAJ* is a cookbook first and foremost. As its title suggests, it brings you spicy recipes from an age long gone. And they are remarkable recipes, as good now as they were then, as I hope you will discover.

But the history of the Raj is equally remarkable and absolutely absorbing, and since there would have been no Raj if it were not for spices, it is completely relevant in a book about spicy food to tell how the phenomenon of the British in India came about.

Even before the Raj was born, my ancestors had made the perilous journey from England to India, hoping to make their fortunes in a new land of opportunity. Their story, of violent ups and downs, is as extraordinary as that of the Raj itself, for it was no easy ride.

In living memory, my mother, uncles and aunts spent a fairytale childhood in India. As kids, they had a wonderful life, blissfully unaware of the politics of empire, and the spine-chilling class system and snobbery which surrounded them. When my grandfather retired to England his brood were still very young. Their anecdotes and memories of India are unsullied by the cynicism of adulthood. The things which happened to them could have happened, and doubtless did, to any Raj family. Much of it was funny.

I was not born in India, so this is not my story, but as a young child the telling and retelling of these memories and anecdotes were my bedtime treats, which held me as enthralled as nursery rhymes. I never tired of them. I am duty bound to share some of them with you.

And if the story which I tell seems larger than life, it is because living in that extraordinary country, India, and living under that extraordinary rule, *was* larger than life. I have no need to embroider it. There has been nothing like it before or since.

That was the Raj.

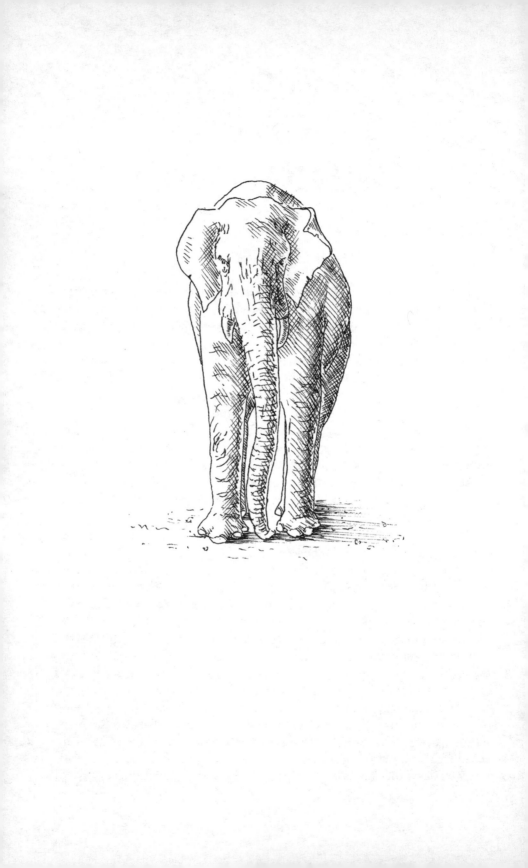

# PROLOGUE

I have been fortunate enough to visit India many times in recent years, yet in over twenty visits, I had never consciously sought out the remnants of the Raj, nor the traces of my ancestors. As I mention elsewhere, unlike them I was not born there. I was born in wartime London. My earliest memories are of the 'blitzkrieg', overhead aerial dog-fights, doodlebugs and choking London smogs. It was as far removed from the trappings of the Raj as could be envisaged. The India I visit so regularly now, is the contemporary India, not one of Empire and history. It had simply not occurred to me to look for something which had ceased to exist so long ago.

Could there be anything left to find? And where to look?

Dominique and I decided to visit three cities, each of great significance to my family, as we shall see. Lucknow, because, my great-grandmother was orphaned there during the 1857 mutiny. Calcutta, because it was where my grandmother's cookbook, the *Indian Cookery Book*, which contributes so much to this book, was published at the turn of the century. And Agra, because my great-grandparents bought a bungalow there in 1903.

One of Lucknow's most evocative sights is the ruins of the 'residency', a complex of buildings set in acres of landscaped parkland, where the British lived in the first part of the 19th century. It was where a significant incident of the 1857 mutiny took place. The British residents became holed up within the residency, whilst thousands of insurgent Indians attempted to destroy the site with cannon. They did not succeed, but my three-year-old great-grandmother, Alice Beatson, whose story appears on page 18, was one of the few survivors. The residency was abandoned in ruins, and it remains today exactly as it was in 1857, left as a memorial to the event. The silence in the traffic-free gardens is broken only by the screeches of parakeets. Its beautiful red brick buildings stand broken, gaping from their wounds, unrepaired and eerie, yet elegant and evocative. Surrounding them in slightly unkempt gardens are the graves of hundreds of those killed. I did not attempt to locate those of Alice's family. It was enough to know they were there somewhere. I had told our guide, Naved Zia, whose family had lived in Lucknow for 250 years, that Alice's mother's maiden name was Lawrence, and that it was also my middle name. Inside the rather faded museum was a picture of the 1857 Chief Commissioner, Sir Henry Lawrence, with whom, I explained, our family has not traced a relationship. This was unnecessary for our guide, who, pointing at the painting exclaimed: '*You have the nose!*'

Despite its reputation, Calcutta is always worth a visit. We did so in the company of Santi Bhattacharya, a philosopher and former school teacher, turned tour guide. His family had lived in the same house for generations, he told us. And they lamented the passing of the British. Sipping beverages in the celebrated Indian Coffee House, on College Road, Santi told us why. '*They united India with one language, and one law and they brought the nation freedom. India may now be free but without them she lacks organisation.*' It's a view I've heard many times from educated Indians. Of course, neither they nor the British have any real desire to return to those old days of ruled and ruler. It is nothing more than a romanticised 'grass-is-greener' notion. Santi had numerous other views. He resented the communist local government, whom he described as corrupt. He praised one British inheritance, Calcutta University, though he pointed out that it is locally known as '*the University of Unemployment, since it creates 450,000 jobless graduates per annum*'. He cursed the fact that another British inheritance, Calcutta's tram system, was falling apart through lack of maintenance. '*It's a Streetcar named Disaster,*' he quipped.

He ruefully told of today's tourists, including one recent couple whose request stunned him: '*Show us Calcutta without leaving the hotel,*' or another couple who upon specifically asking him to show them around the wards of Mother Teresa's hospital, then threatened to sue him, when they discovered the wards contained patients with highly contagious tuberculosis! His anxiety that we may behave likewise turned to relief, when he discovered that my main mission was to visit some of Calcutta's 600 bookshops. I knew that the publisher of my grandmother's cookbook, Thacker and Spink, had ceased trading when the British left India. Santi's eyes lit up. '*I collect their books,*' he said. I explained about the *Indian Cookery Book*. And I quoted some of its more amusing passages, such as the '*knight of the broom'* (see page 32). I described its size and appearance. '*I am sure I too have this book,*' said Santi. '*I bought it for four rupees* [about eight pence] *years ago, but I have never read it through. You must come to my home so that I can check it.*' We did so, and it was indeed the very same book. I was deeply touched at the privilege of being invited to his home, and at the coincidence. I showed Santi the passages that I had quoted earlier. He was flabbergasted that an English tourist would know such a book so intimately, and he promised to read it through from cover to cover.

By the time we reached Agra, the monsoon had ended, though it was still very hot. My mission was to locate my old family bungalow. To help me I had an old photo taken circa 1918, the description given so precisely by my mother (see page 63) and its address, 166 Metcalf Road. I soon found that the street name had changed to something more Indian years ago, but as luck would have it our taxi driver not only lived on that road, he thought he knew the bungalow's location and its present owner very well indeed. Somewhat sceptically we set out to locate them both. Within minutes, I was eating humble pie. It was indeed the right bungalow, though now only its pitched high roof was identifiable. The remainder of the building had been converted into a series of very ugly shop fronts, or handicrafts emporia.

We took some pictures, and were about to depart, when our driver said '*please come*'. He led us behind the bungalow, where a portly cheery middle-aged man was squatting on the lawn with his wife and daughters, who being strict Moslems, fled at the sight of a strange male. Our host turned out to be one Zaki Ahmed, and when I explained that I was trying to confirm that this had indeed been our family home, he burst into animated glee, saying, '*You, sir, must be William Martin.*' Confused, I assured him I knew no one of that name. '*So it must be Alici Lemmoni then.*' he said, without pause. I was stunned. I had not mentioned my great-grandmother's married name. Zaki laughed when he saw my expression. With a clap of his hands, a servant appeared bearing iced drinks. A few words were exchanged, and in a trice the servant reappeared this time carrying a large file of papers. '*This is my hobby,*' said Zaki, opening the file. There before us was the entire history of no.166. There were the deeds and numerous other papers, written in Urdu. But there were other documents in English. The earliest of which says of '*166 in the Cantonment Road: The said estate is bounded in the north by a ravens; on the south by an empty compound and an adjoining property, no. 164, owned by Heera Lal, banker; on the east by a ravine; and on the west by Metcalf road.*' Another document tells us that the area of the property consisted of '*3 vegas, 17 biswas and 10 bisras*', which translated to 10,000 square yards.

It was built for one William Martin, former bailiff of Lahore, in 1893 at a cost of 1,635 rupees. On his death that same year, it was sold to a Babu Mooradi Lal, who himself sold it to my great-grandparents in 1903 for 3,750 rupees. Alice Lemmon died in 1924, and the property was sold for 12,000 rupees to Zaki Ahmed's grandfather.

'*You are the first owner . . . I am the second.*' His brotherly, though inaccurate pronouncement stayed with me as we drove back to our hotel. I was also struck by the quite enormous inflation of the times. 12,000 rupees was close to £1,000, an enormous sum of money for those days. I tried to establish what no.166 would be worth today, and was told 5 crore (50 million rupees), which is around £1million. Without in any way wishing to dispossess Zaki, I could not help wishing I was still the number one owner.

Before we left India, I had some further research to do. I wanted to find out two things: what had happened to that enormous working body of people, the Indian servant, since the departure of the Raj, also what had happened to Anglo-Indian food in the fifty intervening years. I presumed, correctly as it turned out, that the servant was alive and thriving in modern day India. They are all still there, the cooks and the butlers, the waiters and the bearers, the gardeners and the *ayahs* and all the rest. And they don't just work for upper-class and wealthy Indians. Just about every Indian, whatever his or her status, employs servants. Even servants have servants. As ever, of course, the richer the employer, the more servants. Their roles have hardly changed, if at all, since the days of the Raj, and we'll meet them all in this book. An Indian friend of ours told me that the British generally treated their servants well, whereas, '*We Indians treat them like dogs. It's really terrible,*' he went on, '*particularly since it was the British who taught the Indians to respect life.*'

One role which now commands good money, though little respect, is that of the *methar*, the cleaner, still regarded as untouchable in caste. It is this person who cleans the household toilets. And because it is an 'untouchable' job which no Indians will do themselves, modern day *methars* do the job on their terms. They freelance with up to 60 clients on their list, to each of whom they devote a few minutes a day at a rate of 100 rupees (two pounds) a month each. Their gross pay equals that of most managers or teachers, and often exceeds that of their clients. It's a far cry from the old days when, as I explain on page 155, the *methars* would work for scraps of food from their master's table.

As for Anglo-Indian food, my presumption that it had all but died out could not be more wrong. I had met examples of it in Kashmir . . .

delicious clove-studded apple pies and creamy custard and spicy stews still haunt the houseboats, but I thought that was it. Not so . . . I found to my amazement that I was wrong. The whole repertoire of Anglo-Indian food is faithfully served to this day in, amongst other places, the officers' messes of the Indian military, at public schools and convents, and in many an upper-class Indian home. My good friend Karan Bilimoria, son of a recently retired Indian army general, and educated not so long ago in the Indian public school system, confirms this to be the case. '*Much as I loved the endless succession of cutless and rummled egg, and roast meat and boiled carrots, I used to yearn for real Indian food when I was a boy.*'

Our trip to India had yielded a great deal of fascinating material for this book. I wished I could have visited some of the other places where my family had been posted. But there wasn't enough time. The Raj may have ended fifty years ago, but its memory is still very much alive in India. But my greatest surprise was the discovery that the taste of the Raj still exists, preserved in certain circles as if in a time warp. That alone made our trip worthwhile.

# INTRODUCTION

## THE RAJ

I<small>T IS A CENTURY</small> and more since my grandparents were born, and decades since they died. It was to be their lot to live and work in India at the height of the British Raj. They lived during the reigns of six monarchs and saw the total demise of the Empire they so diligently strived to serve. For they were not to know that within their lifetime the Raj would become no more than a memory. This book tells their story. It also paints a picture of life in the old Indian Empire which would be familiar to all who served there.

My great grandmother was born in 1854 in Lucknow, India, into a wealthy and privileged family. Her grandfather was chief constable, a position of some importance. Her mother had married an officer in the Indian Civil Service. With these credentials my family looked destined to live a life of luxury for as far as one could envisage. But it was not to be. Within three years the unthinkable happened and disaster struck. India mutinied. With the exception of my great grandmother, my family was wiped out. She was lucky to survive. The very existence of the British in India was threatened. Yet greater things were still to come. Out of the ashes came the Raj, part of the largest empire the world has seen. But Lucknow signalled the beginning of the end of empire. Within nine decades the British left India for good. To find out how this remarkable rise and equally rapid decline took place, we need to look back in time.

### ROMANS AND NORMANS

It all had to do with spices. Everything did a long time ago, and to understand the whys and wherefores of the British Raj we need to join the story at the dawn of recorded British history. Spices were an everyday commodity for the Romans. They exchanged their gold for spices, their trading links extending to the Middle East and beyond. It is certain that after their withdrawal from Britain, we no longer enjoyed such commodities, but during our Dark Ages Europe continued to use them. Venice and Genoa built up their empires and wealth by specialising in maritime trade connecting all the ports of the Mediterranean.

Britain's Dark Ages came to an end with the Norman conquest. And with the French came a range of culinary spices which had not been seen for six centuries. But spices were not for the masses; they were very expensive luxuries only afforded by aristocrats. Such delights as cloves, cardamoms, nutmeg, cinnamon, ginger, garlic, turmeric and pepper were used in court cooking. Spices were so valuable in those days that they could be used in lieu of money. Pepper, for example, became a trading commodity in its own right. A pound (450g) of pepper in twelfth-century London would buy you several sheep, and it was used to pay taxes and debts. Today the term 'peppercorn rent' means a minimal sum of money. Then it meant rent at the market price, payable in pepper.

Pepper at its source, southern India, was inexpensive and abundant. But by the time pepper and all the other spices from the Orient had changed hands through a succession of Indian, Afghan, Persian, Arab, Venetian and Northern European middlemen, they had assumed considerable value and considerable mystique. The exact origin of most spices was indeed a well guarded secret. But to those Europeans on the edge of the known world, Holland, France, Britain, Spain and Portugal, it was a source of deep annoyance that they were not a part of this lucrative trade. If only the Italian trade monopoly could be broken. By the fifteenth century locating spices at source had become their number one priority. Unable to gain command of the Mediterranean seas, but being maritime nations, they began to turn their attentions to exploration of the oceans.

Monarchs were persuaded to finance small fleets of adventurous mariners. The prizes promised to be great, for both king and captain. The Spanish king had been convinced by Columbus that the enormous wealth of fabled India and China, and their spices, lay just a few thousand miles away across the unexplored Atlantic. In 1492 he discovered America, not realising that another continent and another ocean lay between him and his spices. In 1498, following a century of probing around the African coast, the Portuguese eventually landed in India. Within a few years, they had sourced all their spices, and the world itself had been circumnavigated. The Spanish and Portuguese soon became very rich.

# THE TUDORS

Britain meanwhile had not been a part of this initial exploration. Until then, her ships had only been built for skirmishes across the Channel. Recognising the threat from invasion by a better equipped navy, King Henry VIII started to build a real navy with ocean-going ships, but there was as yet no plan for exploration. During the reign of Queen Elizabeth I the ships were used to plunder Spanish vessels, a ploy which made the monarch very rich. No one was better at this than Francis Drake who, more by accident than design, made the world's second circumnavigation in 1577. This brilliant feat earned him a knighthood and substantial personal wealth. It also made further ventures a top priority. In a concerted effort, the Spanish tried to finish Britain's ambitions off once and for all. But their disastrous 1588 Armada was destroyed by Drake and his more manoeuvrable ships, leaving the seas clear for exploration.

The British had their eyes firmly set on controlling the Spice Islands, the source of the clove and the nutmeg. They even called them the East Indies. Unfortunately the Dutch had the same idea. Neither nation was interested in India. Although it was the best source of pepper, India was regarded as already too overcrowded with European and Arab merchants, and this made it a 'second best' target. True, the East Indies were occupied by the Portuguese, but it was felt, correctly as it turned out, that the Portuguese would be as easy to defeat as the Spanish. The British got into the lead, dispatching their first voyage to the Spice Islands in 1591. However, the expedition was under-financed, and carried insufficient arms and fighting men to defeat even a small, weak Portuguese occupying force. It turned into a maritime and trading disaster. Learning from this, the Dutch set up a trading company called the Dutch East India Company, which had sufficient finance and military strength, and in 1595 they sent their first expedition to the Spice Islands. There they easily ousted the occupying Portuguese, and their first cargo of cloves earned the mission a 2,500% profit.

# THE EAST INDIA COMPANY

This spurred the British into a belated rethink. On the last day of 1600 they established the East India Company, by royal charter. It was financed by Queen Elizabeth but she died before she reaped its benefit. The Company, as it at once became known, got off to a bad start. Its first mission was to remove the Dutch from the East Indies, but in that it failed. Following a number of bloody attempts, the Company did oust the Dutch and set up a warehouse on the islands, but in 1623 the Dutch struck back. They retook the East Indies and executed the entire British contingent there. Despite numerous attempts, the Company was never able to re-establish its base there. Had it not been for this British inability to take the East Indies, there may never have been an Indian Empire. As it was, a minor company representative, one Captain William Hawkins, was first dispatched there in 1608. His mission, given low priority, was to obtain permission for the Company to establish a small trading base at a suitable anchorage.

## THE MOGHULS

Hawkins arrived at the time when India's most powerful dynasty was at its peak of power. In remarkably long reigns, just six great Moghul emperors ruled India between 1526 and 1707. The first of these, Barbur, was related to Genghis Khan, whose Mongolian tribes had terrorised and ruled China 300 years before. If the Mongols were barbaric, the Moghuls were the epitome of civilisation. But such ancestry did Barbur no harm. At the age of eleven, he became king of his small state, and by fourteen he began a series of conquests which eventually led him to control of India. Barbur was cunning, daring and undoubtedly lucky. With an army of just 12,000 men, he pulled off the impossible by defeating an army ten times greater than his own, albeit with the advantage of a new weapon imported from the West, the flintlock gun. Barbur marched into Delhi and declared himself emperor. He then waited for retaliation. To his surprise there was none. To the indigenous Indian population, the fact that Barbur was not of the Hindu religion, and that he was not even Indian, did not bother them. For several hundred years there had been a succession of Moslem invasions in the north, so another Moslem ruler was nothing new. He would probably be no worse than his predecessors. In the absence of any real resistance, Barbur set about empire building. He did so without dethroning any of the incumbent Hindu kings and princes, who were allowed autonomy in their own states, providing they accepted Barbur as emperor, and paid their taxes directly to him. Soon Barbur's power encompassed much of the subcontinent, and so enormous was the wealth the taxes yielded, that it enabled everything the Moghuls did to be magnificent.

Their army consisting of 100,000 men, 10,000 camels and 1,000 war elephants was invincible. Their rule, though austere for their subjects, created a lifestyle unmatched anywhere else on earth before or since. They built, for their own protection and enjoyment, forts, palaces, mosques and mausoleums which were unparalleled, as is witnessed by the world's most outstanding building, Agra's Taj Mahal, built by grief-stricken Emperor Shah Jehan as a memorial to his wife, Mumtaz, on her premature death in childbirth. Their cities were bigger than their counterparts in Europe, a fact not unnoticed by visiting ambassadors. Opulence at court was displayed in magnificent robes, oversized jewels, huge harems, elephant jousting, massive parades, and excess luxury in everything they did.

This was the India the newly formed East India Company's representative William Hawkins discovered in 1608, when he landed at Surat, the small natural harbour on the north-west coast of India, a place highly suitable for the proposed Company base. The fourth Great Moghul Jehangir had just succeeded to the throne. Hawkins journeyed to court to request an audience. There he discovered, to his disgust, that the Portuguese were well ensconced. Having been in India since 1498, some three decades before the arrival of Barbur, they were not only present at court, but had the close ear of the emperor. And they had no reason to help the Company to become trading rivals. Whether or not the court knew the official Company line about India being a second best opportunity, they certainly treated Hawkins as second best. He found himself and the pathetic baubles he had brought as gifts for the emperor a subject of derision. He was kept waiting for three months for an appointment to see Jehangir. In the event, he was only given audience with a minor court official of no higher rank than himself. Since he was under no pressure to return to England, Hawkins persisted, however, and eventually, through his ability to speak Persian, the Moghul court language which the Portuguese never bothered to learn, he became a confidant of Jehangir. Despite that, the Portuguese ensured that it did not lead to permission to trade. Since the Portuguese controlled the seas around India, the first essential was to wrest that control from them.

On his eventual return to England, the message Hawkins gave King James was to send a war fleet, and rather better presents for the emperor who had everything. The advice was heeded. With its lack of success in the East Indies becoming transparent, the Company at last turned its full attention to India. A fleet was dispatched in 1612. Because it was properly equipped, and with its more manoeuvrable vessels, it had no difficulty in defeating the Portuguese fleet off Surat. A new ambassador, Sir Thomas Roe, a better educated, more sophisticated man, was dispatched to India. There he found Jehangir so impressed with the British maritime victory that he met Roe without delay. The Moghuls had never been a maritime power, which made them vulnerable to attack by those who were, and unable to fend them off. Finally here was someone who could. Jehangir was only too pleased to water down Portuguese influence. Their religious fanaticism had reached the stage where even the all-powerful Moghuls were concerned that their Moslem faith would be undermined. In Roe, like Hawkins, he found a pragmatic ally, with no overt religious convictions, just a desire to trade. By 1618, the precious licences were granted, and the long-desired base at Surat was established. Roe for his part saw India through rather less rosy coloured spectacles than Hawkins, and he observed the abject poverty endured by the overwhelming masses. In his prophetic reports he concluded that despite this, the subjects of the empire were not likely to rise up in dissent against British traders. He foresaw a very profitable future for the Company.

## THE DECLINE OF THE MOGHULS

It was not the excessive wealth of the Moghuls, nor the excessive poverty of the population which caused the decline of the Moghuls. Nor was it the presence of the British.

It was, if anything, the fact that here were alien aristocrats who never really took the trouble to understand their Hindu subjects. The closest contact the court had with the people was through its network of spies. These individuals, being invariably Moslem, were easily identified by the people, but their activities were largely regarded with indifference. Providing the people paid their taxes, there was little contact between both parties. This lack of integration by the rulers into the country as a whole did not matter at the beginning of the empire, at which time there was a succession of strong rulers. But the other problem that manifested itself throughout the whole Moghul period was a lack of succession to the throne. It was the double factor that all the great emperors were benign in rule, as well as having very long rules (two of the six ruled for 49 years). Since they were not corrupt there was no real motive to dethrone them, thus great stability resulted. However, without a direct line of succession to the oldest son, there was no heir presumptive. And so no individual was 'groomed' to become emperor.

Upon the death of the current emperor, the job was up for grabs amongst any of the males in the immediate family. As a result, considerable intrigue, rivalry and violence were not uncommon. To prevent bloodshed, the young princes, sons and nephews, were distributed to diverse parts of the empire, to dispense Moghul power as local rulers. To an extent it worked, but the death of Aurangzeb in 1707, following his 49-year rule, heralded a series of wars and skirmishes all over the empire, culminating in the sacking of Delhi, the massacring of its population, and the removal to Persia of much of the Moghul treasure trove by an Afghan shah in 1756. This was followed by a number of tribal wars which culminated in the Battle of Panipat in 1761. Although a weak Moghul emperor was the victor, he next had to face a nationwide mutiny from his army who, not having been paid for the two previous years, quite reasonably demanded remuneration.

# THE GROWTH OF BRITISH POWER

From the granting of their first licence in 1618, the British had gone to great pains to cultivate good relationships with the Moghuls. They paid their rents and taxes and kept themselves, as much as possible, out of sight and out of mind. They had long since stopped regarding India as second best. They rapidly outgrew their trading post at Surat, and in 1640 easily obtained permission to establish a second post at the tiny coastal town of Madras, on the south-east coast. This was followed in 1674 by Bombay, which at the time consisted of nothing more than a fishing village. In 1698 a third base was established in the north-east of India at a place called Calcutta. What these three places had in common were extremely good anchorages, and they were so insignificant that none was even on the Moghul map. Warehouses came first to store the goods that were to be taken back to England in the Company's own vessels. Young men flocked to sign up to the Company and the ships were thus never empty on their return trips to India. Some of my ancestors were amongst them.

Towns quickly sprang up to provide housing both for the newly arrived Company officials and the native workforce. Soon it became clear that strong fences were needed to ensure the security of the goods and the townships. And finally, the fences needed defending by armed soldiers against possible attack. Indeed, such defence was crucial, since attacks ranged from minor skirmishes to major local incursions. The Dutch had been in India in a minor way for the same length of time as the British, but they represented no real threat to them. The French were a different matter. They did not arrive until 1664, and though for a century they became the biggest European rival to Britain, they were never a real threat.

By the time the Moghuls realised it, the British had established their bases as highly fortified cities. In 1757 Clive (of India) in the Battle of Plassey defeated the last serious royal challenge, and the British had become the major power in India.

How did this come about? How did the British, a race and culture far more alien than the Moghuls, and from a land so very distant, succeed not only in seeing off one of the richest and most powerful empires in world history, but in taking over a nation 20 times larger than their own, with a population 30 times larger?

## DIVIDE AND RULE

What the British recognised about eighteenth-century India was that it was no more a single nation then than it is now. It was a country divided, with many religions, fifteen totally different languages, each with their own written scripts, and scores of dialects, none of which could understand the other. There were hundreds of independent princedoms and numerous different ethnic groups, none of whom had anything to do with each other. This pot-pourri was ruled by a declining emperor, whose court language and culture had remained as alien as it was in Barbur's time. It was abundantly clear that there was no Indian contender to the throne waiting to replace the Moghuls. The way was open to anyone who had the ambition and the infrastructure to take over the reins of India. No matter how alien they might be, providing they did not attempt to force a change in religious beliefs, language and culture, and providing they maintained and encouraged the princedoms, they would succeed. Put another way, it was India's very divisions which, if covertly maintained, would help the new contender remain in power, just as the Moghuls had done. Britain was that contender.

At what point Britain's ambitions changed from the creation of profits to the realisation that power was just around the corner is irrelevant. As time went by, wealth came all too easily, and in its wake the thirst for power began to grip the East India Company. The vacuum created by Moghul decline coupled with native apathy was too good to ignore; if the Moghul court had lost the will to rule their empire, and if, being so divided, no native Indians were in a position to take on the challenge, the

British had no such disinclination. They were totally unified and disciplined, and their strategic locations all over the country were better placed and better fortified than those of any potential opposition. They had an unrivalled attention to detail and a desire to do things correctly, something which had never before been seen in India. They had supreme confidence in themselves and total belief in what they did. Above all they had prepared for this move for some time, and they had a hunger to succeed.

From the start they set out to build and nurture relationships with the leaders of the many princedoms, of which there were some 640 all over India. Without this, the Company had no chance of succeeding at any level. Besides, the British have always had an affinity towards royalty, and it gave Company officials a heaven-sent opportunity to rub shoulders with maharajas (great rulers), to whom they always showed enormous respect. For their part, many of the maharajas welcomed British attentions, and so respected did the Company officials become that they began to act as 'honest broker' intermediaries between various princely rival factions who did not speak directly to one another. Whilst not being actively dishonest in such actions, the British soon realised what power this gave them, and they deliberately set out to maintain divisions, rather than remove them. Divide and rule became an effective maxim of the British Raj.

## 'GOING NATIVE'

Officials of the Company were abundant employers of local labour, and invariably they paid on time, and they paid the agreed amount. Under the circumstances they became trusted and respected. Initially the respect was two way and there was considerable integration between British and Indians with little, if any, discrimination. There were so few British women in India at the time that it was not uncommon for cohabitation to take place between a white man and an Indian woman (*bibi*), especially if she had a hint of royal blood, though rarely, if ever, did this lead to marriage. The resultant children of mixed blood were regarded as a normal occurrence. Many Company officials were by now born and bred in India, and 'going native' was so natural to them that they wore Indian native costume on a day-to-day basis, they spoke the various languages fluently, they thoroughly enjoyed spicy food and native culture, and they smoked the hookah.

It went down well with much of the population who were in desperate need of assertive leadership. The British supplied that need with aplomb. Among the considerable benefits for India came peace, stability, law and order. There followed democratic government, education of the masses, medicine and the cure of widespread disease, hospitals, post, telegraph, railways, roads, grand architecture, clubs, Christmas, pomp and circumstance. English became the national language. Though many Indians took to this very actively, not all supported British rule. There were from time to time quite serious insurrections and battles. In each case the British were the victors. Both sides began to believe the British army was unbeatable. It was the same elsewhere in the empire, and at home, with Nelson and Wellington achieving monumental victories.

## THE ROUTE TO MUTINY

In a way it was Britain's military success itself which led to a gradual change of attitude in the post-Napoleonic era. Wherever they were, the British began to believe in their own invincibility. They became arrogant and complacent, and in India as elsewhere, a feeling of racial superiority became the norm. To some extent, this was fuelled by the inability of the indigenous population to contribute towards its own development. However, even then, in the early to mid-1800s, more officials were genuinely pro India and her population than were not. They had an earnest desire to impose what they emphatically believed to be a better system on a less fortunate race. But each successive new governor who arrived from Britain seemed to have ever decreasing empathy with India and her age-old ways. Their brief was to achieve more rapid progress with greater profits, and to achieve it they wanted the old ways and attitudes to change. Before long, cohabitation became outlawed. Company officials who adhered to their Indian dress, friends, food and customs became subject to ridicule. If they persisted, they were quickly and quietly retired, to be replaced by a new breed of official, educated in the English public school system, who had precisely no idea at all of what India was about. It became fashionable for their descendants, those people of mixed race, to be despised. 'Black-blooded', 'half-caste' and 'Eurasian' were three new derogatory terms invented to reinforce this hatred, as was 'Anglo-Indian', a hitherto respectable word meaning a British person who loved India.

Little by little these newer generations of officials eroded the real power of the Indian royals. Furthermore, they did not do this behind closed doors. They did it in ways which caused the Indians to lose face. The early respect and genuine friendship between many Indians and English gave way, over the years, first to dislike, then to deep resentment and open hostility. By the mid-nineteenth century it had become critical. Of the new governors, none was more aloof, nor felt more superior, than the Marquis of Dalhousie. What he believed he saw was an ungrateful Indian race apparently unready for the 'blessings of British rule'.

What the Indians saw were 'new-fangled' ideas, systems and education being foisted upon them by a particularly uncompromising governor. Not surprisingly, they deeply resented the newly applied lack of respect, and the racism. During the 1850s, stress began to build up all over India, resulting in isolated flash points and riots. They were easily quelled by the British army, but since the army consisted of a small number of white officers controlling a large number of Indian troops, this led to unease in the ranks. Indian was being made to fight Indian. True, there was a token number of Indian officers, called *subadhars*, who incidentally never got promoted beyond major, but even these officers found it increasingly difficult to communicate with the troops, and this too eroded respect.

## CHANGE FOR EVER

In 1857, an event took place which changed the course of history. The population of India finally rose up and revolted. It happened over the length and breadth of India. What fuelled it was almost irrelevant. Anything could have caused it. What did cause it was a crass mistake which typified just how out of touch the British were with India. It certainly could never have happened even a few decades earlier. As we have seen, the Indian troops (sepoys) were already unnerved. They were a mixture of Moslem and Brahmin Hindus. Part of their strict religious dogma concerned proscriptions on the eating of certain animals. To the Moslems it was the pig, and to the Hindus it was the cow. A new type of rifle, the Enfield, was being supplied to all troops. As in England, its cartridges were lightly greased. The grease used was dripping made from rendered animal fat. It was inevitably likely to contain pig and beef fat. The mistake was soon spotted, the few cartridges that had been issued were withdrawn, and a new supply, greased with machine oil were supplied. But it was too late. It was the last straw, seen by India, quite wrongly as it happened, as a plot to replace Islam and Hinduism with Christianity. The population rose up. Its aim was to wipe out British rule, and it nearly succeeded.

Of all the places where the mutiny took effect, Lucknow carried the greatest impact. The 2,000 British people there took refuge in the governor's residence, where for several months they were pinned down by the hostile native population. Eventually, the besiegers broke through the walls and indiscriminately massacred the great majority of the British people who were hiding inside in abject terror. The circumstances were particularly violent. One of the few survivors was my infant great grandmother.

The buildup to the mutiny was obvious in hindsight, but it was arrogantly ignored by the powers that be. They certainly did not foresee that as a consequence it would change India for ever. Lucknow was a minor district, *en route* between the East India Company's principal trading post Calcutta, the Moghul centre Delhi, and the north-west frontier. Insufficient troops were stationed at Lucknow, and when the siege took place there was no telegraph nor railway network to facilitate swift communications and troop movements.

## THE DAWN OF THE RAJ

It took months to get a message to England and several more months to get a reply, let alone assistance. The Suez Canal was not to be opened for a further twelve years, taking three months and 5,000 miles off the one-way journey. The 1857 mutiny was the final trigger in a long chain of events in India which led to the demise of the East India Company. The British government had for decades been concerned that the Company was becoming too wealthy and too powerful. In fact, it had had most of its teeth pulled by then. It remained as an administrator, having virtually ceased to trade. But the British used Lucknow as a catalyst. The mutiny was the chance to grab immediate control of India, and their overreaction to the event was to pump in thousand of troops.

Though hundreds of miles inland, Lucknow was relieved in 1858 by the Royal Navy, with its field guns. Their massacre of the, by then, incumbent Indians was even more horrific than the original event, given the navy's superior armaments, numbers and training. But it was all justified by the British feeling of self-righteousness. They saw the mutiny as a personal affront to all they had done for the Indians. To the Indians, it was just another uprising in a centuries-long history of such events. But it did reveal to the Indians that the British were not invincible. The seeds of full independence were planted, although this was still some 90 years ahead, and few Indians really believed it would happen. Certainly no British did and, in the meantime, India was to be taken to the peak of British rule, in the form of a new empire, under new management, with greater power than ever before. This was the start of the British Raj.

In truth the Lucknow mutiny was little more than a symbol. If it was an attempt to scourge India of the British, it had little hope of succeeding. The century of British influence had, as planned, failed to rid the country of its age-old differences. Indeed, once again it was their divide and rule policy which saved the occupiers from being ousted. And for all the flaws, there were many powerful Indians who could see much larger problems in an India without Britain, than one with her. The maharajas, by and large, stayed loyal. The backbone of the army, the Sikhs, Gurkas and Punjabis, also remained loyal. They had been, in any case, unimpressed by animal grease and rumours.

The British did learn a lesson. Over the next two decades scores of British regiments were formed for the purpose of being sent to India. Despite their loyalty, no longer would the new army be soldiered solely by native troops. A hard core of British ranks and NCOs became the norm. This British army in India acquired a new name, the Indian Army. Civil servants, engineers, lawyers and traders also poured in. To ensure that they would never again be caught out by not being able to move troops rapidly around the country to deal with insurrections, construction of a vast national railway network, ten times the size of that in England, took place in just 30 years It had eight systems and five different gauges. The law and government itself was reformed. The first viceroy was appointed. The last Moghul emperor was exiled to Burma. It took eighteen months of bitter and very bloody fighting all over India to put down the mutiny, and it took a further eighteen years to re-establish firm control and to implement the reforms.

## THE HEIGHT OF THE RAJ

To mark its completion, in a massive display of military magnificence, a Great Durbar, Queen Victoria was proclaimed Empress of India on 1st January 1877. The real age of the Raj had begun. In the same year, my grandfather was born.

Many Indians were delighted that their country had again become an empire. They were immensely proud that they had, for the first time, an empress rather than an emperor. They at once named her *Kaiser-i-Hind,*

Maharanee Victoria. When they heard that she had an Indian manservant, the *munshi*, with whom it was alleged she was intimate enough to learn Hindi and share Indian food, they were overjoyed, a view not altogether shared by the then British government. But to many in India, Victoria was seen as a natural successor to Akbar, the greatest Moghul emperor.

It was the arrogance and insensitivity of the British which had caused the uprising. However, the reforms which established the Raj did not sweep away its arrogance. If anything, it intensified it. The British upper class had created a caste system far more subtle than the Indian system. It was impervious to change and was virtually impossible to infiltrate. Top of the pile were the British royal family and aristocrats. Next came civil servants, top of whom was the viceroy and his district commissioners. Senior police officials, the judiciary and cavalry officers came next, followed by other army officers. Exclusive clubs were established for these privileged individuals. Such was the rivalry to join the Indian Civil Service that the few who did win this prestigious appointment were called 'competition *wallahs*' for their first five-year tour of duty by the 'old hands'. Merchants and traders, however, were dismissed as 'box *wallahs*', and no matter how wealthy they were, the clubs were not open to them. Neither were they open to upper-class Indians, not even to the maharajas. Shop owners were 'counter jumpers', engineers 'grease monkeys'. Surveyors were called 'jungle *wallahs*', whilst tea or indigo planters were treated with indifference, and at best looked down upon as self-made men (money, unless inherited, was nothing to be proud of), though jute planters, often Scots, were thought to be even more inferior. Missionaries and the clergy were tolerated, but not encouraged. Creative people such as authors and artists were 'brush *wallahs*' and, being normally impoverished, were regarded as curiosities but with a status lower than 'box *wallahs*'. Almost without status came a huge mass of British men in minor governmental positions, the 'office *wallahs*', and the lowest of the low were the private soldiers in the Indian Army.

## THE BACKBONE OF THE INDIAN ARMY

This unfortunate individual, 'Tommy Atkins', the cannon fodder of many a war, the British Other Rank or BOR, was considered to be in a caste of his own. He was only just above the lowest Indian caste, the untouchable, and was almost ranked equal with people of 'mixed blood', in that he was virtually spat upon by everyone else. He served in India for a seven-year-minimum posting. At least five of those years were on the front line. He had no leave home to England during that period, and what leave he had in India was usually spent in barracks. What else was there to do? Barrack conditions were primitive, each dormitory room shared with some two dozen other BORs. He was permitted few possessions and, unlike just about everyone else in India, he was allowed no servants, so much of his spare time was spent cleaning his kit. There was no mess or club for him, and there were many things he was not allowed. Fraternising with women, Indian or British, was taboo. And certainly the BOR was not allowed to marry in India. He had to be a senior NCO before that privilege was allowed. Since much in the Indian town or city was out of bounds to him, he found himself confined to barracks, or camps, his main relief from tedium being the long marches in between.

Rudyard Kipling, when just a young journalist in the 1890s, wrote of how the lucky ones led a life of 'duty and red tape, picnics and adultery'. On the other side of the coin, he told of how *single men in barracks, most remarkable like you* (the BOR), led a harsh life of underpay and under-privilege. Lady Curzon, wife of the contemporary viceroy, described the BOR in less sympathetic terms: '*The two ugliest things in India,*' she pontificated, '*are the water buffalo and the BOR.*' Perhaps Tommy Atkins was better off not talking to white women, if that was their attitude.

But the BOR was by no means a lonely, dispirited being. He had the companionship of his regimental peers, and that cocky confident spirit with which all Britons of the era were blessed. Furthermore, the carrot of promotion was no idle promise. It was very real and very frequent. Many made it to NCO status, and with it a vastly different, almost unrestricted, world opened up for them. More remarkably, a very select few achieved the 'impossible' by making it into the officer corps. This was no mean achievement for these few, who had to overcome the disadvantage of their working-class upbringing and background, not to mention their regional accent, and above all they had to become accepted by the sahibs and memsahibs into their worlds of silver spoons and servants, innuendo, clubs and *chota* pegs. Surprisingly, perhaps, for such a class-ridden society, it worked, and for at least one BOR it worked supremely. Frank Roberts was born in Cawnpore, joined the army as a private, won the VC in the mutiny, and ended his career as Field Marshal Lord Roberts, Commander-in-Chief Indian Army, 1885–1893. As we shall see, my own grandfather, who just two years earlier joined the Indian army as a BOR, also achieved the 'impossible', going from private to senior officer in his own distinguished military career.

BORs were not the only people to be excluded from society. Indians, with their own complicated caste system, played no part in the real social life of the Raj, no matter who they were and how high their caste. Indians exclusively did the menial tasks for the Raj, and the prize job was to be engaged in service. Even an English bachelor household would boast four or five servants, the average number was ten. The perks for the Indian domestic were plentiful, and far from the obvious as we shall see. But there was yet one more category in the Raj caste system. It was the person of mixed British-Indian blood. We have seen how they came to be despised. It was no better for them post-mutiny than it had been before. The few jobs that were available for them had no prospects, and they were equally despised by Indians and British.

Even if you were British through and through, it was infra dig to be born in India, and worse if you were brought up there. It merely indicated that you had insufficient wealth to avoid the stigma of either, and that put you well down the social ladder. Indeed there were derogatory terms for both these 'conditions'. A Briton born in India was 'country born' and one educated there was 'country bred'.

## THE END OF THE RAJ

Once the dust had settled on the mutiny, and Victoria was proclaimed empress, it seemed that once again the Raj would continue for ever. The problems of religious division never went away, in fact they got so bad that in 1911, the viceroy moved the capital of India from Calcutta to Delhi. The First World War came and went, but despite the intense loyalty of the maharajas, India now got confirmation of what she had long suspected since the mutiny. Britain was indeed not invincible. That the king emperor could not prevent European fighting European was perceived to be a deep weakness. And that Britain so nearly lost the war did not go unobserved, neither did the fact that many Indian sepoys lost their lives for a cause not their own in the battlefields of Belgium and elsewhere. Perhaps there would come a day in the not-too-distant future when the Raj would quit India. It took Mahatma Ghandi to voice those words in his ceaseless and well supported bouts of passive resistance. The British tried to carry on as if nothing had changed. In the early 1920s, they spent an emperor's fortune building sumptuous new government buildings and their new capital city, New Delhi. It was built to last 1,000 years.

But India was not prepared to wait that long. Had it not been for the

Second World War, her independence from Britain might have come in the thirties. As it was, the world had to wait until 14th August 1947.

On that day, the British Raj came to its end.

# SAHIBS, MEMSAHIBS, COOKS AND CROOKS

## FROM RICHES TO RAGS

**M**Y GREAT GREAT great grandfather was born in 1791 in Chunar, not far from Varanasi in India. His name was William Lawrence, but whether his parents, John and Joanne Lawrence, were born in India, and what John's occupation was I cannot tell. But John, or maybe his father, must have been one of those young men who flocked to join the Company, eager to get his hands on the land of opportunities. I can only guess that. All I have to go on is one of many records so diligently searched out by my contemporary cousins. It is a copy of William's baptism certificate, reference Bengal N/1 vol. 4 page 116. It positively puts all three in India in that year.

Proof that John and Joanne must have had upper-class, well-heeled families, comes to light on William's daughter Sarah's baptism certificate, which lists her father's occupation. William achieved the exalted rank of Chief Constable of Lucknow, and such a position was denied to all but the privileged. More evidence of high status comes from Sarah's marriage certificate, which shows she married one Abraham Beatson, an officer of the Indian Civil Service, a supreme position indeed in 1852. This marriage also took place in Lucknow. For both it was their second marriage. I do not have the record of the cause of death of Abraham's first wife, but Sarah's first husband, John Petrie, had contracted 'jungle fever' and died while she was still young. Fatal illness was common enough in those days. Everyone lived in fear of it. '*Two monsoons are but the age of man*' was a saying that echoed around at the time. Even educated people universally believed that such diseases as cholera and tuberculosis, smallpox, malaria and the measles were caught by inhaling invisible vapours while they slept. Second, third and even fourth marriages were not unknown. Plenty of ambitious men took lifetime engagements with the East India Company, but there was a chronic shortage of British women in the India of the time, so it was perfectly acceptable to marry a widow.

## ALONE AND ORPHANED

Two years later, in 1854, Sarah and Abraham gave birth to a daughter, my great grandmother, Alice Henrietta Beatson. She looked set to live a life of luxury. But in 1857, when she was barely three, fate conspired to strike a cruel blow. The most serious and bloody uprising the British had ever encountered erupted across India. And the place which suffered most and longest was Lucknow. We saw on page 12 how, in a siege which lasted for nearly a year, almost the entire British population of 2,000 was wiped out.

When the residency was eventually relieved by British forces, one of the few survivors found miraculously alive was the helpless baby, Alice Beatson. Her parents, brothers, sisters, aunts, uncles and cousins were dead. When it became clear that she had no immediate family left, she was taken to the British Military Orphanage at Sanawar, near Simla.

It was here that Alice Beatson grew up for the next fifteen years. An orphanage is an austere establishment with little love, and this army version would have been no exception. I have no record of what my great grandmother thought of those awful years. The place was at least warm and safe, but divested of her upper-class background and her former wealth, of which fortunately she would have remembered little, the best Alice could look forward to was a lifetime of derision from her former peers. For Alice was impoverished. And worse! She was a domiciled European, 'country born' and 'country bred'. It took her from the top to the bottom of the social ladder.

## HUMBLE STOCK

Alexander Lemmon had the same qualifications. His family had left Britain long ago and had been domiciled in India for several genera-tions. Unlike Alice, they were of humble stock. His father, John, was a sergeant major in the 11th Infantry Regiment. At sixteen, Alexander started work as a clerk at the telegraph office. At 24 he was getting to the age when he needed a wife. Eligible unmarried English women were scarce. The wealthy and the upper classes could afford to send their children back to England to educate them, and have them return later to search for wives, but this was out of the question for ordinary working-class folk. The problem had become so acute in the India of the 1870s that young single women were encouraged to come out to India at the beginning of each new 'season'. They were known to the old hands as 'the fishing fleet'. Men in search of a suitable wife would trawl through them until they found the partner they could tolerate. Not even this ghastly system worked for everyone. The few women who had not been lucky enough to receive a proposal by the end of the season, were sent home with the description 'returned empty'. Being of too low a status to be allowed to make contact with the 'fleet', Alexander Lemmon had decided on his own rather novel way to find a wife. He decided to choose one from the nearby orphanage. Alice Beatson was eighteen when they married. The year was 1873.

# GRANDFATHER

Four years later, and 5,000 miles away, my grandfather William Henry Hawley was born in Plumstead, South London. His father, a Yorkshireman originally from Penistone near Barnsley, was a wheelwright at the nearby Woolwich army base. His mother was a strict, uncompromising woman. Young William Henry hated her and he hated home. At thirteen she tried to make him follow her father's trade and become a tailor. He had no interest in that. He wanted to follow his brother into the army. So he ran away. He went to the army garrison at Woolwich and, pretending to be sixteen, signed up for a seven-year enlistment as a private (BOR, see page 14) in a British gunnery regiment, the York and Lancaster Regiment, about to be sent out for duty in India. The year was 1891. To Private Hawley, it mattered little where he served. India was as good as anywhere as long as it was far enough away from his mother. A BOR was a BOR wherever he was. But he didn't remain in the ranks for long. The regiment moved around India and my grandfather gained rapid promotion through the NCO ranks, until he became regimental colour sergeant. In 1901, the regiment became based in Agra.

# GRANDMOTHER

Alexander and Alice had several daughters and sons. Grace was their fourth child. Alexina, their sixth, my grandmother, was born in Lahore in northern India in 1884. Some time after that, Alexander's work took him to

Agra. He had worked his way up to telegraph master, and thus could afford to buy the family a bungalow there. In 1901 Grace was proposed to by one of the colour sergeants from the newly arrived York and Lancaster Regiment.

The wedding took place in due course with Alexina as a bridesmaid; William Henry Hawley was best man. They soon became engaged, and in the next year they too got married. With marriage came an entitlement to standard army married quarters, in this case, of sergeant-major status: a bungalow with four bedrooms, half an acre of garden, and a complement of six servants.

One perk available to a senior Indian Army NCO was furlough, leave of absence from military duty. The couple's first child, my uncle Bill, was two when, in 1905, Grandpa paid his first return visit to England since he had run away from home fourteen years earlier. My grandmother had never been there. They were visiting his mum in Plumstead. One day they went shopping in the market and Bill got lost. Eventually his distraught parents found him safe and sound at the local police station being thoroughly spoiled. The police were mightily confused with their tiny charge, however. For every question they asked, he replied '*nay malum, nay malum*'. It means 'don't know' in Hindi, and it seemed perfectly logical to the wee tot to answer in the language of his *ayah* (nanny) even though she was thousands of miles away.

# SAHIB

When the army found that my grandfather had an aptitude for figures, they transferred him to the Indian Army Pay Corps, where he was soon carving out a promising career. It was hardly a dashing and glamorous army role, but it was one which affected all personnel, and Grandpa was greatly respected. He was fluent in both Urdu and Hindi. That he was good at his job was confirmed when in 1916 he was commissioned from the ranks to become a sahib – an unusual occurrence then, and a difficult transition to make amongst the snob-riddled attitudes of the Raj. But my grandfather handled it well. He was a clever man and had a strong personality. Not for him airs and graces and affected ways. His direct Yorkshire manner, with his strong Yorkshire accent, must have ricocheted through the officers' messes and clubs of the day.

My grandparents were experiencing the best of life in the Raj at its peak. Yet it wasn't all a gravy train. As an ordinary military family, they endured the regular postings and the upheavals of many moves. As was the norm in those days, they had a huge family of nine children, which their income never seemed enough to support. It was a hard life, especially since both had to move upwards from the working class. Even as late as 1925, whatever one's status, there was no electricity. Lighting was by oil lamps, cooking in the cookhouse by charcoal-fired stoves. There was no running water, and no bath. The showers were rather crude but effective tin boxes into which the water, always lukewarm all year round though never artificially heated, was poured by the *bhisti* (water carrier). There was no radio, of course no television, no record players, no phones and no motor cars. The first aeroplane my mother saw was in 1923 when she was a schoolgirl in Jubalpore. So important was the occasion that it was billed in advance, and all the schools shut down for the day, to enable all the kids and teachers to witness the arrival of the first aircraft in central India.

But their quality of life steadily improved, made ever easier by the strength of the Raj. As and when the officers in the Indian Army got promoted, so their perks, not to mention their expenditure, increased *pro rata*. The bungalow was bigger with more rooms, the compound larger with more 'go-downs' (outbuildings) and gardens. And of course to look after the ever increasing burden, ever more servants were required. By the time my grandfather reached the rank of major, his wife, as the '*Burrah Memsahib*', would have had at least twenty servants to control. More entertaining was expected of one of such senior rank. Years before, Grandpa had acquired a bicycle. He loved it dearly. He used it daily and it took him hither and thither. Like him, it was practical and unfussy. He especially liked it because it was a solo vehicle. Try as they would, it couldn't be servant-driven. Sadly the authorities considered it undignified for a senior-ranking officer. Transport more befitting was issued, like it or not (and Grandpa didn't), in the form of a phaeton, a horse-drawn trap, complete with a *syce* (groom/coachman) both of which lived in the 'horse and trap house'.

## MEMSAHIB AND BOBAJEE

The elevation to the world of memsahib was the hardest transition my grandmother had to make, but she had many advantages over the *keehais* (see page 98) and the blue-chip girls of the fishing fleet, who may well have been born and bred in the right place, but who were totally lost and inept in India. Not so my grandmother. She knew India and its ways, and could speak several of its languages. She also had known from her youth how to run an Indian household, with all its wily servants.

And none was wilier than the cook. This individual was always male, generally in his forties, and a man of some considerable power, or so he thought. As he was rarely literate, and he certainly could not read English, a new recipe would have to be demonstrated to him. Thus the shrewd memsahib had good reason to enter the cook's hallowed empire, the kitchen. We'll meet it on page 29. Suffice to say, it was invariably detached from the main house and was in a small outbuilding, a go-down, on its own at the bottom of the compound called, appropriately enough, the cookhouse.

The cook and his family had a small dwelling supplied, alongside the cookhouse. As it was an Indian kitchen, cooking was done over coals on a simple stove and on the floor. A table was provided, more for the memsahibs than the Indian cook, the *bobajee*, who like all his kind, was more comfortable in the lotus position on the floor. A charcoal-fired clay oven, though not a tandoor, was standard. Fetching and carrying, washing and cleaning were done by the assistant cook, or helper, the *musolchi*. There was no running water; it was brought in liberal supplies by the water carrier in clay pots. The job of cooking was learned by observation and then by eventually doing. The helper finally became a cook in his own right, going off to his own household.

The cook's power came about not so much because he fed the household, but because he did the food shopping at the bazaar. He held the purse-strings for this operation. And it was he who could run an inexperienced memsahib into the ground. Mrs Beeton observed: '*It is absolutely necessary to look after the cook* bobajee, *who will probably be the marketer. It is best to give him his orders overnight, that he may go early to the bazaar to buy. There is a tariff of all articles sold at the bazaar, regulated by the bazaar master and cantonment magistrate: therefore, having mastered the value of the various coins and a few words for everyday wants in the way of food, it should be difficult for your bobajee to excercise his proclivities for defrauding you.*'

The likes of the Beetons and Steels undoubtedly instilled into the weaker memsahib the certainty that she would be cheated at every step. In fact, the better memsahib had no such illusion and learned to handle her cook with courtesy and respect, but with a no-compromise attitude regarding discipline. The cook generally responded quite well to his female boss, even though she might be half his age.

He was the most respected servant in the household, even more so than the *khansama* (butler) who fancied himself as the head man, because he was nominally responsible for all the other servants. All, that is, except the *bobajee*, who daily had the memsahib's ear and rupees. Rivalry between butler and cook was legion, but in truth, if the memsahib couldn't handle her cook, then all the servants would run rings round her. Jobs would not be completed, or they'd be done badly. In the worst cases they wouldn't even get started. Timekeeping would slip, and all sorts of excuses would be put forward for why servants were incompetent, or even absent, or why possessions would get broken or would disappear. Cleaning standards were the hardest to maintain. The clue which gave away a weak memsahib was the standard of cleanliness of her table setting, in particular, cutlery and plates. And the other memsahibs' gossipy tongues didn't miss a trick when it came to running down one of their own kind, no matter how good her pedigree.

My grandmother had no such problems. She hated such gossip, and wanted to help the weaker women. From the moment she became a memsahib herself, she was often called upon to put things right in other households, even though she was younger and of more junior rank than many of the wives. She believed that it all began with the daily shopping routine. Unlike Mrs Beeton, who never visited India herself, she preferred to give orders on the day in question. At about 7am, after breakfast, the *bobajee* had to present himself in the parlour. There today's and, if visitors were expected, tomorrow's meals would be planned. Then the shopping list for today's cooking, along with any required pantry stores, was agreed and handed to the cook, along with the sum of cash the cook said he needed.

Herein lay the rub. It had been tradition for as long as the British had been in India to allow the *bobajee* a little extra cash, called the *dastur*, as a bonus for doing the daily chore of shopping at the bazaar. In return he was supposed to achieve better than the asking price for produce, and to ensure that it was top quality. There was widespread inexperience among many memsahibs, most of whom who couldn't speak more than a few words of the language of their servants, and their reluctance to venture into the bazaars bordered on paranoia. It was not surprising that there was widespread exaggeration by the cooks to their memsahibs about bazaar prices. It was easy for them to invent today's prices, and to trot out the same story to their memsahibs, since all the *bobajees* met and compared notes at the bazaars every day.

My grandmother knew the bazaars inside out. She was quite capable herself of haggling over the price of a chicken or a vegetable in virtually any language the trader cared to try on her. And every so often, she'd do it, taking a couple of the more timid young wives with her. On more than one occasion she exposed crooked servants, who were ripping their memsahibs off beyond belief. But it was rare, and far from the norm. Instant dismissal was the price and this was serious. Without references, no servant would ever be employed again. So it was a warning first, then if the individual persisted, the inevitable happened. Needless to say, word soon got around among the *bobajees* and the *keehais* that here was a memsahib to be reckoned with.

## RETIREMENT

My grandparents retired in 1930 and brought the family back to England, thus ending an association with India that went back over 150 years. It was a sad period in their life, and a story in its own right which I offer as the Postscript on page 197. In common with nearly all who served there, they brought back to England with them a deep love and nostalgia towards India, and a craving for spicy food.

I was quite a young lad when, in the 1950s, they both came to live with my mother at our Ealing home. I used to enjoy their reminiscences. They had witnessed the arrival of electricity, the aeroplane, the car, the telephone and radio. They had learned to mix with maharaja and field marshal on the one hand and untouchable *methar* (house cleaner) and army BOR on the other. Grandpa thrilled me with his tales of the Raj. I could picture him a slim blond Yorkshireman, with his piercing blue eyes not missing a trick. Now his blond hair was silver but his wit and memory remained as sharp as steel. Granny also enthralled me with her stories of India, but it was her cooking which was to leave its lasting memory on me.

So little remains now. A few faded sepia photographs and trinkets, some second-hand memories, for they are not my memories. Some aged books, their pages frail, their bindings cracking and disintegrating. In the way of all things, nothing lasts for ever. And this is not my story. But before it all slips from view, I feel duty bound to preserve those memories, and to keep alive those fabulous tastes, their food.

I am proud that generations of my family, including my mother, uncles, aunts, grandparents, and their ancestors too, were 'country born' and 'country bred', and of their working-class background. Their marriage certificates tell of butchers, farriers, soldiers, tailors, hospital porters, nurses, clerks and wheelwrights. For all I know, we have 'black blood' too. And if we do, I'm proud of that; it would have been more than likely back in the 1760s. Our family tree becomes a bit obscure around then, and I'm certain those old Company men would have 'gone native'. I'm proud of them and their resistance to disease, and of my great grandmother for surviving the mutiny, and going from the upper to the working class. And I'm proud of my grandpa, for making it from private to senior officer, of my gran for being such an inspiring cook, and of my mum for keeping all those memories alive. It was grit like this that made India the 'jewel in the crown'. I hope they are proud of me for telling their story.

# RAJ READING MATTER

THE MEMSAHIBS relied on four or five cookbooks, most of which unashamedly attempted to reproduce European food in the totally unsuitable conditions of India. Some were openly hostile to Indian cookery, referring to it disparagingly as 'native' food. Others were more appreciative, but this shows how divided attitudes were in the Victorian Raj about whether to hate and ignore Indian food or whether to enjoy it. Of course, their authors were all taken seriously at the time. And they took themselves seriously too, poking fun at the 'natives' and with pompous attitudes. Viewed today with our more enlightened outlook, some of this material is comical, some unintentionally so, and I have no hesitation in offering you some wonderful quotes in the pages of this book.

The best known author, even in India, was the inevitable Isabella Beeton, who was the Delia Smith of her day. Her mighty tome *Mrs Beeton's Book of Household Management*, first published in 1861 and still published today by Ward Lock, contained, as such books of the time did, advice on just about everything from the duties of the household to the rearing of children, and of course there are hundreds of Victorian recipes too. Although Mrs Beeton never visited India herself, it did not prevent her from proffering advice and recipes in a small fifteen-page section on Indian Cooking (well under one per cent of the book). Her comments and recipes are interesting, but one senses a distaste for India, and more literally for Indian cookery, which in every way typified the attitude of the Briton who had never been there.

Someone who not only had been there, but who led a successful career, unusual for a memsahib, as an architect, schools inspector, author and pontificator was Flora Annie Steel. Being neither country born nor bred, she arrived in India from Blighty, a fresh innocent young memsahib, and she was an inveterate snob. When she was in her fifties, in 1898 she wrote the highly influential *Indian Housekeeper and Cook* (assisted by Grace Gardner). This book, incidentally, was *the* best seller for 20 years on cooking in India, and it proved beyond doubt that there were two schools of thought about the benefits of Indian food. Her book devotes just one and a half pages (out of 400) to what she dismissively calls: '*Native Dishes – added by request*'. She condescendingly goes on: '*It may be mentioned incidentally that most native recipes are inordinately greasy and sweet, and that your native cooks invariably know how to make them fairly well.*'

On the other side of the coin was *Culinary Jottings from Madras* by 'Wyvern'. The author of this turned out to be a regimental colonel with such an eye for culinary detail that he set up a cookery school in England after he retired from the Raj. Wyvern is totally sympathetic to India and its food, and he laments the fact, as we shall see on page 36, that curries were being relegated to the back seat by people like Mrs Steel. For a book written originally in 1878, and which was also a popular favourite, remaining in print for over 30 years, Wyvern's attitude to food is thoroughly modern (a 1994 reprint of this interesting book is published by Prospect Books). Equally modern, and thoroughly sympathetic, is his attitude to the Indian servant, as seen through the eyes of 'Ramasamy', Wyvern's all-purpose, do-everything, and probably invented (a kind of amalgam of all typical servants of the day) cook/butler.

A book which was not a cookbook, but which was definitely a Raj favourite, was *Behind the Bungalow*, written in 1895 under the pseudonym 'EHA', who later disclosed himself to be one Edward Hamilton Aitken. His highly amusing writings, in this case about the servants of the Raj and especially about his cook Domingo, were sensitive and never derogatory, and displayed a remarkable understanding of human nature. EHA was as popular an author as Kipling at the time.

Another astonishingly interesting reference book (though again not a cookbook), which was as certain to be in a Raj bookcase as the Holy Bible, was simply entitled *Hobson Jobson*. First published in 1886, it describes itself as: '*A Glossary of Colloquial Anglo Indian Words and Phrases*'. Its 1,000 pages provided the sahibs and memsahibs with such a wealth of definitions and information that the work was regarded as essential reading. A reprint was published by Routledge in 1985.

A popular book was the *Indian Domestic Economy and Receipt Book* by one Dr R. Riddell, who for many years held a '*high appointment in the Nizzam of Hyderabad's service*'. It devotes about one eighth of its 640 pages to what he calls '*Oriental Cookery*', or the '*culinary processes followed by the Muslims and*

*Hindus of Asia'*. The book is for the most part comment free with useful workman-like recipes. Most of Riddell's observations are not derogatory, although he does become patronising on more than one occasion. Having highly praised the qualities of servants, for example, he goes on to say: '*Their principal vice is an intolerable habit of lying.*' To bring you the flavour of the times, I have drawn on these books from time to time throughout my recipe introductions and elsewhere.

The one book which proves that Indian cookery was alive and well and enjoyed by certain Raj families, and which was undoubtedly my grandmother's favourite, was the *Indian Cookery Book*. It was written by '*a thirty-five years resident*' (probably another male, who like so many authors in this field wished to remain anonymous) and first published in Calcutta by Thacker and Spink in 1877, coincidentally the year my grandfather was born. Interestingly it had the longest publishing history of all the specialist Raj cookery books, the last (6th) edition being published as late as 1944. This astounding life of nearly 70 years proved that the Raj really did like curry no matter how desperately the snobs tried to belittle its supporters. My grandmother's edition was published in 1902. It was her eighteenth year, and the year she was married in Agra. It was a wedding present from her mother, and probably one of her most treasured possessions. Certainly it was one of the few items she brought from India with her when she retired. Its pages are well thumbed and brown with age. It was well used.

It still is. I have it in front of me now. It is one of my most prized possessions too. It was given to me by my Aunt Alice many years ago when she realised just how much I adored spicy food. It is probably not worth much on the second-hand market. It is not a first edition, and its original cover was lost long before it was rebound a few decades ago. None of this matters. What are important are its recipes and its positive attitude to India, the servants, and the food.

My grandmother had no need to cook herself. There were always servants to do the work, but she had a deep interest in cooking. Fortunately, she not only learned how to cook curries in the Indian way, but she in turn passed on to her cooks methods for making English food. She had only been to England briefly once, some 25 years before her retirement. Most of her repertoire was learned from her family, friends and associates. The women of the Raj, the memsahibs, relied a great deal on word of mouth to collect recipes, in much the same way that one does today. What evolved was a unique combination of English food, adapted to match the range of available ingredients by generations of Indian chefs. Its 'east meets west' style could not be more appropriate for the 21st century.

The useful blank pages which appear throughout the book are crammed with my grandmother's tight, concise, handwritten recipes, now almost faded away and quite hard to read. In this way, she collected from her friends a lifetime of recipes which are on loose paper. They are all gems.

So is her *Indian Cookery Book* by its 'thirty-five years resident'. It had been a long time since I had opened it. When I recently did so, I remembered with nostalgia and mouth-watering pleasure just how delicious its contents are. The book begins with observations about Indian money, the bazaars, the seasons and, of course, the servants. But it is humorous and not dismissive. It then moves swiftly on to a sizeable and very useful chapter on curries. Then follow all those Anglo-Indian dishes I remember my grandmother used to cook so well. Wonderful rissoles, or chocolate pudding, beef olives, stuffed hearts, fish moolies and lamb chilli fry. I loved her Christmas cakes and her curries, her fudge and apple pies, and so much more. I knew the time had come to pass on this wealth of material through the pages of a book of my own.

My first task was to organise the recipes into chapters. First and foremost in my mind came curries. Nearly every Raj household soon came to love curry, and it was usually served several times a week. For one thing the cook had to make it several times a day for himself and the other live-in Indian servants, but in any case it was popular on the family dining table. I have devoted a complete chapter to curry and, just as in the *Indian Cookery Book*, I have given it a place of honour and importance as Chapter 1. And if you look carefully through many of the other chapters, you'll find more curry dishes sneaking in there too!

For the remaining chapters, I have followed the order of the day. First comes breakfast, then tiffin (lunch) and afternoon tea recipes. Next, I have included the celebrated *chota* peg, the pre-dinner snorter, without mention of which the eating habits of the Raj would be incomplete.

The next five chapters are main-course recipes. They would have appeared at the Raj dinner table. This meal was an elaborate affair, as it was in Victorian Britain. Five courses were not unheard of, even in an ordinary home. Soup would be served first, followed by fish. The main course would consist of roasts, meat pies, casseroles or stews, accompanied by several vegetables. The fourth course was pudding, and the fifth was a small canapé-style savoury. And as if all that was not enough, a sixth course called the dessert ended the meal. It was all washed down with considerable amounts of alcohol.

My grandparents' family was quite large, and there was never enough spare money to allow for overindulgence. Apart from the inevitable entertaining, meals at home rarely exceeded three courses and were as simple as one would eat today, with alcohol reserved for a special occasion. But this was no puritanical household. They had a lot of fun, and especially so at the Indian Christmas. It was always a time of great festivity for the Raj. My grandmother's homes were no exception, judging by her collection of Christmas recipes, a few of which conclude the chapters in this book. I used to look forward to her Christmas cake every year, and it never failed to live up to my expectations. I recommend you to try it.

Indeed, I recommend you to try all of these Raj recipes. You'll find many a delightful adaptation of familiar English dishes. Nothing could be more contemporary. A pinch of spice here, a touch of flavouring there, and a well-known favourite dish becomes transformed into something new, exciting and quite glorious. It becomes just a little larger than life. But then that was the Raj.

This book is my tribute to that era, and to a lifestyle now long gone. I hope you enjoy the quotes and the anecdotes that make up that story. But, more than that, I hope you'll enjoy trying the recipes, because if you do we'll have kept alive the taste of the Raj.

It's almost time to start tasting, but just before we do let's set the scene and step back a century or two into the stygian hell that was the Raj kitchen.

# THE RAJ INDIAN KITCHEN

WHAT SO MANY British Victorian observers of the Raj failed to understand was that it was *they* who were aliens in a subcontinent that had been civilised for centuries before Britain had emerged from the Dark Ages, and even longer before their bigoted eyes arrived on the scene. It was not the Indians who could not cope with the situation, it was their colonialists, attempting to impose their own culture upon a population who had their own ways of doing things, which had remained unchanged for as long as anyone could remember. Ironically, dress, hygiene, technology, behaviour, attitudes and even the food of medieval and Tudor Britain were not so different from that of India. We even shared the eating habit of using no cutlery. It was Britain which subsequently changed with its quest for invention, propriety, and exploration.

The Indian population tried extremely hard to adapt to the changes required of them, and nowhere more so than in the food requirements meted out to them. They had every right to be incredulous at the mountains of unfamiliar dishes they were expected to turn out daily. And who could blame them if they resented being referred to by some as inferior, stupid, lying, cheating, dirty savages? The great majority were none of those things. And since they did not see dirt as a problem, their standards of cleanliness were, quite simply, different from those of their 'masters'. That the Indian servants achieved anything at all is a miracle. They did it on a shoestring budget, and for the most part were totally ill-equipped. That they did it, at least in our family, almost invariably loyally, honestly, diligently and cheerfully, says more for them than it does for those who criticised them. But criticise they did.

There was no bigger critic than Flora Annie Steel who said: '*The kitchen is a black hole, the pantry a sink. The only servant who will condescend to tidy up is a skulking savage with a reed broom. With regard to the kitchen, every mistress worth the name will insist on having a building suitable for this use and will not put up with a dog kennel. She must (with sinking heart) begin the daily inspection of pantry, scullery and kitchen. A good cook will ask to have the cook-room walls thoroughly whitewashed. If the floor is of mud, relay it with broad flat bricks, nicely joined with mortar.*' It was all a case of control which some of the memsahibs did and others simply ignored.

Mrs Major Clemens in her book *The Manners and Customs of India*, published in 1841, wrote: '*Few people think it necessary to visit the cook-room* [so that] *none of the disagreeables of that department are ever seen; perhaps the sight of the place, and of the manner in which many a dainty dish is prepared, might affect the delicate stomachs of our countrywomen.*'

Mrs Beeton observed that: '*Housekeeping in India is totally different from housekeeping here* [by which she meant Britain; remember she was never in India]. *The mistress cannot undertake the personal supervision of her kitchen, which is not in the house or bungalow, but outside, and often some distance away. She will also soon learn (that is supposing she has been accustomed to English housekeeping) that it is impossible to treat Indian servants in the same manner as those on whom she has been accustomed to depend for daily service. Indian servants are good, many of them: but they cannot be trusted and will cheat if they have a chance.*'

George Atkinson in his book *Curry and Rice on 40 Plates*, published in 1859, talked of 'slaves' and 'niggers' (I have cut those references) and despite his attempt at a non-patronising conclusion, his condescending attitude shows through. He said: '*Is there not a luxury in the very contemplation of a kitchen, the fragrant smells of savoury good things insinuate themselves up the stairs, and through the crevices of the doors, arrest the senses, and whet the appetite?*

'*Look into that Oriental kitchen. If your eyes are not instantly blinded with the smoke, and if your sight can penetrate into darkness, enter that hovel, and witness the preparation of your dinner. The table and the dresser, you observe, are Mother Earth. The preparation for your dinner must therefore be performed in the earth's broad lap, like everything else in this Eastern land. As a matter of course, you will have curry, the standing dish of the East. There are the servants busy at its preparation. The chase for the fowls has terminated in a speedy capture. Already the feathers are being stripped, and the mixture of the spicy condiments is in course of preparation. There, on his hams, and a not over-alluring object, is the head of the culinary department, grinding away the savoury stuff which is soon to adorn that scraggy chicken, and to excite the palling appetite. Thus you perceive, simplicity is the prevailing feature in an Indian kitchen. A spit, two native saucepans, a ladle, and a knife, comprise all the requirements of an Eastern cook. And if the cooks of the West have more costly and more extensive appliances, and laugh to scorn the rude apparatus, let him come at once, and we will prove to him what really good things can be got.'*

Wyvern, considerably more tactfully, put the blame where it always belonged, with the householders: *'Remembering the cheerful aspect of the English kitchen, its trimness, its comfort and its cleanliness . . . how is it that we are aware that the chamber set apart for the preparation of our food is, in ninety-nine cases out of a hundred, the foulest in our premises, yet we are not ashamed?'*

Apocryphal stories abounded at the servants' expense, of bearers cleaning only the top side of the dinnerplate *'because no one eats from its underside'*, of chamber pots being used by the bearers to serve soup in, while soup tureens were used to wash their feet in, of ayahs dosing their charges with opium to make them sleep at night, of cooks sleeping on the chopping table, and of their helpers using the sahib's socks to strain food through, and being proud of the fact that the master had worn them first.

I am relieved to say that my grandmother's cookbook, the *Indian Cookery Book* of 1877, gave the most positive advice about the kitchen, without innuendo or condescending comment. This, unedited, is what it had to say:

## OBSERVATIONS ON THE KITCHEN AND ITS REQUIREMENTS

*'The kitchen should be roomy, light, and airy, with contrivances, in the shape of shelves and other conveniences, for laying out in order all utensils and other necessaries inseparable from the kitchen. The oven and all the fireplaces should be constructed of fire-bricks, and not of the ordinary clay-bricks so generally used in Indian kitchens, requiring constant repairs, to the great annoyance of the cook and hindrance of his work.*

*'A good supply of reservoirs or large earthen jars (jallahs) for fresh water is*

*essential. Of these there should be two at least, both to contain equally good clean water, but yet to be applied to two widely different purposes – the one for washing, and the other exclusively for cooking the victuals. Those who can afford the expense ought to have a reservoir on the terrace of the kitchen, and the water brought down by means of a pipe, with cock attached; which would effectually prevent dirty and greasy hands being put into the reservoirs.*

*'The drainage should be well constructed, with a sufficient incline to carry away easily all washing and offal; and the doors and windows provided with finely made bamboo chicks, to keep out the flies, which at some season are more troublesome than at others.*

*'Great cleanliness is necessary throughout the kitchen: the flooring as well as the ceiling, the walls, and every nook and corner ought to be kept constantly in familiar acquaintance with the whisk, and the knight of the broom called in occasionally to aid the cook in the work of a thorough turn-over. There are very many kitchens in India the ceilings of which are cleaned only once in three years, when the triennial repairs to the premises oblige it to be done.*

*'The very best recipes, however, for ensuring a perfectly clean kitchen, well-tinned utensils, and fresh water, are the frequent visit of the lord and lady of the mansion to the cook. On these occasions expressions of satisfaction should never be withheld, if deserved, at the mode of cooking or serving up; where not merited, the one or more instances should be particularised, and such modification as may appear necessary be gradually suggested. Attention should next be directed to the order and cleanliness of the kitchen etc: let there be no sparing of praise, if well deserved – such treatment is encouraging, and then if need be, anything disorderly or unclean can be pointed out more as a passing remark than as one of complaint or censure.*

*'The cook should be kept well supplied with dusters, of the commonest kind, for cleaning and wiping pots and pans, and two dozens of a better, yet coarse, description, for straining soups, gravy etc. There ought always to be a supply of twine for tying up roast meats, etc.*

*'A quarterly reckoning should be taken of all the kitchen property in charge of the cook; this is more particularly necessary in houses where there are frequent changes of cooks and servants.*

*'Finally, one other suggestion is of no little importance, viz, cats, dogs, and sweepers, as a rule, have no business in the kitchen. The sweeper, or, as he is elsewhere called, the "knight of the broom" should only be admitted either before the operations of the day have commenced, or after their final termination. Ninety-nine sweepers out of a hundred know that intrusions in the kitchen are against all established rules throughout the length and breadth of India; and yet, if the master or mistress be indifferent, not only the knight, but his lady also will indulge their fingers in many a savoury pie. It is no uncommon thing to find them constantly in kitchens of*

*houses of gentlemen ignorant of the rule, peeling potatoes, shelling peas, and performing other offices for the cook, in expectation of some return for such assistance or service rendered.*

*'Never quarrel with a good cook if his only fault be that of eating from your kitchen; all cooks will do so, and a good one will eat no more than a bad one.'*

Darned good advice that! Let's get on with the cooking.

## CHAPTER ONE

# RAJ CURRIES

W E SAW ON PAGE 4 that it was not until 1608 that the first
Englishman, a Captain William Hawkins, was officially sent to
India. He soon came across 'native Indian food'. In *Hobson Jobson* (see page
26) Hawkins' encounter is described thus: '*Indian food consists of some cereal.
In the North this is flour, baked into unleavened cakes, elsewhere it is rice grain,
boiled in water. Such food, having little taste, some small quantity of a much more
savoury preparation is added as a relish.*' Hawkins called this preparation
curry, although he doubtless did not coin the word himself. Neither did
any 'native' Indian. In fact the word did not, and still does not, appear in
any of India's fifteen languages and the derivation could be attributed to a
number of words (see Glossary). Hawkins went on: '*Curry consists of meat,
fish, fruit or vegetables cooked with a quality of bruised spice and turmeric, called
masala. A little of this gives a flavour to a large mess of rice.*' And so the word
curry was born.

The early Company men took to curry as ducks to water, as we saw on
page 9. But the newer generations of Company men had less regard for
things 'native'. This may have been the fault of the memsahibs, who
allegedly despised curry. It was just another obstacle to be overcome in
India's rich tapestry, such as dust, heat, disease, dirt and servants. Curry
was perhaps the easiest to dispose of, under the illusion that it was a danger
to her digestive system. Even before the mutiny, curry had been relegated
to the second division, and that was certainly the case when my grandfather first arrived in India, in 1891. At first he wouldn't touch any 'native'
food. Little by little he became used to army-mess-style Anglo curries,
little more than stews with curry powder and sultanas added. It was not
until he married that real curry figured at all in his life. According to

Wyvern in his contemporary *Culinary Jottings from Madras* from around this same period: '*Curries now-a-days are only licensed to be eaten at breakfast, at luncheon, and perhaps at the little home dinner, when they may, for a change, occasionally form the pièce de résistance of that cosy meal.*' He goes on: '*Having thus lost caste, so to speak, it ought hardly to surprise us that curries have deteriorated in quality. The old cooks who studied the art, and were encouraged in its cultivation, have passed away to happy hunting grounds, and the sons and grandsons who now reign in their stead have been taught to devote themselves to more fashionable dishes.*'

Wyvern was not entirely correct, of course. In the homes of less elevated circles, such as those of my grandmother, curry, the real thing, was alive and well. Being born and bred in India had some advantages. Indeed, her principle reference work, her *Indian Cookery Book*, devoted many of its pages to the real thing. Wyvern knew that really. He admits: '*While it cannot be denied that the banishment of curries from our high art banquets is necessary, there can be no doubt that at mess and club dinners, at hotels and at private houses, these time honoured dishes will always be welcome.*'

There's an ironic postscript to the family story. After 40 years of service in the Indian Army, my grandfather finally retired. He said, on arrival in Portsmouth, '*Thank goodness for proper English meals and no more curries.*' But after about a month, he began to get withdrawal symptoms, and turned to my grandmother, saying, '*No curry?*' Anticipating this, she had already been round to the chemist to order her spices and ground masalas. The very next day she cooked her first curry in England. It was to be the first of many, and I was privileged enough to enjoy many of her curries in later years. She cooked it in the authentic Indian way, using spices correctly and avoiding dollops of raw curry powder.

It is appropriate, I think, to make curries the subject of the first chapter in this book. The recipes are based on those in the *Indian Cookery Book*. The results are not the pallid, insipid offerings of the Anglo canteen, they are truly Indian, with thick, creamy, tasty gravies as good as you'd get anywhere.

# CURRY MASALA MIX
## *Curry Stuff*

For this first recipe I make no apology for the fact that it has appeared in some of my previous curry books. Virtually this recipe first appeared in 1877 in my grandmother's *Indian Cookery Book*, although its weights are described in chittacks (see page 70). I have converted it for our use into measures we more easily understand. To the Indians a mixture of spices is called a 'masala'. The British called it 'curry stuff', curry condiments or curry powder. Whatever it is called, it has earned itself a poor reputation, probably not helped in 1861 when Mrs Beeton pronounced: '*Some persons prefer to make* [it] *at home; but that purchased at any respectable shop is, generally speaking, far superior.*'

She was decidedly wrong then, and she is now. It is infinitely better to make your own. That way, you know exactly what has gone in. Most of the recipes in this book do not require this Masala Mix. The individual spices they use are listed as required. But we do need this mix from time to time, and it is handy to keep in the store cupboard for use when required.

My grandmother's book advises us that: '*A curry stone and muller (pestle and mortar) are necessary for the preparation of condiments for daily use. The first cost of this of large size will not exceed one rupee, but will require re-cutting every three or four months, at a cost not exceeding one anna.*' fortunately we can use an electric spice mill or coffee grinder. The book goes on: '*However high prices may range, one rupee worth of mixed condiments, including hotspice, will suffice for a month's consumption for a party of from four to six adults, allowing for three curries per day, cutlets and made dishes included.*'

Devoted though they were to curries, even my family didn't manage three per day! There were thirteen rupees to the pound in 1900. I'm afraid it will cost you rather more to make this batch, which I imagine will last you a little longer. It is given in metric measures only, since it doesn't translate well to imperial, nor to chittacks. A heaped teaspoon gives you 5g of spices on average.

MAKES: 250G CURRY STUFF

| | |
|---|---|
| 60g coriander seeds | 20g garam masala (see page 39) |
| 30g white cummin seeds | 5g dry ground curry leaves |
| 20g fenugreek seeds | 5g asafoetida |
| 25g gram flour | 5g ginger powder |
| 25g garlic powder | 5g chilli powder |
| 20g paprika | 5g yellow mustard powder |
| 20g turmeric | 5g ground black pepper |

1    Roast the first three spices. To do this heat up a wok absolutely dry on the stove. Add the three spices (together) and stir continuously. Within seconds they will start to give off their wonderful aroma. Keep stirring. They will be 'roasted' enough after about 30 to 45 seconds. They must not burn. Remove them from the wok to cool down, then grind them as finely as you can.

2    Mix everything together and store in an airtight lidded jar, preferably in a dark place like a cupboard.

NOTE: *To make a dish for four you would need about 25g (1 oz) of this masala, so this amount would give you ten portions. It improves with age, and it will keep well for about eighteen months, but after that it will need replacing. It loses flavour and can go bitter.*

CURRY PASTE: You can make a paste from some or all of the above masala using water, which you then fry. The *Indian Cookery Book* is very interesting about making it into a preserved paste. The reference to the Cape is South Africa, of course. It is interesting to note that the Suez Canal opened in 1869, thus turning a four-month journey into one of just one month. The book says: '*Condiments prepared with water will not keep good for any number of days; if required for a long journey round the Cape therefore, as presents for friends at home, the best English vinegar should be substituted for the water and mixed with the masala to the consistency of thick jelly. Then warm some good sweet oil* [blended mustard oil] *and when bubbling, fry until the mixture is reduced to a paste. Cool and bottle.*'

# GARAM MASALA

Garam masala is an important, but not universally used, spice mixture. *'Garam'* means hot, and *'masala'* means mixture of spices, the heat coming from the peppercorns. But the point of it is to use aromatic whole spices in the masala, which is then added to a dish towards the end of its cooking. That way the aromatics are retained and not cooked away earlier on. To release these aromatics, or volatile or essential oils, which are locked inside each spice, it is necessary to cook them. In this case we apply heat to the spices without oil or water. The process is called 'roasting', and it can be done in the oven, or it can be done under the grill. However, the simplest and most economical way to roast spices is to cook them dry in a pan or wok on the stove.

Some of the recipes in this book require you to roast this or that spice. The technique is the same as for this recipe. As in the previous recipe, it is only practical to give metric measures here. Don't worry that your quantities are not precisely measured. There are as many recipes for garam masala as there are cooks, so there is enormous flexibility in what spice you might choose to use. Next time you may wish to vary the contents to suit your taste.

———————— MAKES: 400G SPICE MIXTURE ————————

140g coriander seeds
110g white cummin seeds
50g black peppercorns
30g cassia bark

30g brown cardamoms
15g mace
10g bay leaves (about 20 leaves)
15g dry ground ginger

1 Mix together all the items except the ground ginger. They now need roasting. To do this, heat up the wok absolutely dry on the stove. Add mixture and stir continuously. Within seconds the spices will start to give off their wonderful aroma. Keep stirring. They will be roasted enough after about a minute or two. They must not burn. Remove them from the wok to cool down, then grind them as finely as you can in an electric spice mill or coffee grinder.

2 Add the ginger and mix everything together. Store in an airtight lidded jar, preferably in a dark place like a cupboard.

# CHICKEN GRAVY CURRY

For this 'everyday' curry, the *Indian Cookery Book* tells you to: '*Take the usual full-sized curry chicken, the price of which has latterly ranged from three to four annas* [in those days there were 52 annas to the pound] *and divide it into sixteen or eighteen pieces.*' The recipe could equally be applied to kid, veal, beef, mutton, duck and young pigeon, the prices of the former three ranging from three to four annas and the latter four to six.

Here I will use chicken breast, which is readily available skinned and boned, its cost several hundred times more than it was in the Indian bazaars a century ago!

SERVES: 4

700g (1lb 9 oz) chicken breast, skinned and filleted
4 tablespoons ghee
2 to 4 cloves garlic, finely chopped
2.5cm (1 inch) ginger finely shredded
225g (8 oz) onion very finely chopped

1 tablespoon coriander, roasted and ground
½ to 2 teaspoons chilli powder
350ml (12 fl oz) chicken stock or water
2 teaspoons garam masala (see page 39)
2 tablespoons finely chopped fresh coriander leaves

1   Cut the chicken breast into bite-size chunks
2   Heat the ghee in the wok. Add the garlic and ginger and stir-fry for about 30 seconds. Add the onions, and lowering the heat, fry for about 12 to 15 minutes or until such time as the onions are browned, stirring from time to time.
3   Add the chicken, ground coriander and chilli powder, and stir-fry until the chicken is fully sealed, i.e. it doesn't look raw any more.
4   Add the stock or water little by little, simmering the chicken on a lowish heat for about 30 minutes, until the meat is quite tender and the liquid is reduced to half its quantity.
5   Add the garam masala and the fresh herbs, and salt to taste, simmering for about 5 more minutes, then serve.

# DOOPIAJAS

'*The literal translation of doopiaja,*' says the *Indian Cookery Book*, is '*two onions and the term is probably correctly applicable, as it will be noticed that besides the first quantity of onion, it is necessary to put in about an equal quantity of fried onion, thereby doubling the quantity. Doopiajas are more piquant curries,*' the book continues, '*and they are cooked with more ghee and less water than gravy curries.*'

I particularly like this superb piece of advice: '*It is necessary to impress upon the amateur artist, the importance of paying particular attention to the firing. A brisk fire will dry up the ghee and the water before the curry is half cooked, and necessitate the addition of more water, which in every instance will spoil the doopiaja, although the addition of a little water, if such be necessary when the curry is nearly cooked, will do it no harm.*'

So whether you are an amateur artist or not, let's get to work!

SERVES: 4

700g (1lb 9 oz) lean meat (any type) divested of all unwanted matter
3 tablespoons ghee
225g (8 oz) onion thinly sliced
3 tablespoons blended mustard oil
3 to 4 cloves garlic, finely chopped

110g (4 oz) finely chopped onion
250ml (9 fl oz) meat stock or water
2 or 3 fresh red chillies, shredded (optional)
2 tablespoons finely chopped fresh coriander leaves
2 teaspoons garam masala
salt to taste

SPICES

2 teaspoons roast and ground coriander
½ teaspoon ground cummin
1 teaspoon turmeric
1 teaspoon chilli powder

1   Cut the meat into cubes about 4cm (1½ inches) in size, remembering that they will shrink during cooking as the liquids come out.
2   Heat the ghee in the wok, and on a lowish heat stir-fry the sliced onions until they are brown and set aside in a casserole dish of about 2.5 litre (4½ pint) capacity.
3   Using the same wok, heat the mustard oil and stir-fry the garlic and

finely chopped onion for 3 to 4 minutes. Add the spices and continue to stir-fry for another couple of minutes.

4  Add the meat and fry for a few minutes to seal it.

5  Put the wok items into a casserole pot, cover and put into the oven, preheated to 190°C/375°F/Gas 5.

6  After about 15 minutes, inspect and add the stock or water, and optional chillies, and return it to the oven for a further 20 to 25 minutes.

7  Inspect again, this time adding the fresh coriander and garam masala. Return to the oven for a final 25 to 30 minutes, or until the meat is perfectly tender and the liquid is reduced to a thick consistency, about half its original quantity. Salt to taste and serve.

# KEEMA CURRY
*Mince*

I've based the recipe on one from the *Indian Cookery Book*, which tells you to: '*Get rather more than two pounds of good fat beef . . . rejecting all veins and scraggy portions, and if desired put up a broth of all the rejections.*' The *bobajee* (cook) had the onerous task of making mince by pounding the meat to a coarse texture. If it was pounded further, it was called 'forcemeat' and was used to make balls and kebabs, as in the next two recipes. Incidentally, the *bobajee* had patois names for everything. Mince was called 'eemince' and forcemeat 'farce'.

Here we'll use rather less than two pounds of best quality beef, already minced, and it will be lean, and minus scraggy portions! It will also be delicious, especially if you try it with some peas and pickle.

SERVES: 4

4 tablespoons ghee
225g (8 oz) onion, finely
  chopped
3 cloves garlic, finely
  chopped
1 or 2 fresh green chillies,
  chopped
450g (1lb) coarsely ground
  lean minced beef
150g (5½ oz) carrot
  chopped into small cubes

200g (7 oz) tinned plum tomatoes
1 tablespoon tomato ketchup
200g (700ml) tinned tomato soup
3 tablespoons finely chopped
  fresh coriander
2 teaspoons garam masala (see
  page 39)
1 tablespoon dried fenugreek
  leaves (optional)
salt to taste
225g (8 oz) mashed potatoes

SPICES

2 teaspoons freshly roasted
  and ground coriander

1 teaspoon turmeric
1½ teaspoon ground cardamom

1   Heat the ghee in a wok or frying pan. Add the onions, garlic and chillies, and stir-fry for about 4 to 5 minutes, by which time it will be nicely translucent.

2   Add the spices and a splash or two of water to keep things mobile, and stir-fry for a couple more minutes. Mix in the mince and stir-fry until it browns.

3   Put the stir-fry into a lidded casserole dish of a least 2.3 litre (4 pint) capacity, and place it, covered, into the oven, preheated to 190°C/375°F/Gas 5.

4   Cook for about 20 minutes, then add the carrot, tomatoes, ketchup and soup, stirring it all in well.

5   After a further 20 minutes in the oven, stir in the coriander, garam masala and fenugreek, and salt to taste.

6   Cook it for a final 20 minutes or so, then it is ready to eat.

NOTE: *this recipe is great in its own right, served with Indian breads or rice. It is also the base as stuffing (or, as the* bobajees *called it, 'estarffin') for curry puffs, page 78, shepherd's pie, page 80, and potato mince rissoles, page 151.*

# COFTA·KA·CAREE
## *Forcemeat Ball Curries*

We call forcemeat 'mince' these days, but in the days of the Raj it was called 'farce' by the *bobajees*, who had the job of pounding it to a pulp. The spelling of kofta curry is interesting too. Kofta or cofta means balls, and there are meat or vegetable versions. Recipes are given in the *Indian Cookery Book* for the usual beef, mutton and chicken. Additionally there is one for liver and udder which I have no wish to try.

I like the one for crab: '*Select 10 to 12 gheewalla kakrahs which are crabs full of red coral.*' About prawns the book says: '*It is impossible to quote any prices, the fluctuation being almost incredible. Fine large (bagda) prawns may be obtained one day at 2 annas for 20, and the very next day they will not be procurable at less than 8 annas for the same number.*'

About lobsters, it says: '*According to their size, take 8 or 10 lobsters.*' The book doesn't give their bazaar price, unfortunately, but at today's prices we are looking at half a week's pay just for the lobsters. Uniquely this recipe adds bay leaves and lemon grass. Fish is not overlooked either: '*Best for fish coftas are left overs, the remains of hermetically sealed fish, such as salmon and mackerel removed from dinner, are well adapted for making cofta curries. Some cooks add to cofta curries, ground hot spices, which are fried with the curry condiments, and are suited to most tastes.*'

I am one of those cooks whose taste is suited, and here I am using king prawns.

---

SERVES: 4

THE COFTAS

---

600g (1lb 4 oz) shelled cooked king prawns
4 cloves garlic
1 fresh red chilli
1 tablespoon roast, ground and crushed coriander seeds
1 teaspoon coarsely ground pepper

1 tablespoon finely chopped fresh coriander
3 tablespoons finely grated breadcrumbs
1 egg
½ teaspoon salt
some gram flour for rolling

3 tablespoons blended
   mustard oil
spices
2 cloves garlic, finely
   chopped
200g (7 oz) onion, finely
   chopped
1 or 2 fresh green chillies,
   chopped

600ml (1 pint) thick fish stock or
   water
2 teaspoons garam masala (see
   page 39)
2 tablespoons finely chopped
   fresh coriander leaves
salt to taste

SPICES

2 teaspoons curry masala
   (page 37)

1 teaspoon coriander
¼ teaspoon turmeric

¼ teaspoon chilli powder

1   Pulse the prawns and the cofta ingredients to a coarse purée in the
    food processor. Roll into balls about the size of a large walnut. Roll in
    gram flour.
2   Heat the oil in the large wok. Stir-fry the spices for about 30 seconds,
    adding a splash of stock or water to keep things mobile. Add the garlic
    and the onion and stir-fry for a further 3 or 4 minutes.
3   Add the coftas and stir-fry for about 3 more minutes to start to brown
    them.
4   Add the stock or water and allow to simmer for about 12 minutes,
    stirring as required.
5   Add the garam masala and fresh coriander, and salt taste, then serve.

# TICK-KEEAH KAWAB

By my reckoning *tick-keeah* means tikka. Tikka means a piece and it should,
I think, be the title of the next recipe and vice versa.

However the *Indian Cookery Book* requires us: '*to pound the meat, mix with
the condiments, form into balls of equal size, flatten them, pass them onto iron or*

*plated skewers about 18" long, rub well over with ghee, wrap them in a plantain banana leaf and roast or broil over a charcoal fire. Serve them hot, removed from the skewer. They are usually eaten with a chappattee.'*

Not bad instructions those, particularly if you like pounding, have a banana leaf to hand and charcoal fired up and running. We'll use the food processor, kitchen foil and the oven or grill. But they do make great barbeque food.

———————————— SERVES: 4 ————————————

450g to 600g (1lb to 1lb 4 oz) lean steak, divested of all unwanted matter

1 tablespoon natural yoghurt

1 tablespoon very finely chopped onion

1 teaspoon very finely chopped ginger

1 teaspoon very finely chopped garlic

1 teaspoon very finely chopped fresh chilli

1 teaspoon crushed peppercorns

½ teaspoon turmeric

1 teaspoon garam masala (see page 39)

½ teaspoon chilli powder

1 egg

1   Chop the meat into manageable pieces, which you then pulse through the food processor until you achieve a glutinous smooth texture.

2   Then, as the book says, mix in the 'condiments', i.e. the remaining ingredients.

3   Roll into balls the size of golf balls, and press flat to make a disc.

4   The kebabs can be oven baked. Put them on an oven tray, and into the oven preheated to 190°C/375°F/Gas 5 for 10 to 12 minutes. Or they can be grilled. Preheat the grill to medium heat. Line the grill pan with foil (to catch the drips and save on cleaning). Put the kebabs on the pan rack and slide the pan to the midway position. Grill for 10 to 12 minutes, turning once. Only if you barbeque them do they need to be covered with foil to prevent them drying up too much.

5   Serve hot or cold with salads and chutneys.

# SEIK KAWAB
## 'Curry on Skewers'

Today we know seik kawab, or sheek kebab, as ground meat on skewers (see previous recipe). The *Indian Cookery Book* describes this one as a: *'Hindoostanee curry . . . Pass the squares of meat, which have been marinated in the condiments, onto a silver plated or other metal skewer, and roast or broil over a slow charcoal fire, basting the whole time with ghee, to allow the kawab to become of a rich brown colour without burning or being singed in the basting. Remove from the skewers and serve hot. Seik kawab is usually eaten with chappatee* [sic] *or hand bread, and only occasionally with rice.'*

SERVES: 4

450g to 600g (1lb to 1lb 4 oz) lean steak, or leg of lamb or poultry
2 tablespoons mustard oil
4 tablespoons very finely chopped onions
1 tablespoon very finely chopped ginger
1 tablespoon very finely chopped garlic
2 teaspoons very finely chopped chilli

2 teaspoons roast and ground coriander seeds
1 teaspoon garam masala (see page 39)
1 teaspoon salt
½ teaspoon turmeric
6 to 8 tablespoons natural Greek-style yoghurt
juice of 1 lime
a little ghee

1   Chop the meat into squares of equal size, say 5cm (2 inches). Mix the remaining ingredients and marinate the meat for between one and six hours, covered in the fridge, turning it over occasionally to absorb the mixture.

2   Alternatively put the marinated meat chunks onto skewers. These will probably be bamboo skewers, about 20cm (8 inches) long. Give them a one-hour soak in water before use. This retards any burning of the bamboo.

3   Preheat the grill to medium heat. Line the grill pan with foil (to catch the drips and save on cleaning). Put the skewered kebabs on the pan rack and slide the pan to the midway position. Grill for 10 to 12 minutes, turning once. Baste with any spare marinade during the grilling.

4   Serve with salads and chutneys, and indeed 'chappatees' if you wish.

# HUSSANEE CURRY
## *'Curry on a Stick'*

This recipe is a follow-on from the previous one. Could this perhaps be the precursor of the now world famous tikka masala curry?

The *Indian Cookery Book* says: '*Small cubes of meat are threaded onto six silver pins, five inches long* [125cm] *or, in the absence of these, six bamboo pins.*' It goes on: '*Half a dozen sticks will be ample for four hearty diners.*' Since it requires us to serve up the dish without removing the sticks, one wonders how 'hearty' the diners remained when it came to dividing six by four!

---

SERVES: 4

450g to 600g (1lb to 1lb 4 oz) seik kawab (see previous recipe)

4 tablespoons ghee or light oil

2 to 4 cloves very finely chopped garlic

1 teaspoon very finely chopped ginger

200g (7 oz) very finely chopped onion

100g (3½ oz) Greek-style natural yoghurt

200ml (7 fl oz) stock or water

salt to taste

2 teaspoons garam masala (see page 39)

1 tablespoon very finely chopped fresh coriander leaves

1 tablespoon very finely chopped fresh mint leaves

---

SPICES

1 teaspoon coriander

½ teaspoon cummin

½ teaspoon chilli powder

½ teaspoon turmeric

---

1  Cook the kebabs following the previous recipe for Seik Kawabs

2  Before and/or during their grilling, make the gravy. Heat the ghee in the large wok. Stir-fry the spices, garlic and ginger for 30 seconds, then add the onion and continue to stir-fry for about 5 minutes.

3  When this is beginning to sizzle into a golden colour, add the yoghurt, and stir-fry this mixture until it starts to thicken.

4  Little by little add the stock or water, maintaining that glossy thickish texture. Salt to taste.

5  By now the kebabs are cooked. Simply transfer them, still on their skewers, to the gravy, and amalgamate them thoroughly. Add the

garam masala and fresh leaves, stir in and simmer for a final minute or two. Serve more or less at once with a dish of spicy rice and pickles.

6   Alternatively, remove the kebabs from their long skewers and pin each chunk of meat with cocktail sticks.


# KURMA OR QUOREMA CURRY

Whichever way you spell it, this dish was the favourite of the Moghul emperors. But here's a challenge from the author of the *Indian Cookery Book*, who said of this dish: '*This is without exception one of the richest of Hindoostanee curries, but it is quite unsuited to European taste if made according to the original recipe, of which the following is a copy.*' Well let's see now! Here are its ingredients, unexpurgated, apart from the conversions in brackets which are mine:

'*2lb* [900g] *meat, 1lb* [450g] *tyre or dhye* [yoghurt], *2 chittacks* [110g] *garlic, 1 dam cardamoms* [about 6], *4 chittacks* [225g] *bruised almonds, 4 mashas* [3 tablespoons] *saffron, juice of 5 lemons, 1lb* [450g] *ghee, 4 chittacks* [225g] *sliced onion, 1 dam cloves* [4 or 5], *1 chittack* [60g] *pepper, 4 chittacks* [225 ml] *cream, ¼ tsp gd garlic.*'

Well, Mister 'Thirty-Five Years Resident', I've got to admit, you were right. It's rich. More than that, just the saffron content alone would poison a Moghul emperor! Never mind the cost and never mind the amount of pepper and the ghee! And where are the vital aromatic spices? Actually, I think he certainly has got his weights wrong. None of the classic kormas I have come across in my travels in India would have been so excessive.

To be fair, he does give an alternative recipe, which does work. But strangely, he uses lemon grass in it. One statement which he did make is interesting. He wrote: '*Most Europeans give the preference to fowl quorema.*' Given that chicken korma is the second most popular dish at today's contemporary Indian restaurant (behind the modern invention of chicken tikka masala), it shows that tastes do not change much over the centuries.

Here is my absolutely delicious version of the classic Korma Kurma or Quorema.

SERVES: 4

675g (1lb 8 oz) fatless, boned
  lamb, cubed
2 teaspoons sugar
1 teaspoon salt
225g (8 oz) natural yoghurt
4 tablespoons butter ghee
  or vegetable oil
½ teaspoon turmeric
2 teaspoons coriander
2 tablespoons finely
  chopped garlic

1 tablespoon finely chopped
  ginger
8 tablespoons finely chopped
  onion
20–30 strands saffron
4 tablespoons ground almond
175ml (6 fl oz) single cream
akhni stock or water
2 teaspoons chopped fresh
  coriander leaves

WHOLE SPICES

15cm (6 inches) cassia bark
12 green cardamoms

10 cloves
8 bay leaves
1 teaspoon fennel seeds

GARNISH:

**some fresh coriander leaves**
**toasted flaked almonds to garnish**

1   Trim the meat of any gristle etc.
2   In a non-metallic mixing bowl, mix the sugar, salt, yoghurt, meat and whole spices, cover and marinate for 6 to 48 hours in the fridge.
3   Preheat the oven to 190°C/375°F/Gas 5.
4   Heat the ghee, then stir-fry the turmeric and coriander for 30 seconds. Add the garlic, ginger and onion and stir-fry for 10 minutes.
5   Combine this spice mixture with the lamb, place in a casserole and cook in the oven for 25 minutes.
6   Remove, inspect and stir, then mix in the saffron, ground almond and cream. Return to the oven for 20 more minutes.
7   Remove the casserole from the oven, inspect and, if necessary add a common-sense amount of stock or water if it looks too dry. Taste for tenderness. Judge how much more casseroling you need to reach complete tenderness. The meat should melt in the mouth. It will probably need at least 10 minutes more. It can be served straight away, garnished with the fresh coriander leaves and the flaked almonds, or reheated next day (some people prefer that, as it gives it more time to marinate). It can also be frozen.

# MALAY CURRIES

Malaya became British in 1786, when Penang was acquired from the local sultan. And Raffles established Singapore at a strategic point on the Malay peninsular. The indigenous population were of Indian descent, and their curries were coconut-based. The *Indian Cookery Book* gives recipes for Malay curries, which are quite authentic, using lemon grass, although the statement '*the seeds of coriander and cummin must on no account be put into Malay curries, or the delicate flavour of the cocoanut will be destroyed*' is a bit sweeping. Quite why the book gives no coconut-based curries from south India is a mystery in an otherwise definitive book on curries. That aside, this is a good recipe. So is the advice about making coconut milk, which fortunately we are spared thanks to tinned and powdered products:

'*It will be necessary to provide what the natives call a 'narial-ka-khoornee', which if interpreted means 'coconut scraper'. It is a small circular flat piece of iron, about the size and thickness of a Spanish dollar, the edges being notched. It is of rude construction, and fixed on a conveniently shaped wooden frame, also of rude construction. The best kind can be purchased for 2 annas. The nut is scraped or rasped with the aid of this tool, into very fine particles. It is then put into a deep vessel, and boiling water is poured over until it covers it. After allowing it to steep for 15 minutes, it is carefully strained through a clean napkin into another vessel or cup. This is cocoanut [sic] milk. The pulp is thrown away.*'

Without further rudeness, let's make a Malay prawn curry!

---

SERVES: 4

---

24 or so large raw king prawns each weighing about 30g (1 oz) in its shell
300ml (½ pint) tinned coconut milk
2 or 3 stalks lemon grass
18cm (3¼ inch) cinnamon stick
4 to 6 cloves
4 tablespoons sunflower or light oil

1 teaspoon turmeric
4 to 6 cloves garlic, thinly sliced
6 or so spring onions, bulbs and leaves, chopped
1 to 4 red chillies, shredded
8 to 10 fresh or dried curry leaves (optional)
salt to taste
some chopped fresh basil leaves for garnish

---

FACING PREVIOUS PAGE  TIFFIN OR PICNIC: Salgamundi Salad (page 83), Fruit Salad and Curry Puffs (page 78).
FACING PAGE  AFTERNOON TEA: Cucumber Propers (page 92) and Pickle Sandwiches (page 96), a selection of Pickles, Lemon Cheese Tarts (page 97), Mysore Coffee and Hindustanee Chupattis (page 100).

1   Peel the prawns, discarding the heads and tails. Cut the veins away from their backs, then wash the prawns thoroughly and dry them.
2   In a smallish non-stick saucepan, heat the coconut milk, the lemon grass, cinnamon stick and cloves. Bring it to the gentlest simmer, and allow it to reduce and thicken a little, by simmering for about 10 minutes, stirring occasionally.
3   Meanwhile, heat the oil in a large wok. Fry the turmeric for just a few seconds, until it goes a little darker, then add a tablespoon of water. Once that is sizzling, add the garlic and stir-fry for 30 seconds. Add the onions, and chillies and stir them to the sizzle.
4   Add the prawns and keep on stir-frying until they go pink. Add the curry leaves, then transfer this mixture to the saucepan.
5   Simmer for 10 minutes, stirring as required. Add minute quantities of water should it thicken up too much. Remove and discard the lemon grass. Salt to taste. Garnish with the herbs and serve with plain rice.

# PORTUGUESE CURRY
## *Vindaloo/Bindaloo*

Anyone who has not heard of vindaloo, must have come from another planet! It's the archetypal benchmark for today's curry restaurant's hot curry, and the butt of many a journalistic cheap joke. How many times have you tired of hearing about lager louts and their vindaloo habits?

The real thing was around long before the restaurants reinvented it to be just a hot curry, and though their interpretation included potato (*aloo*), this had no place in the original dish. The *Indian Cookery Book* says of it: '*This well known Portuguese curry can only be made properly of beef, pork or duck.*' And the book proceeds to give recipes for each. It also gives a recipe for vindaloo pork pickle, which culminates in the instructions: '*Put the pickle into a dry stone jar with patent screw top. Screw down the lid and cover it with a good sound bladder to render it perfectly air tight.*' Good sound advice, I'll be bound. But the book does not tell us of the dish's origins (partly because the British preferred not to admit to the Portuguese presence in Goa throughout their occupation of India). The dish, correctly pronounced 'Vin-dar-loo' (emphasis on the second syllable) originated in Portugal as *Vinho e Alhos,* where pork was marinated in wine and vinegar (*vinho*) and garlic (*alhos*). It did not take Goan Indians long to add chilli and call it 'Vindaloo'. In Goa pork is still the most frequently used ingredient, but the book is right. Duck and beef work equally well. Here it is with pork.

— SERVES. 4 —

675g (1lb 8 oz) lean leg of pork, off the bone, any fat, gristle and skin removed
3 tablespoons ghee or vegetable oil
4 to 6 garlic cloves, chopped

225g (8 oz) onions, finely chopped
2 tablespoons lemon juice
1 tablespoon garam masala (see page 39)
1 tablespoon chopped fresh coriander
1 to 4 fresh red cayenne chillies, finely chopped

salt to taste

— MARINADE —

200ml (7 fl oz) red wine
2 tablespoons red wine vinegar
4 to 6 garlic cloves, crushed
1 to 3 tablespoons finely chopped red chillies

1 teaspoon roast and ground coriander seeds
½ teaspoon roast and ground cummin seeds
1 teaspoon salt

— SPICES —

2 or 3 bay leaves
10 cloves
6 green cardamon pods

5cm piece (2 inches) cassia bark
1 teaspoon cummin seeds

1   Cut the meat into cubes about 4cm (1½ inches) in size, remembering that they will shrink during cooking as the liquids come out.
2   In a large non-metallic bowl, mix the meat and the marinade. Cover and refrigerate for up to 60 hours.
3   To cook: heat the ghee or oil in a karahi or wok. Stir-fry the garlic and the spices for a minute, then add the onions and continue to stir-fry for 5 to 8 minutes.
4   Using a 2.25 to 2.75 litre (4 to 5 pint) lidded casserole, combine the fried

ingredients, the pork and its marinade and place in an oven preheated to 190°C/375°F/Gas 5.

5    After 20 minutes, inspect and stir, adding a little water if it is becoming too dry.

6    Repeat 20 to 25 minutes later, adding the remaining ingredients. Add aromatic salt to taste. Cook for a further 20 to 25 minutes or until the pork is completely tender.

# EGG CURRY WITH GREEN PEAS

This, according to the *Indian Cookery Book*, was '*a favourite with some families in winter when English green peas are procurable*'. We can procure perfect frozen ones at any time, but shelling fresh peas is fun in season. The book tells us to use the doopiaja recipe (see page 41) and I am doing that, modifying it for this curry.

SERVES: 4

3 tablespoons ghee
225g (8 oz) onion, thinly sliced
2 tablespoons blended mustard oil
3 to 4 cloves garlic, finely chopped
110g (4 oz) finely chopped onion
250ml (9 fl oz) meat stock or water

2 or 3 fresh red chillies, shredded (optional)
2 tablespoons finely chopped fresh coriander leaves
2 teaspoons garam masala (see page 39)
6 to 8 hard-boiled eggs, halved
450g (1lb) frozen and thawed peas, or cooked fresh peas
salt to taste

SPICES

2 teaspoons roast and ground coriander seeds
1 teaspoon turmeric
1 teaspoon chilli powder
½ teaspoon ground cummin

1    Heat the ghee in the wok, and on a lowish heat stir-fry the onions until they are brown and set aside in a casserole dish of about 2.5 litre (4½ pint) capacity.

2    Using the same wok, heat the mustard oil and stir-fry the garlic and finely chopped onion for 3 to 4 minutes. Add the spices and continue to stir-fry for another couple of minutes.

3    Little by little add the stock or water, maintaining a bubbling simmer and a thickish texture. Add the optional chillies, fresh coriander and garam masala.

4    Keep simmering and stirring as needed until the liquid is reduced to a thick consistency, and is about half its original quantity.

5    Now add the eggs and the peas, and salt to taste. Once everything is good and hot, serve with rice and/or breads.

# SEAM ALOO MATTAR CHAHKEE CURRY
*Bean, potato and peas curry*

The *Indian Cookery Book* states: '*Chahkee is a term applied to vegetable curries, some of which are deservedly popular, and one in particular, using runner beans (muckun seam), potato and peas which many families have daily during the season these vegetables are procurable* [October onwards] *and yet never tire of.*'

Other popular vegetables are cauliflower, carrots, pumpkins, gourds, artichokes, and aubergines.

SERVES: 4

4 tablespoons blended
   mustard oil
½ teaspoon turmeric
2 or 3 cloves garlic,
   chopped
225g (8 oz) onion, very
   finely chopped
1 to 3 fresh red chillies,
   shredded
20 runner beans, de-stringed,
   and cut into 3

4 large cooked potatoes,
   quartered
250g (8 oz) frozen peas, thawed
1 tablespoon chopped fresh
   coriander leaves
1 tablespoon chopped fresh mint
   leaves
2 teaspoons garam masala
   (see page 39)
cup water
salt to taste

1   Warm the oil in the large wok. Add the turmeric, and stir-fry for about 20 seconds. Add a splash of water and the garlic, onion and chillies and stir-fry for about 5 to 8 minutes, by which time it will have begun to go brown.

2   Meanwhile, de-string the beans, and chop them into 3. Blanch them until they are almost tender then add them to the wok.

3   Add the potato and peas, herbs and garam masala, and stirring carefully, add the water little by little over about 3 minutes on a heat high enough to maintain the texture of the curry.

4   Salt to taste and serve with plain rice or bread.

NOTE: *A tasty variant is to add 6 tinned plum tomatoes with 2 or 3 (to taste) tablespoons of tamarind at the same time as the other vegetables.*

# BURTAS
*Spicy Mashes*

The *Indian Cookery Book* tells us: '*Burtas are mashes of potatoes and other vegetables with or without cold meat, fish etc. They are palatable and much liked by most Europeans as accompaniments to curry and rice.*' Of course, this minimally spiced dish makes a wonderful accompaniment to anything savoury, and it's quick to make.

---

SERVES: 4

---

8 or 10 well-boiled potatoes
2 or 3 tablespoons butter
juice of 2 limes
3 or 4 tablespoons cream

1 pink onion, chopped
2 fresh green chillies, shredded
1 teaspoon garam masala
(see page 39)

salt and pepper to taste

---

1 Mash the potatoes with the butter, lime juice and cream until you achieve the texture you require.
2 Add the remaining ingredients, including salt and pepper to taste. Serve hot or cold.

# DAL CAREE
*Lentil Curry*

In 1877 when the *Indian Cookery Book* was first written '*half an anna's worth of any dal will suffice for a party of four*'. The book tells us there are 16 annas to the rupee and research shows us there were 13 rupees to the pound sterling. So this curry would have cost just one two-hundred's of a pound, or an old penny! Fantastic value even in those days. The indomitable Mrs Beeton had a view about all this, of course. She wrote: '*Food in India is not dear, and the fact of only having to provide for the family and not for any servants makes a very great difference in the trouble of housekeeping. Indian cooks are clever, and will turn out a good dinner with simple materials which an ordinary English cook would waste or convert into the plainest meal.*' This is a rather different opinion from the Mrs B who declared that all Indian servants were cheats (see page 30). But even the mighty Isabella wasn't always right. All the live-in servants were fed by the household, especially the cook and his family. She was right about the cook, though. And this recipe proves it. Dal is highly nutritious, very filling and, served with plain rice and pickles, it is a fabulous meal. Even today this is probably the most economical curry there is.

## SERVES: 4

175g to 225g (6 to 8 oz) red lentils (massoor dal), split and polished
3 tablespoons ghee or oil
3 teaspoons black mustard seeds
1 teaspoon white cummin seeds
1 teaspoon turmeric
1 tablespoon curry masala (see page 37)

4 or 5 cloves garlic, sliced
450g (1lb) onion, sliced
2 to 4 fresh green chillies, chopped
20 fresh or dried curry leaves (optional)
2 teaspoons garam masala (see page 39)
3 or 4 tablespoons cream
salt

### GARNISH

some onion tarka (explained in the recipe)
some fresh coriander leaves

1   Pick through the lentils to remove any grit or impurities. Rinse them several times, then leave them to soak in water for a minimum of about 20 minutes, maximum 4 hours.

2   To cook, drain and rinse the lentils, then measure an amount of water twice the volume of the drained lentils, and bring it to the boil in a 2.25 litre (4 pint) saucepan. Add the lentils, and simmer for about 30 minutes, stirring from time to time. This should be enough water, but if the dal gets too dry add a little more water as required.

3   During stage 2, heat the oil in the wok. Add the seeds and stir-fry for about 10 seconds. Add the turmeric and curry masala and continue stir-frying for a further 30 seconds, adding splashes of water as needed.

4   Add the garlic, onion and chillies, and stir-fry on low heat for at least 10 minutes, preferably double that time, to achieve a tarka (well-browned spicy mixture). When you have, add the curry leaves and garam masala, stirring in well, then take the wok off the heat.

5   At the end of stage 2, add the cream. The dal should have cooked down to be quite well puréed. You can improve upon this by applying the electric whisk for a few seconds, if you wish.

6   Add most of the stir-fry items (keeping a few tablespoons behind) and mix them in well. Salt to taste.

7   Garnish with the remaining stir fry items, now called the tarka, and the leaves. Serve hot with plain rice and pickles.

# CHAPTER TWO
# BREAKFAST

THE RAJ DAY BEGAN at dawn to avoid working in the heat. A piping hot cup of tea and biscuits would be served on trays to the family in bed by the *khansamah* (butler) at the unearthly hour of 5.30am. This was called the *chota hazree* or little breakfast.

Most sahibs and some of the memsahibs would then go for a brisk horse ride to catch the cool of the morning air. Then they and the children would assemble on the verandah for breakfast proper.

Flora Annie Steel sniffily decried breakfasts in India as: '*horrible meals, being hybrids between English and French fashions. Then the ordinary Indian cook has not an idea for breakfast beyond chop, steaks, fish and quails.*' I believe she was alone in these views. And although at the turn of the twentieth century, breakfast could be a fairly massive meal, with a choice of several heavy meat dishes, such indulgences were by that time on the way out. My family recall a 'self-serve' style of breakfast with fresh exotic fruit or juice, and cereal, often oatmeal porridge with thick creamy milk from the household buffalo, followed by a choice of eggs, bacon, fish or kedgeree. Mrs Steel rants on: '*If the mistress is wise, servants are not allowed to stay in the room at breakfast. It is not necessary to have a tribe of servants dancing round the table ready to snatch your plate away at the least pause.*' Wrong again! The *khansamah* would be mortified if he were not allowed to bring in the hot bread and to pour the tea, coffee or hot chocolate. Toast, incidentally, was rarely requested, being an unpalatable, smoky affair because it was cooked over charcoal.

More adventurous families, the 'old hands', were not averse to Hindoostanee breakfasts, not every day, but from time to time. Chupattis, sweetened yoghurt and light curries such as a mooli were considered to be a breakfast treat. My selection of breakfast recipes here omits those with which we are still familiar, but includes the ones which are now rarely encountered. They are delicious at breakfast or as a snack at any time. If you cannot face curry at breakfast, try these recipes at another time of day.

# RUMBLE TUMBLE
*Buttered Eggs*

This recipe is a traditional Victorian favourite. Eggs are slowly cooked until they achieve a creamy consistency, whereupon it becomes a sandwich spread. It is, of course, a version of scrambled eggs, though it should be much creamier. Traditionally it should be spread onto hot buttered toast, while it is still hot, then allowed to cool.

Appropriately, for the first recipe in this chapter, it appears in my grandmother's cookbook as a note, written in her own concise, left-sloping handwriting. She called it Rummled Egg. The word rumbled is a great example of Raj 'servant-speak' or patois. Their tongues couldn't get round the word 'scrambled', and 'rumbled' passed into the language of both cultures. '*Stir one way with silver spoon,*' she wrote.

I've changed nothing, except to go metric and use a non-stick pan for the 21st century.

SERVES: 2

2 tablespoons butter
2 eggs
1 tablespoon single cream
salt

pepper
4 thin slices buttered white bread
  hot toast, crusts removed.

1   On a low heat, melt the butter in a non-stick frying pan.
2   Whisk the eggs then add them to the butter, with the cream, and salt and pepper to taste, stirring constantly until the mixture becomes thick like butter. To achieve smooth creaminess, do not allow it to become too hot.
3   Spread, whilst hot, onto hot buttered toast. Serve hot or cold.

NOTE: *Prior to spreading you can optionally add one, some or all of the following: chilli purée, tomato purée, corned beef, chopped anchovies, etc.*

# SCANDAL DOGS
## *Scrambled Eggs, Hindoostanee-style*

Between 1902 and 1908, my grandfather and the family were posted to Agra. The barracks where he worked were located within the walls of the Moghul Red Fort, which one could see across a *maidan* (common) a few hundred yards down the road from their bungalow. The father of the kids' best schoolfriend was the military horse vet, and a favourite pastime was to feed titbits to the Fort's horses. The 7th and 14th Hussars were stationed there at the time, and there was an alley where the kids would sit on a wall and watch the soldiers at bayonet practice in their colourful uniforms.

The bungalow was set in three acres of ground. At the rear, the compound went downhill to a lake where men walking waist deep would collect the green *singaras* (water chestnuts) and sell them in the bazaar. The kids would be sent by Granny with a few pice to buy fresh *singaras* from these men. They would then take them to my grandmother's cook, Thumbi, who boiled them until they went gun-metal grey.

From the compound at the rear you could just see the dome of the Taj Mahal, perhaps a mile away. A pathway curved around the lake and led directly to the world's most famous building. In those days no one seemed to mind that the kids climbed up the minaret towers, and even up inside the dome. One minaret had a sign saying 'no entry – walls unsafe'. That, of course, was the cue for the kids to climb up to the top, totally oblivious to the fact that the entire minaret might collapse with them inside into the nearby river Jamuna.

The compound was home to a number of clucking, plump brown hens who wandered around, laying their plump brown eggs wherever the mood took them. Thumbi had his own recipe with its own name for scrambled eggs. The spicing is really quite light, and it makes the eggs taste divine.

SERVES: 4

| | |
|---|---|
| 2 tablespoons butter | ⅓ teaspoon ground black pepper |
| 1 small onion (about 110g/ 4 oz) | ⅓ teaspoon turmeric |
| 1 clove garlic | sprinkling parsley or coriander leaves |
| 1 green chilli | salt and pepper to taste |

1   Heat the butter in a small non-stick saucepan. Peel and finely chop the onion, garlic and chilli, then stir-fry them in the butter with the pepper and the turmeric for about 10 minutes, until the contents are golden.
2   Add the eggs, mix in well, and stir-fry until you have the texture you require.
3   Season it with salt and pepper, and serve it with hot buttered crusty bread or toast, or as a sandwich filler, garnished with chives, parsley or coriander.

# EGGY SOLDIERS

Surely everyone's had fun with this true Victorian recipe. In fact it's not so much a recipe as a way to make the kids enjoy their food. Upper-class kids in Britain had their nanny in their nursery; Raj kids, their ayah. Pronounced eye-er', she was a servant of importance. She looked after the children. She was always married, sometimes with children of her own, and sometimes she performed the role of lady's maid as well. She was never a wet nurse, the *dhye* did that. She never lived in, since she had her own home and family to care for. When the children went off to boarding school, her job was finished.

Us ordinary mortals who had neither nanny nor ayah can just enjoy Eggy Soldiers anywhere, any time. But what better time than at breakfast. What better way to be spoilt than having your loved one bring them to you in bed. Hence the portion for a romantic twosome!

So, what are Eggy Soldiers? They are sticks of buttered toast which you dip into your soft-boiled egg. No recipe needed, but for those who say 'it's as easy as boiling an egg' there are a number of observations to make about egg boiling.

There are seven EC size grades, ranging from Grade 1, which is 70g or over; to Grade 4 which is 55–60g; to Grade 7, which is 45g or under.

To prevent an egg cracking when boiling it should be at room temperature, not straight from the fridge. Do not waste salt, oil or vinegar in the water. Simply prick the blunt end of the egg with a pin, piercing only just through the shell. This allows the air in the air sac to escape as it expands when immersed in the boiling water.

To hard-boil a Grade 1 egg, immerse it in boiling water. Remove after exactly 15 minutes and cool at once in cold water. Longer cooking results in a blue ring around the yolk. To soft-boil a Grade 1 egg takes 5 minutes. Smaller eggs take less time. A quail egg takes 4 minutes to hard-boil.

# JOLLY BOYS
*Egg fritters*

Until they were eight, the kids went to the local Military School. Each day they were collected and delivered in a bullock *ghari*. This lumbering form of transport, still prevalent in today's India, was the main form of transport then. The *ghari* is a two-wheeled cart, with seats on either side, enough for eight passengers. It is pulled by two bullocks, usually a pretty silvery grey in colour, their curved horns often gaily painted and adorned with colourful ribbons. It all sounds picturesque, but lively seven-year-old Frank managed to fall off and was lucky to escape being run over. Another form of transport, now mercifully extinct, was the 'dandy', a litter on poles, between which was perched the occupant, hauled by two strong servants. My grandfather hated having to use them. He preferred his horse, and later his bicycle. Whatever they travelled in, the family enjoyed Jolly Boys.

They are a kind of fritter, made with a seasoned egg and flour batter, which is fried like an egg. Served with lashings of crispy bacon, they were breakfast favourites. Thumbi, by the way, would prefer to add chilli and garlic, and a pinch of ground cummin. And so can you, if you wish.

| | |
|---|---|
| 2 eggs | ½ teaspoon salt |
| 60g (2 oz) corn flour | 6 tablespoons vegetable oil or |
| 175ml (6 fl oz) milk | clarified butter (ghee) |

1　Beat the eggs with the flour, milk, and salt (and Thumbi's extras, if required) to achieve an easily pourable batter.

2　Heat the oil or butter on a medium heat.

3　Spoon in a quarter of the batter, shaping it with your spoon so that it is a circular disc. Repeat with the other three quarters. Fry for about 3 minutes, spooning hot oil over the tops.

4　Turn them over and fry for a further minute or two, until they are as crispy as you want them.

5　Serve with crispy, hot bacon crumbled over them.

# POTATO BACON CAKES

On the *maidan* (common land) which was alongside the family bungalow, a goatherd (*buckri wallah*) used to bring his animals to graze. One day, having got very thirsty romping around, and since the goats were on the *maidan*, with the herder nowhere to be seen, my mother and her brothers Frank and Jim decided to help themselves to some 'free' milk. Undaunted by not having milked a goat before, Jim grabbed an unsuspecting nanny, while the others started attempting to squeeze the contents of the udders into their mouths, without a great deal of success. Not surprisingly, the goat was uncooperative. It leapt into the air emitting a huge bleat. At that precise moment, the goatherd reappeared. He too was uncooperative, and with a series of bloodcurdling yells he gave chase to the rapidly disappearing youngsters.

They'd have probably got away with it, except for the fact that one of my grandfather's peons (orderlies) happened to witness the entire scene from a nearby office window. Recognising the perpetrators, he reported the incident to Grandpa. The kids got a good military ticking off, and were grounded for some time.

This dish is a great way to use up left-over cooked potato at breakfast time. It is a breadcrumbed fried rissole, made of mashed potato at the centre of which is chopped ham and/or crispy bacon.

SERVES: 4

2 tablespoons finely chopped ham
2 tablespoons finely chopped crispy bacon

12 tablespoons mashed potato
1 egg
2 tablespoons golden breadcrumbs

1   Mix the ham and bacon, and divide it into four.
2   Divide the mashed potato into four. Take one of these quarters and carefully wrap it round the ham/bacon. Shape it into a rissole.
3   Repeat with the other three quarters.
4   Whisk the egg, put it into a saucer, and coat each rissole with it.
5   Dab each rissole in the breadcrumbs, achieving an even coating.
6   Heat the oil in a frying pan. Fry the rissoles until golden.

# SIDNEY'S KIDNEYS

When she was eight, my mother attended Agra's Jesus and Mary convent school. The year was 1918, and the horrors of the Great War had just ended. That was a long way from India, and eight-year-old kids knew nothing about horrors. But one of the war stories which did the rounds amongst the kids at school was about a Major called Sidney. No one can now remember whether this was his surname or his Christian name. Nor does it matter. Before the war he'd served in Agra, but volunteered for the Flanders trenches. There he lost a leg before returning to Agra to retire in some considerable pain. He also had something wrong with his kidneys, or so it was said. A favourite breakfast Raj dish was devilled kidneys. Since the unfortunate Major was a near neighbour, he was frequently on Grandpa's verandah complaining of his pains. And since Thumbi would have nothing at all to do with the devil, this dish became known to our family as Sidney's Kidneys, under which pseudonym it was transformed into Raj magic by Thumbi!

Liver or a combination of liver and kidney is equally good.

SERVES: 4

350g (12 oz) lamb kidney
3 tablespoons butter
1 clove garlic, finely chopped (optional)
1 or two fresh red chillies, deseeded and chopped

1 teaspoon yellow mustard powder
½ teaspoon chilli powder
2 tablespoons tomato ketchup
2 teaspoons Worcester sauce
salt to taste

1   Halve or quarter the kidneys, and plunge them into boiling water for one minute. This removes the bitter taste. Drain them and rinse them to remove any scum.
2   Chop the kidneys into tiny pieces.
3   Heat the butter in a frying fan, add the garlic and chillies, and stir-fry for about 30 seconds.
4   Add a tablespoon or two of water, being careful about the splutter, then add the mustard and chilli powder, stir-frying for a further 30 seconds.
5   Add the kidneys, and stir-fry for about 3 minutes. Add the tomato ketchup and Worcester sauce, and stir-fry until it is all cooked. About 3 to 5 more minutes will do it.
6   Salt to taste and then serve on hot buttered toast

# KHUMBI THUMBI
*Devilled Mushrooms*

This was the family name for a celebrated dish of the day, devilled mushrooms. There were several 'devilled' things which Thumbi was suspicious of. Devilled kidneys, he didn't mind, because they had a different name. Devilled Ham was rather different. It came from the stores in tins. All it contained was potted, peppered ham, but Thumbi, who was a Hindu and not a Moslem, and was partial to a little ham or pork now and again, would never open that tin until the label was removed. His friend, a *bobajee* at a neighbour's bungalow, who was a Goan Indian and a Christian to boot had much to tell Thumbi about pork, the Portuguese and El Diablo. Since Hindus have many gods and many devils, Thumbi thought it circumspect not to tempt fate by cooking one. Why risk life and limb, especially over an ingredient as mundane as a mere fungus. So the family christened the dish Khumbi Thumbi. Since mushroom in Hindi is *khumbi*, no one was more pleased than Thumbi. And since honour and safety first were both satisfied, Thumbi always turned out delicious devilled mushrooms from then on.

SERVES: 4

450g (1lb) mushrooms, any type
3 tablespoons clarified butter (ghee)
2 cloves garlic, finely chopped (optional)
½ teaspoon shredded ginger (optional)
1 or 2 fresh green chillies, thinly sliced

1 to 2 teaspoons anchovy sauce (optional) or salt to taste
1 teaspoon Worcester sauce
1 teaspoon coarsely ground black pepper
½ teaspoon chilli powder
1 or 2 tablespoons port or Madeira
2 or 3 tablespoons single cream

GARNISH

some parsley leaves
some snipped chives

1  Wash the mushrooms, and only peel them if they need it.
2  Heat the butter in a medium-sized saucepan. Add the garlic, ginger, and chillies and stir-fry for about 30 seconds.
3  Add the mushrooms, anchovy sauce (or salt to taste), the Worcester sauce, the pepper and the chilli powder, and stir-fry for about 3 or 4 minutes.
4  Add the port or Madeira and the cream. When well integrated, garnish and then serve with crusty fresh rolls or bread.

# KITCHRI HINDUSTAN

The first written reference to this dish was by the Moroccan explorer Ibn Battuta, on his eight-year voyage to India. He said, in 1342: '*The munj (moong dhal) is boiled with rice and then buttered. This is what they call Kishri, and on this they breakfast every day.*' In 1590, the Moghul emperor Akbar's chronicler, Abul Fazl gives a recipe: '*Take 5 seer each, rice and split dal and ghee, and ⅓ seer salt. This gives seven dishes.*'

My grandmother's cookbook helpfully tells us about dry weights in the bazaar, that 1 seer is 16 chittacks, 5 seers is 1 pusseree, and that 8 pusserees equals 1 maund. Liquid measures, on the other hand, are as follows: 5 siicas are 1 chittack, 4 chittacks are 1 pow, 4 pows are 1 seer.

But if you happen to be in Bengal, all weights are different. Equally when buying grain, remember 5 chittacks equal 1 coonkee, which equals ¼ raik, where 1 raik equals 1¼ seer. And we haven't yet defined tolas, mashas, rutees, pallies, soallies or khahoons! No wonder the new memsahibs found this new world strange enough to drive them round the coonkee!

In her own handwriting Grandmother noted that 1 seer equals 2lb. But she was used to the bazaar. And she would have remarked that Fazl's recipe would have fed 170 not 7!

Here is her truly authentic kitchri recipe from 1902, taken as printed. My only adjustments are to reduce the onion content from 12 to 2. You may wish to reduce the ghee content. Otherwise it is a truly workable and fascinating recipe.

---

SERVES: 4

---

| | |
|---|---|
| 300g (10½ oz) ¾ *coonkee* basmati rice | 1 or 2 teaspoons shredded ginger |
| 150g (5½ oz) ½ *coonkee* red split lentils (massoor dal) | 1 teaspoon black peppercorns |
| | salt to taste |
| 450g (1lb) onion | 10 cloves |
| 110g (4 oz) 2 *chittacks* ghee | 3 or 4 cardamoms |
| | 6 bay leaves |
| 6 small sticks cassia bark | |

---

1 Take rather more than three quarters of a coonkee of bassmutee [sic] rice and a half coonkee of dal.

2 Take 2 large curry onions, and cut them up lengthways into fine slices.

3   Warm up two chittacks ghee (but before doing so, be careful to warm the pot) and while bubbling, throw in the (washed) dal and rice.

4   Fry until the dal and rice have absorbed all the ghee, then add the onion, a few slices of green ginger, some peppercorns, salt to taste, a few cloves, 3 or 4 cardamoms, 6 bay leaves, and as many small sticks of cinnamon (cassia bark).

5   Mix well together. Add as much water only as will cover over the whole of the rice and dal. Put a well-fitting cover on, and set over a slow fire, reducing the same from time to time as the water is being absorbed. Care must be taken not to allow the kitcheree to burn, which may be prevented by occasionally shaking the pot, or stirring its contents with a wooden spoon.

6   Serve up quite hot, strewing over it the fried onions, which serve both as a relish and garnish of the dish.

⁂

## KEDGEREE
*Breakfast rice with fish*

One of the greatest of all cookbook writers wrote under the name Wyvern at the peak of the Raj. His major opus *Culinary Jottings from Madras* is a lively and brilliant social account of the gastronomic times. Wyvern was later discovered to be an Indian Army colonel named A. R. Herbert Kenny, whose accounts of his servant Ramasamy's activities totally accord with all other Raj servants. They had a '*patois which is easily acquired, and you will soon find yourself interpreting the mysteries of Francatelli or Gouffé in the pidgen English of Madras with marvellous fluency. You will even talk of "putting that troople", "mashing bones all", "minching", "chimmering" etc etc without a blush. There can be no doubt that in Ramasamy we possess admirable materials out of which to form a good cook. We should, moreover, remember that a dish once successfully presented will not necessarily appear so again unless the artist be reminded of the secrets of its composition.*'

One dish which Wyvern's Ramasamy, EHA's Domingo and our Thumbi needed no reminding about was kedgeree. Wyvern describes it as the English type of kitchri, being composed of boiled rice, chopped hard-boiled egg, cold minced fish (usually smoked haddock) and a lump of butter. These are all tossed in the frying pan with pepper, salt and any minced garden herb you can get your hands on, such as cress, parsley or marjoram, and served smoking hot.

SERVES: 4

4 tablespoons butter
500g (18 oz) cooked boiled rice
2 hard-boiled eggs, chopped

50g (1¼ oz) cooked smoked haddock, chopped
1 teaspoon coarsely ground black pepper
½ teaspoon salt

2 or 3 tablespoons chopped fresh herbs (see above)

1   Using a medium-sized saucepan, heat the butter, then add the rice and stir until it is hot.
2   Mix in the remaining ingredients, and serve at once.

# LHASSI
*Yoghurt Drink*

In my grandmother's day, cowrie shells were still traded in India as money. 4 cowries made 1 gunda, 5 gundas made 1 pice, 4 pice made 1 anna, and 16 annas made 1 rupee. Then there were thirteen rupees to the pound sterling. To get an idea of value, her *Indian Coookery Book* advises, that '*it is not unusual to see tables groaning with viands, the most costly a few unpretending fresh green chillies in a small glass urn with water, particularly on breakfast tables, the actual cost of which never exceeded four cowries.*' Consider too that the cook's wages would be between 7 and 30 rupees a month.

This is a favourite drink in India now, as it was in the days of the Raj. It is a mixture of yoghurt, crushed ice and water (optional). Two versions are both excellent at any time of day, especially breakfast. To the savoury version, lhassi namkeen, add pepper, chilli and salt. To the sweet version, Lhassi meethi, add sugar and rose water. Both take just a few seconds to make.

SERVES: 4

8 ice cubes
225g (8 oz) plain Greek-
style yoghurt
up to 300ml (10 fl oz water)
(optional)

½ teaspoon ground white pepper
⅓ teaspoon chilli pepper
(optional)
salt to taste

1 Crush the ice in an ice-crusher and transfer to a tall glass.
2 Put everything in a liquidiser and blend together. Pour into the glass, over the crushed ice, and serve.

NOTE: *For a sweet yoghurt drink, in place of the water use milk as an alternative, and in place of the salt, chilli and pepper, use sugar to taste, and a few drops of rose water or orange water if you have some to hand.*

# CHAPTER THREE
# TIFFIN (LIGHT LUNCH OR SNACKS)

ONE OF THE BIBLES of the Raj community was the publication *Hobson Jobson*. It appeared first in 1886 and was a glossary of colloquial Anglo-Indian words and phrases (see page 26). It describes tiffin as deriving from an English slang term, 'tiffing', eating or drinking outside of meal times, and a 'tiff', a draught of liquor or beer. By the time of the Raj, the word had fallen into disuse in England, but in India it had come to mean a light lunch taken, it seems, at any time between 1 o'clock and 5 o'clock. But sometimes, tiffin was no light meal.

Wyvern wrote: '*There are luncheons large and luncheons small, the former elaborate, very pleasant, and sociable, yet, alas, a little too alluring, and fatal in their effects for the rest of the day.*' He also bemoaned a change in fashion: '*An old standing dish to commence a luncheon party, used to be mulligatawny (soup). I say reserve it for your luncheon at home when alone, enjoy it thoroughly and nothing more.*'

Flora Annie Steel, decreed that '*heavy luncheons or tiffins have much to answer for in India. People at home invariably eat more on Sunday, because they have nothing else to do; so in the hot weather out here people seem to eat simply because it passes the time. If the object of the luncheon party is to have a really pleasant time for sociable conversation, stuffing the guests into a semi-torpid state certainly does not conduce to success.*'

On weekdays my grandfather was typical in that he would have his lunch on the hoof at his desk, or sometimes literally on horseback visiting outlying stations. Wyvern again: *'The office snacklet is, as a rule, a sandwich followed by a slice of cake, itself acceptable at every kind of luncheon; in fact cakes were invented for that meal, for five o'clock tea, for weddings and for schoolboys.'* Not surprisingly, sour-puss Mrs Steel did not agree: *'Many people do not care for cakes.'*

The word tiffin is still universally used in India. It is the norm to see special purpose, round stainless steel dishes which stack one on top of the other, three or four high, neatly clipped together, being carried by the men, going off to their place of work in the morning. Each container holds a different curry, rice or bread and are eaten at lunchtime. They are called 'tiffin carriers'.

Sometimes when the children were away at boarding school and my grandfather was visiting outlying stations, or at the mess, Grandmother would be on her own. At the other extreme, when the family was assembled, the bungalow would be full to bursting. No matter which, tiffin would always be served at precisely one o'clock. Here are some family favourites. They are ideal as light snacks at any time.

## OLIVE SANDWICH

Their sahib's wealth was a matter of paramount concern to all Raj servants, since their status amongst their peers was determined by it. Tinned provisions and sauces were some of those luxuries by which wealth was measured. They were, according to Wyvern, often part of a *'vast collection . . . which resided in the store room'*. He goes on: *'A butler's ideas about stores are, on the whole, very mixed: he worships 'Europe articles' and delights in filling the shelves of the store room with rows of tins, of which some may perhaps be useful, but many . . . remain untouched and lumbering the shelves of the cupboard.'* Olives and olive oil were in those days considered out and out luxuries. Olives themselves appeared, as they do now, as accompaniments to drinks. Olive oil wasn't actually all that popular.

But here is a vintage recipe using both. It could, for all the world, have come straight out of a modern trendy restaurant's menu. It's worth putting into your repertoire. Best enjoyed with a salad and a glass of something sparkly.

SERVES: 4

24 to 30 stoned olives, any unstuffed kind
1 or 2 fresh green chillies, finely chopped

1 clove garlic, finely chopped
4 to 6 tablespoons extra virgin olive oil

1   Chop or mash the olives. Mix together with the chillies and garlic.
2   Heat the olive oil in a pan. Add the mixture, and stir-fry for about 2 minutes.
3   Cut a crusty baguette in half longways and spread the mixture onto it, liberally dousing it with more olive oil if the mood takes you.

# SALMON CHILLI

Raj military children became well used to boarding schools, though they didn't always like them. For my mother and her sister Alice it started when they were tinies in Agra. During the First World War, when my grandfather was posted to southern Persia, my grandmother went to stay with her mother in Agra. The two girls were sent to Agra's Jesus and Mary convent. But since this was at the other side of the city, it was felt safer to make them boarders. Alice hated it, and taking Mum with her she tried to abscond by scaling the convent wall in broad daylight. The *mali* (gardener) ran and told the nuns, who ran out *en masse* in a state of shocked horror. When my grandfather heard of this he had the girls moved to Jubalpore, where their brothers were, and everyone was much happier. The kids always had tuck boxes, with such luxuries as canned fish for treats. Any canned fish such as salmon, pilchard, herring or tuna will do for this recipe. By adding the spicing, the contents are transformed into a really delicious snack, served with salad or in a sandwich.

SERVES: 4

1 small onion (about 100g/ 4 oz)
400g (14 oz) can of salmon

2 tablespoons vinegar, any type
1 tablespoon mayonnaise
salt to taste
chilli powder to taste

1  Finely chop the onion.
2  Open the can and inspect the salmon, discard any bones, then mash all the ingredients together.
3  Serve with salad on toast, or as a sandwich filling.

༺✤༻

# CURRY PUFFS

༺✤༻

Curry Puffs are, perhaps, one of the best examples of east meets west, or Raj meets Indian, that I can think of. They are a kind of sausage roll where, instead of sausage meat, the filling is minced curry. When I was a kid at boarding school, I used to ask my mother to make me a supply of Curry Puffs to take back with me at the beginning of term. She used to make a flat oven tray's worth, about what you'll get from this recipe. When cut into pieces, it made about 36. I used to eat one a day, and being very careful not to let my friends know I had them, let alone share them, they'd last me about a month. I remember that by that time they tasted a little musty. How they didn't go off, I'll never know. They certainly weren't refrigerated! Please use yours up within a few days kept in the fridge. They will freeze, of course, but they're so good piping hot (or, as I prefer them, cold) that I doubt there will be any left to freeze.

MAKES: 36 CURRY PUFFS

400g (14 oz) frozen puff pastry (or homemade)

THE FILLING

about 500g (1lb 2 oz) cooked Keema Curry (see page 42)

1   Allow the pastry to thaw, then divide it into four equal pieces.

2   Carefully roll out one piece to about 22 cms (9 inches) square by 3mm (⅛ inch) thick (a). Then cut the square into three strips each about 7.5 cms (3 inches) wide (b).

3   Put a line of filling down the centre line of one of the strips (c).

4   Wet one side of the strip, then fold the pastry over the filling, pressing the edges firmly together.

5   Brush with a glaze of water or egg white, and spike the roll a few times to let the air out when it cooks.

6   Repeat until all the strips are finished. You can freeze them now, if you wish.

7   To cook, put the 12 strips onto a greased, flat oven tray, and into the oven, preheated to 190°C/375°F/Gas 5. Bake for about 20 minutes, or until the pastry is well browned.

8   Cut each strip into three (d). Serve hot or cold with salad and chutneys. They can be frozen when cold.

(a)                        (b)

(c)                        (d)

# SPICY SHEPHERD'S PIE

This was a good old standby of every Raj family. It was simple for the cook to make, and was a reliable way to use up left-overs from the night before. At its simplest, of course, it is a minced meat base, topped with mashed potato.

The *bobajee* (cook) wasn't content with doing it the bland old English way. He always added spices. This version uses a traditional keema (mince) curry, and is absolutely amazing as a variant to curry and rice. Incidentally, the pronunciation of this dish was another tongue twister to the *bobajee*. It was known universally as '*Essepad Spy*'. Try it with peas and pickles for a change.

### SERVES: 4 TO 6

450g (1lb) mashed potato
2 or 3 tablespoons thick
  double cream
1 egg yolk
salt to taste
ground black pepper to
  taste

450g (1lb) cooked Keema Curry,
  see page 42
the white from the 1 egg
a knob or two of butter
chilli powder
some snipped chives

1  Preheat the oven to 190°C/375°F/Gas 5.
2  Mix the potato with the cream, egg yolk and salt and pepper to taste.
3  Using a suitable size oven pan or casserole dish, put the curry in first, then top off with the mashed potato. The *birwachi* enjoyed making artistic swirls with his well-licked fingers. You may prefer to do so with a fork! Brush on the egg white for a glaze.
4  Place the pan the middle of the oven and bake it for 20 to 30 minutes, or until the potato crust is suitably golden.
5  Garnish with the butter, a sprinkling of the chilli powder and the chives. Serve it on the table, piping hot from the pan.

# FRIAR TUCK'S MOCK VENISON PASTRY PIE

Pies were a great Victorian institution, and contained anything savoury or sweet, particularly left-overs. They were good hot or cold, and were therefore ideal for Raj lunches. Of course, they are a meal in themselves, and are as good for the evening meal as well. As for mock venison, i.e. lamb, there is no reason why you cannot use the real thing. Even in Mrs Beeton's day, 1861, it would have been common. She says: '*Generally speaking, India abounds with game. Deer of many species are to be found in different parts of the country, and most of them afford excellent venison. High up in the Himalayas the ibex (wild goat) and the ovis amon (wild sheep) are to be found, and wild boar too. The bison is shot, and affords beef. Bears in great variety are found in the hills, and hunters appreciate the hams and stewpans prepared in the Russian fashion.*'

I do not know how Friar Tuck got into this recipe. But it's there in the *Indian Cookery Book*, and I'm sure it was a family favourite. By the way, in the book, the previous recipe is for Alderman's Mock Turtle Pie. This is what it tells you to do: '*Make an extra rich hash of a calf's head. Make an extra strong stock with 8 calfs' feet.*' You can experiment with that if you wish. Meanwhile, here's the mildly modified bear-free recipe for Friar Tuck's pie.

————————— SERVES: 4 TO 6 —————————

450g (1lb) diced stewing steak or lamb or venison
a cupful of flour
3 tablespoons ghee or oil
175g (6 oz) onion, chopped
1 tablespoon finely chopped ginger
1 to 4 cloves finely chopped garlic
1 or 2 fresh red chillies, chopped (optional)

4 beef or pork sausages
6 strips streaky bacon
3 tablespoons finely chopped fresh coriander
500g (1lb 2 oz) shortcrust or puff pastry
some melted butter for the pie dish
1 beaten egg

## SPICES

| | |
|---|---|
| 1 teaspoon garam masala (see page 39) | 6 small sticks cassia bark |
| 2 blades mace | 12 crushed allspice seeds |
| | 1 teaspoon white pepper |
| 1 teaspoon salt | |

## THE GRAVY

| | |
|---|---|
| 300ml (½ pint) chicken or vegetable stock | 1 or 2 teaspoons Worcester sauce |
| 3 to 6 tinned oysters (optional) | 125ml (4 fl oz) port |
| ⅓ teaspoon nutmeg | 1 tablespoon fresh lemon or lime juice |
| | salt to taste |

1   Dredge the meat well in the flour.

2   Heat the ghee or oil in a wok or saucepan. Stir-fry the onion, ginger, garlic and chillies for about 5 minutes. Add the meat, sausage and bacon, and stir-fry until it is well sealed, i.e. for at least 6 to 8 minutes, adding just enough water to keep things mobile.

3   Add the spices and the fresh coriander, lower the heat and simmer for about 10 to 15 minutes, stirring and adding enough water to make it creamy, not dry.

4   Meanwhile, roll out the pastry. Line a buttered pie dish with a thick layer of pastry, building up the sides and edges of the dish with it. Leave enough pastry for stage 5. Add the meat mixture and its stock.

5   Top off the pie dish with a layer of pastry, sealing the edges thoroughly. Trim round the edge to release spare pastry, which is best made into a decoration on the pie top (flowers or strips). Make a hole in the centre with a knife tip, to allow hot air to escape while cooking, and brush on the egg for a glaze.

6   Bake for around 1 to 1½ hours in the oven, preheated to 190°C/375°F/ Gas 5.

7   Heat the stock and the oysters in a saucepan. Simmer for about 20 minutes, stirring from time to time, until it starts to reduce.

8   Add the remaining ingredients and continue the reduction until it is as thick as you wish it to be. Serve the pie, hot or cold, with a selection of vegetables and gravy.

FACING PAGE   THE CHOTA PEG AND SAVOURIES: The Commander-in-Chief Punch (page 107), Sherry Cobbler – in the cocktail glasses (page 110), Russian Eggs (page 178), Turkish Toasts (page 178), Cheese Crab (page 179).

# SALGAMUNDI
## *Decorative Salad*

This is described in *Larousse Gastronomique*, 'the world's greatest cookery encyclopaedia', as: '*an elaborate salad laid out on a large flat round dish with each ingredient minced (ground), shredded, or sliced, and arranged attractively in small rings or rounds of contrasting colour. Cold meats, fish, cooked vegetables, salads and pickles – anything can be used. The word is also used figuratively to mean a miscellaneous collection of things.*' All this suited the *bobajee* very well. As we have seen on page 71, this dish gave him all the opportunity in the world to do his adored '*mashing bones all*', '*minching*', '*chimmering*' and '*chredding*'. As to arranging miscellaneous things in rings of contrasting colours . . . ! It was all a gift for using up the left-overs. Here we are using egg, prawns, salmon, carrot, coleslaw, sweetcorn, peas and beetroot. There is no limit to what your imagination will dream up.

### SERVES: 4

4 hard-boiled eggs, sliced
4 tablespoons mayonnaise
milk
salt to taste
pepper to taste
chilli powder to taste
150g (5½ oz) prawns in brine
½ teaspoon paprika
100g (3½ oz) soured cream
100g (3½ oz) tinned red salmon

2 tablespoons tomato ketchup
1 teaspoon Worcester sauce
½ teaspoon chilli powder
1 tablespoon vinegar
200g (7 oz) tinned sweetcorn
2 or 3 tablespoons plain Greek-style yoghurt
85g (3 oz) shredded carrot
85g (3 oz) coleslaw salad
85g (3 oz) peas
60g (2 oz) beetroot

### THE BEDDING

your choice of lettuce leaves, radiccio, chicory, rocket, watercress, and/or chives

FACING PAGE DINNER DISHES: Delicious Curry Soup (page 115), Beef Olives (page 140) with Roast Onion Surprise (page 157), and Mango Fool (page 172).

some onion rings
some juliennes of cooked
   sliced ham and/or beef
some olives

your choice of finely chopped
herbs, such as sorrel,
horseradish leaf, chives, mint,
red chillies etc

1   Mix the hard-boiled eggs with the mayonnaise and enough milk to make it still thick but mobile. Season with salt, pepper and chilli powder.
2   Drain the prawns from their brine. Mix them with the paprika and soured cream. Season as above.
3   Mix the tinned salmon with the ketchup and Worcester sauce, the chilli powder and vinegar.
4   Mix the sweetcorn with the yoghurt and season as above.
5   Arrange the lettuce and leaves as a bed on a large serving plate.
6   In any configuration or pattern of your choice, arrange the already made up items above, along with the shredded carrot, coleslaw salad, peas and beetroot.
7   Garnish and keep chilled in the fridge until ready to serve.

# SPICY LIVER

This is quite delicious, and so simple. It's ideal at lunchtime or for a snack or starter. Note the brandy, for fun, and the use of Worcester sauce, with which Wyvern was not impressed. He said: *'All native cooks dearly love the spice box, and they all reverence "Worcester sauce". Now I consider the latter too powerful an element for indiscriminate use in the kitchen, especially where our cooks are inclined to over flavour everything. If in the house at all, the proper place for this sauce is the cruet stand where it can be seized in an emergency to drown mistakes, and assist us in swallowing food that we might otherwise decline. But it should be preserved from Ramasamy with the same studious care a bottle of chloroform from a lady suffering from acute neuralgia.'* On the subject of spices, Wyvern evidently shared the earliest views of my grandfather that his food should be minimally spiced: *'Spice, if necessary, should be doled out in atoms. The cook ought never to have it under his control.'*

Well, there's no mistake with this recipe. Who knows, you might even want more Worcester sauce to pep it up further!

SERVES: 4 AS A SNACK

450g (1lb) lamb liver
25g (1 oz) butter
1 tablespoon olive oil
1 or 2 cloves garlic, finely chopped
100g (3½ oz) onion, finely chopped

1 fresh red chilli, shredded
½ teaspoon chilli powder
50ml (2 fl oz) brandy
1 teaspoon Worcester Sauce
1 tablespoon tomato ketchup
salt to taste

1. Chop the liver into bite-size pieces.
2. Heat the butter and oil in the wok. Add the garlic and stir-fry for about 30 seconds. Add the onion, chilli and chilli powder and continue to stir-fry for a couple of minutes.
3. Add the liver, and stir-fry for about 5 minutes. Add a few judicious splashes of water to keep things mobile, as needed.
4. Cut through a large piece to check whether it is cooked right through.
5. Once it is, add the brandy, Worcester sauce and the ketchup, stir-frying until it is all amalgamated.
6. Serve piping hot with crusty or Indian bread and pickles.

# ESTARFEGS
*Stuffed Eggs*

Here the hard-boiled eggs are stuffed with another of those Raj luxuries, tinned sardines. Other traditional stuffings included cooked shredded chicken or turkey, or ham, or prawns. Thumbi, like all *bobajees*, liked the notion of stuffing (estarffin) things. It is very tactile, of course, but finger licking must be avoided during the process, the avoidance being not a notion greatly approved of by Thumbi and his kind. The other contribution he made to the recipe was the addition of garlic and chilli, both optional if you wish, but both sensational!

——————————— MAKES: 8 EGGS ———————————

8 hard-boiled eggs, shelled
4 tinned sardines in oil
1 or 2 tinned anchovies
1 fresh red chilli, finely
  chopped (optional)

1 clove garlic, finely chopped
  (optional)
mayonnaise
Greek-style plain yoghurt
salt and pepper to taste

1   Carefully cut the top off each egg, and scoop out the yolk. Cut a sliver off the bottom of each egg to make it stable enough to stand up.
2   Chop up the egg whites (the tops and bottoms) and mix with the yolks.
3   Remove the sardine bones and mash them with their oil.
4   Finely chop the anchovy.
5   Mix together with all the remaining ingredients to achieve a thick paste.
6   Fill the empty egg white cases.
7   Serve with salad and crusty bread.

# PAKORA

An onion bhaji by any other name! And that's what a pakora is, another name for onion bhaji. It's a special kind of fritter, and it's today's 'Top of the Pops' starter dish at the Indian restaurant. There's nothing new about it, not to the Indians. It had been around in that country for centuries, long long before the English arrived. And it's still one of the country's most popular snacks. Naturally it became equally popular as a Raj snack at lunchtime. It makes a good starter for a main meal too.

Its first secret, which must never be varied, is its use of gram flour in the batter. The filling here is onion, but any dry vegetable will do, such as cauliflower florets, peppers, chillies, potatoes, carrots, or mushrooms. Equally good are small pieces of raw chicken breast, or small prawns. The next secret is to use the ingredient of your choice raw, even chicken. Ten to 12 minutes in the deep fryer will cook it to perfection. The final secret is to use clean, deep-fry oil at exactly the right temperature: too hot and it burns, too cool and the pakora becomes an unpleasant soggy mush. Get it just right and the result is a dry, not oily, fritter which is crisp on the outside and soft and cake-like on the inside.

---

MAKES: 8 PAKORAS

## clean vegetable oil for deep-frying

THE FILLING

### 225g (8 oz) onion

THE BATTER

110g (4 oz) gram flour
  (besun)
1 teaspoon coriander
  roasted and ground
1 teaspoon ground cummin
1 teaspoon garam masala
  (see page 39)
½ teaspoon turmeric
½ teaspoon chilli powder

1 garlic clove, finely chopped
1 teaspoon salt
1 teaspoon bottled mint
3 tablespoons natural plain
  yoghurt
2 tablespoons finely chopped
  fresh coriander
sufficient water to make a thick
  batter

---

1   Chop the onion into thin strips, about 2.5cm (1 inch) in length.

2   Mix the batter ingredients together, then use just sufficient water to achieve a thickish paste which will drop sluggishly off the spoon. Let it stand for at least 10 minutes, during which time the mixture will absorb the moisture.

3   Next mix the onion in well. Again leave it for a further 10 minutes or so, to absorb.

4   Meanwhile, heat the deep-frying oil to 190°C/375°F (chip-frying temperature). This temperature is below smoking point, and will cause a sliver of batter to splutter a bit, then float more or less at once.

5   Inspect the mixture: there must be no 'powder' left, and must be well mixed. Then scoop out one eighth of the mixture and place it carefully into the oil. Place all 8 portions in, but allow some seconds between each one so that the oil maintains its temperature. Fry for 10 to 12 minutes, turning at least once. Remove one from the oil, drain well on kitchen paper and cut it in half to ensure that the middle is fully cooked. If not, return both halves to the oil and continue until all are cooked.

6   Sprinkle with salt and garam masala and serve piping hot with salad and chutneys.

## HAM TRENCHERMAN

The three bachelors who lived in the bungalow next door to the Mhow bungalow were sergeants. They often played with the kids, and on one occasion took them to their very first cinema outing. The year was 1918. The film was a melodramatic comedy, and even 80 years on my mother remembers the sad look on the heroine's face when she was being bullied. She would remember it. Not because it was the first movie she had ever seen, good enough reason in itself, but because the actress's name was Wanda Hawley, and Hawley was, of course, the family name. Mum doesn't remember the name of the film, but a little research indicates that it was most probably Ms Hawley's first film, a silent called *Old Wives for New*. In the interval the sergeants bought the kids lemonade. A trencher, by the way, is an old word for a wooden platter, or chopping board, or it is a person who enjoys the pleasures of the table, i.e. a hearty eater. Needless to say, the chaps would have been trenchermen, and like all members of the Raj, they liked their egg with toast. This recipe is a spicy, hammy scrambled egg, an easy enough thing to make, especially at lunchtime.

SERVES: 4

| | |
|---|---|
| 2 tablespoons butter | 1 teaspoon English mustard |
| 3 eggs | 3 or 4 leaves sage, chopped |
| 2 or 3 slices of cooked ham, finely chopped | 1 clove garlic, finely chopped |
| | 1 fresh chilli, finely chopped |
| salt to taste | |

1 Heat the butter in a non-stick pan. Put the eggs in and stir gently.
2 As soon as it starts to set, add the remaining ingredients, and stir until it sets sufficiently to your taste.
3 Serve hot, on hot buttered fingers of toast.

## A NICE WHET

Major Sidney's dog had puppies. The family took one in because it was small, sweet and wriggling. Soon it grew up to be huge, snuffling and snoring. It was a bloodhound. One day it bit Frank on the calf, and it had to go. The neighbouring sergeants loved it, and took it to become their regimental mascot. Another dog bit my mother on her thigh, a monkey bit Bill on the wrist, a snake was observed eating a frog, and a stripy squirrel gave birth to a litter on top of the ceiling broom, a delicate brush on the end of a tall slender cane.

Pests were more common than pets. Flying ants were a menace, especially during the monsoon. They smothered the oil lamps so that the rooms went dark. Huge scorpions walked across the rooms with impunity. Chiplees, a sort of anaemic lizard, were 'glued' to the walls and ceilings. Well, almost. One fell into Mum's hair one time, much to her consternation. On one memorable occasion, the family was shocked to see the tail of a deadly poisonous greensnake wrapped around my grandfather's tennis racket and walking stick. When challenged, it raised itself up and hissed. The servants all went running, leaving Grandpa to knock it down the verandah steps and kill the four-foot monster.

This is a simple little dish, with a funny name. It's a kind of variation on Welsh rarebit. Traditionally they were served with good old Indian beer in the pint bottle. Maybe that's where the funny name came from.

SERVES: 4

**8 small slices white or brown bread**

THE TOPPING

100ml (3½ fl oz) soured
  cream or crème fraîche
125g (4½ oz) grated
  Cheddar cheese
2 teaspoons gentleman's
  relish (optional)

1 teaspoon English mustard
½ teaspoon Worcester sauce
1 teaspoon chilli powder
salt to taste

1   Mix the topping ingredients together.
2   Remove the crusts from the bread if you wish. The Raj would have!
3   Toast the bread on both sides.
4   Whilst still hot, spread on the topping.
5   Put them under the grill, preheated to medium heat.
6   They are ready when they blacken a bit. Serve piping hot.

# CHAPTER FOUR
# AFTERNOON TEA

Tᴇᴀ ᴘʀᴏʙᴀʙʟʏ originated in India, but it was exported to China centuries before Christ, where it was called Char-i-khitai. The King of China was partial to a herbal hot water infusion called Char or Tey in AD 851. Centuries later the East India Company brought back tea to Britain, and it became a popular beverage in the seventeenth century. In a 'coals to Newcastle' operation, the British took tea back to India, where they established enormous plantations mainly in Darjeeling, Nilgiri, Assam and Ceylon. By the time of the Raj tea was the major hot infusion. The Hindi name for tea is Chai and it entered the English language, immortally, as the slang Cuppa Char.

Tea planters lived a charmed life in beautiful, though isolated, surroundings. They may have been looked down on by the snobs, but afternoon tea was an important ritual in all the households of the Raj. Flora Annie Steel said: '*Afternoon teas are outclassed by tennis parties, though these are a form of entertainment suitable to the limited purses of most people.*' What she meant was that it was far cheaper and easier to do one's main entertaining at this hour, than at dinner. Coffee plantations were established in the Mysore area, and Mysore coffee was as popular then as now, and was drunk as much at tea time as any other time.

At tea time the memsahibs met and exchanged recipes, views and gossip. Many a reputation must have been made or lost in these gatherings, for once the memsahibs formed an opinion about something or someone, neither heaven nor earth could change that view – only the memsahibs had the power to do it.

My grandmother's cookbook gives no clue as to her own involvement in such circles, and I suspect she had little time for the gossips. She had her own circle of like-minded, down-to-earth friends, and she loved making cakes (see page 193). Her book is filled with handwritten recipes for her afternoon tea sessions. Here are some of them.

## CUCUMBER PROPERS

Raj folk were regarded as less than proper when they returned home to Blighty, especially when they started cooking their weird food. Friends of our family related how, when they went on a long holiday (furlough) to England, they took their curry masalas with them. The first time they cooked with them, it was not long before there was a knock on the front door. Two policemen had been called by neighbours because of the peculiar smell coming from the house. The friends took the policemen into the kitchen, where they could see for themselves that no body burning or other weird ritual was in progress. Mind you, this was in the 1920s, and Indian food was rare enough to be confined to just one restaurant, Veeraswamy's in Piccadilly, at that time. A far cry from the 10,000 restaurants which exist today!

Cucumber propers suffered no such racism. They are the very sandwiches which graced the drawing rooms of Victorian England. They are simply thin slices of white bread, with the crusts removed (because they said crusts were hard to eat while remaining dignified), thinly spread with soft butter, and filled with thin slices of cucumber, with the green skin removed (because they said it gave you indigestion). Simply season, and add a little chilli powder too to make it Raj. And that's that, and quite delicious and proper they are too. By the way, to make it more proper still, don't forget to keep your little finger in the air!

# FANCY NANCY

My late Aunty Alice was the 'glamour girl' of the family. She was a snappy dresser, and fancied herself at all the new dance styles, like the Charleston. It was Alice who, years later, spotted my love of curry and gave me one of her prize possessions, my grandmother's *Indian Cookery Book*. Back in the twenties, one essential family servant who visited the bungalow daily was the *nappi* (the barber) who was responsible for wet shaves and haircuts. Seventeen-year-old Alice's current boyfriend had a thoroughly fashionable waxed moustache, of which he was exceedingly proud. One day he came to spend the weekend at the family's bungalow. Alice said to the *nappi*, '*I hate that matchstick moustache. Cut it off.*' Servants obeyed orders. The *nappi* was no exception, and he did it. Off came the moustache while its proud owner was asleep in bed. Needless to say, that was the end of that relationship.

Fancy Nancy, by the way, is a sort of savoury biscuit, which was an age-old standby in case the fresh bread man, the *roti wallah*, didn't show up.

MAKES: 4 BISCUITS

250g (8 oz) strong white flour
200ml (7 fl oz) milk

2 teaspoons baking powder
1 teaspoon sesame seeds
1 teaspoon wild onion seeds
1 teaspoon salt

1 Mix the flour together with the milk and all the ingredients to make a pliable dough. Knead it, then let it rest for about 20 minutes, then knead it again and divide it into four balls.

2 Flour your worktop, then roll out each of the balls to a circle about 1.25cm (½ inch) in diameter.

3 Put them onto a non-stick oven tray and into the oven preheated to 190°C/375°F/Gas 5.

4 Bake for about 15 minutes, or until golden brown.

5 Eat hot or cold with lashings of butter.

# BROWN GEORGE

If Alice was a glamour girl, my mother was a tomboy. As an eight-year-old in Mhow, she wanted to play with her brothers. Bill, Frank and Jim were all older, of course, and did not take too kindly to a little girl becoming attached. And they didn't make it easy for her. But Trudi was not to be deterred. She learned to throw stones like the boys, and to whistle with her fingers in her mouth. I wish I could do that. At over 80, she can still hail a London taxi more effectively than anyone I know. And she climbed into, and fell out of more trees than anyone could count. The kids had a childhood the like of which one cannot imagine. They scrambled around the jungle countryside, jumped across rivers and prowled the valleys, braving jackals, snakes and foxes, and got up to all sorts of pranks, unbeknown to any adult. It was all good fun, and probably far less dangerous than it seemed to eight-year-olds. Trudi could pack a punch too. On one occasion when Billy Austin, the little boy next door, called her a sissy, she punched him in the face, which earned her a parental scolding, but the eternal admiration of the brothers. She became a fully fledged member of their tribe.

---

### MAKES: 4 BISCUITS

250g (8 oz) stoneground wholemeal or ata flour
200ml (7 fl oz) milk
4 tablespoons double cream
¼ teaspoon salt

2 teaspoons baking powder
1 tablespoon ghee or butter
1 tablespoon sugar
½ teaspoon fennel seeds
¼ teaspoon lovage seeds

---

1   Mix the flour together with the milk, cream and all the other ingredients to make a pliable dough. Knead it, then let it rest for about 20 minutes, then knead it again and divide it into eight balls.
2   Flour your worktop, then roll out each of the balls to a circle about 1 cm (½ inch) in thickness.
3   Put the circles onto a non-stick oven tray and into the oven preheated to 190°C/375°F/Gas 5.
4   Bake for about 10 minutes, or until golden brown.
5   Eat hot or cold with lashings of butter.

# CINNAMON TOAST

When one of my grandmother's best friends, a Mrs Thackeray, became prematurely widowed, a common occurrence in the Raj because of the ever-present threat of disease, she had to give up the life of memsahib, to become governess to the Maharaja of Indore's son. On more than one occasion, my mother, who was the same age as the young prince, was invited to stay at the maharaja's Palace. She recalls the splendour of the buildings, the massive ornate gardens, hundreds of servants in gorgeous uniforms, and the sheer wealth. She especially loved the outings, called *machan*, on the backs of elephants. The maharaja had his own private zoo, Mum recalls, complete with tigers and many rare animals. The young prince discarded many a toy, and Mrs Thackeray would often bring the kids such first class toys as dolls, a toy pram, a dolls' house, a toy railway, model soldiers, complete with fort, the lot!

This was a common Raj afternoon tea offering, where cinnamon was mixed with sugar, spread on toast, and then lightly grilled. The notion of spicing up honey with cinnamon was an interesting variant.

MAKES: 4 SLICES

1 tablespoon brown granulated sugar

1 teaspoon ground cinnamon

4 slices white or brown bread

some unsalted butter

1  Preheat the grill to medium heat.
2  Mix the sugar and the cinnamon together.
3  Lightly toast the bread, and while the toast is still piping hot, butter it, then spread one quarter of the sugar mixture onto each slice.
4  Put the toast back under the grill until the sugar melts. Serve at once.

## SPICY SANDWICHES
*Ham Combo*

The ever sensible Wyvern adored sandwiches, and some of his suggestions are as good now as they were in 1885, when he first suggested them: '*Ham and beef sandwiches should make your nose tingle with mustard. Any potted meat, worked up with butter, pepper, a touch of mustard, and a little chutney. Pound a slice of cheese well with a little fresh butter, mustard, pepper, and anchovy. Pass it through a sieve, and spread it on your bread, with a dusting of Nepaul [sic] – chilli – pepper. Fill a sandwich with chopped sardines and some bits of pickle here and there; or with mixed chicken and tongue, a lettuce leaf and some mayonnaise, shallots and a dust of chilli. Fillets of anchovy with slices of olive, embedded in pounded hard-boiled egg and butter with Nepaul pepper compose a very eatable sandwich.*'

The combination of ham, chicken and cheese was a favourite of my family, and is a favourite of my wife Dominique. Another of her favourite combinations is turkey and a soft cheese like Brie and cranberry jelly. Both of these are considerably enhanced by the addition of hot mango chutney or a pickle. A lettuce leaf adds a little crunch.

## PICKLE SANDWICHES

Any Indian pickle, such as lime, brinjal, mango, chilli, or prawn ballichow etc., is just wonderful as a sandwich spread. You don't need butter, but you can add mango chutney or a curry paste to boost things.

# LEMON CHEESE

It's lemon curd by another name. I don't know why the Raj called it lemon 'cheese'. It doesn't resemble cheese in any way. A possible explanation is that 'cheese' was an Anglo-Indian slang expression, which *Hobson Jobson* says is used to describe *'anything good, first-rate in quality, genuine, pleasant or advantageous'*. They believe its derivation is from the Persian and Hindi word 'chiz' meaning 'thing' or 'good thing', and this recipe is certainly that.

MAKES: ABOUT 500G (1LB 2 OZ)

| | |
|---|---|
| 6 egg yolks | 110g (4 oz) butter |
| 3 egg whites | 450g (1lb) caster sugar |
| juice of 3 lemons | |

1  Beat the eggs.
2  Melt the butter and the sugar over a low heat.
3  When they are well melted, using a whisk, add the eggs and whisk until it starts to thicken.
4  Add the lemon juice. Take off the heat and allow to cool.

# LEMON CHEESE TARTS

Even if you haven't got the time to make the lemon cheese or curd in the previous recipe, and pastry, you can make these delightful little tarts using shop bought, bottled lemon curd and ready made short crust pastry.

MAKES: AT LEAST 16 TARTS

| | |
|---|---|
| 150g (5½ oz) shortcrust pastry | 100g (3½ oz) butter |
| or | 2 tablespoons caster sugar |
| 150g (5½ oz) plain white flour | 16 teaspoons lemon cheese or curd |

1    If you are using ready made pastry, skip to stage 4. To make your own pastry, sieve the flour into a cool bowl to aerate it.

2    Cut the butter into little knobs, add it to the flour. Rub both together using your fingertips. Cold hands work, hot ones don't. Add the caster sugar, mixing with a spoon. Add cold water little by little, mixing it until it starts to combine. Using your fingers as little as possible (to keep it as cool as possible) make it into a cohesive ball of pastry.

3    Now cool the pastry down as much as you can by covering it and putting it into the fridge for a couple of hours or so.

4    Flour your worktop and roll out the pastry until it is about 5mm (¼ inch) thick. Cut it into discs with a pastry cutter. Place them into a tart tin.

5    Prick the top of the pastry to allow the air to escape.

6    Put the tart tin into the oven preheated to 190°C/375°F/Gas 5, and bake for 12 to 15 minutes, or until the pastry is golden.

7    Dollop on the lemon curd.

8    Serve hot with clotted cream, or cold on their own.

# DARJEELING TEA

Author Jennifer Brennan, herself a memsahib of the final generation, tells us in her memoirs *Curries and Bugles* published by Viking in 1990: '*The British who spent their entire lives in India became, in their advancing years, "old India hands" (that is to say somewhat opinionated experts on all things Indian). Seasoned and weathered by floods, riots, droughts, insurrections and deaths of both friends and enemies alike, they resembled venerable oak trees surviving in alien soil. It was their custom, upon entering a house (theirs or anyone else's), to throw their topee (pith helmet) on to the hall table and shout "Keehai" – meaning literally "who's there?" But in truth, the peremptory call was a demand for the nearest Indian servant to come running. This idiosyncrasy earned for them the not always affectionate nickname "old keehais".*'

Thanks to our association with India, the British today are the world's greatest tea drinkers, consuming on average 1,650 cups a year per head. In these days of blended tea bags, it is easy to forget how good tea is. Here are a few hints on how to produce a really good cup of tea.

1  Use only freshly poured tap water from the cold tap. This ensures maximum oxygen in the water.
2  Boil more water than you need.
3  Pre-warm the teapot while the kettle boils (use the hot tap).
4  As the kettle comes to the boil, empty the teapot of hot tap water and put in your tea.
5  The minimum is one teaspoon or tea bag per cup, plus one or two 'for the pot' if you like it stronger.
6  Add the boiling water. Put any spare in the cups to warm them.
7  Allow the tea to stand in the teapot brewing for 3–5 minutes, then empty the cups just before serving.

## HINDOO CHAR

You can be sure to find this milky, sweet, cardamom-flavoured beverage wherever there are Indians. Certainly the *bobajee* would keep a constant brew going in his kitchen. EHA's Domingo (see page 26) would have been sure to have one to hand as he composed a menu for his sahib in the patois of the *bobajee*: '*Soup: Salary soup; Fis: Heel fiss fry; Madish: Russel Pups and Wormsil Mole; Joint: Roast Bastard; Toast: Anchovy Poshteg; Puddin: Billimunj and Ispunj Roli*'.

It's almost a shame to translate. If you'd like to have a go yourself, cover up the sentence below and ponder it while you sup a cuppa char!

Celery; hilsa fish; made dish: small rissoles and vermicelli à la moelle, i.e. with beef marrow; roast basted; poached egg; blancmange and sponge roll.

──────────── PER CUP: ────────────

| | |
|---|---|
| tea leaves or tea bags (as normal) | 1 cinnamon stick |
| | evaporated milk |
| 4 crushed cardamom pods | sugar |

1   Prepare ingredients for the number of cups you wish to serve.
2   Put the right number of full cupfuls of half cold water and half milk into a saucepan and add the ingredients.
3   Bring to the boil and simmer for 3 minutes.
4   Serve with evaporated milk and sugar to taste.

# HINDOOSTANEE CHUPATTIS

This simple recipe is a great example of the combination of the two cultures. Here Indian bread, the flat unleavened chupatti, is served with butter and sprinkled with sugar or spread with jam. The cooks could, and often did, make both chupattis and homemade jam, and the combination was the Raj children's favourite.

The *roti* wallah (bread man) was a daily visitor to the bungalow and the family looked forward to seeing him. On his head, he carried a large tin box. Inside were fresh, hot English loaves and biscuits. Granny would make her selection, and the kids would clamour for an immediate taste. One particular treat was especially popular. The twice-daily milk supply was always boiled before it was consumed. When it cooled, a thick cream formed. The kids used to take it in turn at teatime to spread the cream on their bread, and eat it with lashings of jam. Canned jam (the now defunct IXL brand sent by post from Calcutta's Army and Navy store) was their favourite. Try any of these ideas, especially the chupattis. Serve with Mysore coffee or piping chai (Indian tea) from the previous recipe.

———————————— MAKES: 8 CHUPATTIS ————————————

**225g (8 oz) ata or wholemeal flour**
**water**
**butter or clotted cream**
**jam**

1   Put the flour into a bowl, and add enough water to make a pliable
    dough. Knead well for 5 minutes.
2   Set aside and leave for 20 minutes, with a damp cloth covering.
3   Re-knead the dough and divide into eight equal parts. Sprinkle flour
    on a board and roll out each of the dough parts into a 15cm (6 inch)
    disc.
4   Dry cook the chupatti in a hot dry frying pan for about a minute on
    each side. Whilst piping hot, spread with butter or cream and jam.

# CHAPTER FIVE
# THE *CHOTA* PEG

MRS BEETON OBSERVED: '*Drink is the greatest expense in housekeeping in India. The climate is a thirsty one, and the water is bad, and so filled with animalculae that it cannot be drunk with safety unless it is boiled and filtered. Then it is so flat and unpalatable that it is necessary to add something to make it more pleasant to the taste. One of the most refreshing drinks is lime juice and water, and iced tea is another very pleasant beverage. Bottled beer is a favourite drink, but this, as well as draught beer, is expensive. Still, drinking is, after all, more of a habit than a necessity: and those in India who wish to preserve their constitutions should drink as few "pegs" (as the brandies and sodas and other drinks are generally denominated) as possible.'*

The strict rule was that alcohol was never served before 6pm. That was the time when the sun set below the 'yard arm', originally a nautical term for a particular mast. The peg was indeed the measure. It was a finger width in the bottom of the glass. The members of Grandfather's mess used to joke that the best combination was small glasses and an *abdar* (wine waiter) with large fingers. The other joke was that each 'peg' was a peg in your coffin! The *pau* peg was a 'small measure' (one finger width), dismissed as ridiculous, '*even for the memsahibs*'. Best liked was *chota* peg or the 'little snort' and it was precisely two fingers of spirits. The *burra* peg was a 'large measure' of three fingers.

Some of the functions at the officers' mess were glittering occasions. Grandpa recalled that assembly for the formal dining night would usually be at 8pm. After an hour or so of the 'peg', the glamorous assembly in mess kit and long gown would move (stagger?) into the dining room for dinner. The *abdars* and bearers were always smartly dressed in dazzling white Indian 'pyjama' suits, with royal blue turbans and matching cummerbunds, adorned with brass regimental badges. The drinks were served in beautiful cut glasses on silver salvers. Canapés accompanied the drinks on more salvers. Examples today might include olives, nuts, curry vol-au-vents, and Bombay mix.

The drinks themselves included well-known subjects like sherry, rum, whisky, vermouth and gin. In around 1860, tonic water and bitter lemon were invented by the drinks firm Schweppes. Both contained quinine, thought to be good for the prevention of malaria, and ginger ale and ginger beer were also created in India. Beer, or rather ale, was imported from England as early as the 17th century. From early next century it was brewed in India under the brand name East India Pale Ale. A drink which was extremely popular, but now forgotten, was the gimlet, gin and fresh lime. The *Indian Cookery Book* has some other long-forgotten homemade concoctions, some of which I have reproduced here. Cheers!

# GIMLET

Gimlet is gin served with concentrated lime juice. The latter can either be the juice of fresh limes (*nimboo*) or it can be Rose's lime cordial, very popular indeed in the latter days of the Raj. Fresh juice gives a tarter, fresher taste, and sugar or sugar syrup was often added with soda water to lengthen the drink. Old Indian hands would sometimes add salt to the fresh juice version (instead of sugar) as part of their daily salt ration. Salt was needed to replace what was lost through perspiration, especially in the heavy uniforms and dress they all wore. Failure to do so would result in very painful cramps.

Gimlet rather faded into obscurity with the demise of the Raj, which is a pity because it is a most refreshing drink.

SERVES: I

**1 measure gin**
**½–1 measure fresh lime or lemon juice, or**
**Rose's lime cordial**

1   In a mixing glass, combine the gin and juice.
2   Add salt or sugar to your taste.
3   In a cocktail glass add crushed ice, and pour the drink into it.
4   A slice of lime or lemon finishes it off nicely.

## MINT BEER

The book *The Queen's Empire* (see page 183) tells that: '*Wherever the Briton may go, he will in a very brief space of time, start a Club of some sort. Whether it be on an Equatorial lagoon, or in some half-frozen fjord within ten degrees of the pole . . . it is the nature of things that the British resident takes full advantage of the facilities which the country* [he is in] *offers for a peculiarly British recreation.*'

My grandfather was a member of a number of clubs, as befitted his status, and as was typical in the Raj. He played a lot of tennis, and professed to be a great cricketer. On one occasion he took my mother to witness his prowess with willow and leather. For thus tempting fate, he was bowled out first ball for a duck! Evening entertainment was homemade and often involved card games. Grandpa's favourite was cribbage, which he played on many an evening at the club, or at home with Mr Wadsworth, Mum's godfather.

A cooling pick-me-up on the verandah in the height of the Indian heat, this will go down equally well on our summer's days, perhaps even at cricket matches.

MAKES: ENOUGH FOR 4

| | |
|---|---|
| 30 or so fresh mint leaves | 500ml (18 fl oz) fizzy lemonade |
| 500ml (18 fl oz) lager | 500g (1lb 2 oz) crushed ice |

1   Bruise and tear the mint leaves and put them into a large container.
2   Add the lager and lemonade and the crushed ice. Allow to stand in the fridge for about 20 minutes, to allow the mint to infuse. Top up the ice, then serve.

# GINGER BEER

Immensely popular with the Raj, indeed invented by them as a way to actually drink the endless supply of fresh ginger.

It can be purchased, ready made of course, but it's easy enough to make, and I do believe this homemade version is far better.

───────── MAKES: ENOUGH FOR 4 ─────────

100g (3½ oz) fresh ginger, finely shredded

500ml (17 fl oz) lager
500ml (17 fl oz) fizzy lemonade

500g (1lb 2 oz) crushed ice

1   Soak the ginger in water in the fridge for 24 hours.
2   Press it through a strainer, saving all its juice in a container.
3   Add the remaining ingredients, and serve at once.

# GINGER POP WITH ALCOHOL

Reggy Craven lived in the bungalow opposite when the family were posted in Mhow, in around 1914. He and his cousin Rex both came to school with the kids in the bullock *ghari* (cart). Rex's dad ran a soda water bottling factory some distance away. In those days, the bottles were machine capped with small glass marbles which were held into position by a rubber washer. Rex always shared his fizzy water on the way to school, in fact he was quite generous with the amount of bottles he brought. There was an incentive, of course. My grandmother used to make this ginger pop for the kids, using Mr Craven's soda water, with some yeast for extra fizz. She needed the empty bottles to put the pop into.

Here, I'm using alcoholic beverages which are already fizzy to make an adult version!

MAKES: ENOUGH FOR 4

400ml (14 fl oz) water
100g (3½ oz) finely
  shredded ginger
175g (6 oz) sugar

2 or 3 limes, chopped
100ml (3½ fl oz) kirsch or vodka
1.5 litres (2¾ pints) sparkling
  white wine

some fresh mint leaves

1   Bring the water to the boil then add the ginger, the sugar and the lime pieces.
2   Simmer for about 20 minutes.
3   Strain it, discarding the solids, and allow it to cool.
4   Chill it in the fridge.
5   Add the kirsch or vodka, the sparkling white wine, a mint leaf or two, and then serve.

# THE COMMANDER-IN-CHIEF

Who was this named after, one wonders? Was it the tipple of some irrascible Trevor Howard-type field marshal, from *The Charge of The Light Brigade*, whose every growl in the mess increased the terror of the subalterns? My grandmother's cookbook had no cure for that, though it does offer a cure for the '*hiccough or hiccup*'. It says: '*This spasm is caused by flatulency, indigestion, and acidity. It may generally be relieved by a sudden fright or surprise* [the entry of the Commander-in-Chief, perhaps?]. *Also by swallowing two or three mouthfuls of cold water or a teaspoon of vinegar, or by eating a piece of ice, taking a pinch of snuff, or anything that excities coughing.*'

Talking of a commander, one of the family's neighbours in Mhow was a recent widower, a Colonel Ross, C.O. of one of the Hussar Regiments. One day he knew that there was a drinks party happening in one of the bungalows, but he could not remember which one. He got into his *phaeton* (horse-pulled carriage) and said to the *syce* (coachman), '*Take me to the bungalow which is lit up. That's where the party will be.*' The coachman drove all round Mhow's military quarters. All the bungalows were dark. Mystified, they eventually arrived back home to find his own bungalow bright with lights, carriages and people. The drinks party was in full swing. All the regimental officers and their wives were there. Colonel Ross had forgotten it was he who was hosting the party.

─────────────── MAKES: ENOUGH FOR 4 ───────────────

150ml (5 fl oz) red or white wine
500ml (17 fl oz) sparkling mineral water
100ml (3½ fl oz) curaçao

750ml (1½ pints) sparkling white wine
sugar to taste (optional)
500g (1lb 2 oz) crushed ice
some fresh mint leaves

1  Empty into a punchbowl the wine, mineral water, curaçao, and the sparkling white wine. Add the sugar to taste if wanted, and the crushed ice.
2  Garnish with some bruised mint leaves. Serve at once.

# REGENT PUNCH

The *Indian Cookery Book* refers to quarts of champagne here and glassfuls of brandy there and 'old Jamaica rum' everywhere! Remember, they didn't worry about drinking and driving then. As a matter of fact, they didn't have motor transport at all. It's really amazing they had the energy left to get the Raj together at all!

─────────────── MAKES: ENOUGH FOR 4 ───────────────

750ml (1½ pints) sparkling white wine
75ml (3 fl oz) brandy

75ml (3 fl oz) rum
150ml (5 fl oz) cold strained fragrant tea
sugar to taste

1  Mix the wine, brandy, rum and the tea. Add sugar to your taste. Chill and serve.

# NEGUS

Naina Tal means nine lakes. It was, and still is, a beautiful hill station. The family bungalow in 1925 was a military one, and a big one, since my grandfather had gone up in rank once more. Grandpa only had to cross the courtyard to reach his offices. The bungalow overlooked the largest lake, and had a huge terraced garden where two *malis* (gardeners) grew fruit and vegetables. By this time some of the kids had left home, and the new tribe consisted of Frank, my mother and Alec. There were many things to do, not least of which were boating and school hockey. The bungalow had glazing all around the verandah, which made it very cosy during the bitter cold winters. This is a warm, spiced alcoholic punch-type beverage, ideal for the cool evenings in the hill stations and anywhere else.

### MAKES: ENOUGH FOR 4

150ml (5 fl oz) water
⅓ teaspoon ground nutmeg
6 to 8 crushed cloves
6 to 8 green cardamons

2 or 3 cinnamon sticks
1 lime, cut into thin slices
750ml (1½ pints) red wine
350ml (12 fl oz) port
150ml (5 fl oz) brandy

sugar to taste (optional)

1   In a large saucepan, bring the water to the boil with the nutmeg, cloves, cardamoms, cinnamon and lime. Simmer for 5 minutes.
2   Then add the wine, port and brandy, and optional sugar to taste. Allow it to become warm enough to drink comfortably, but not to boil. Serve, straining off the spices if you wish.

# FLASH

A monkey entered my grandparents' bedroom one evening when the family was at supper. My uncle Edwin, then the new baby, was fast asleep in his cradle after his early evening feed. The station was Kasauli, a quiet and peaceful cantonment where you could hear a pin drop. My grand-mother must have heard it drop, or it was sixth sense. Leaving the table for no apparent reason she ran to the bedroom to find the monkey cradling Edwin in its arms. The frightened animal could so easily have taken the baby with it. Fortunately it gently put Edwin back into the cradle before making its exit. To get in, it had managed to remove the metal mosquito screen and undo the catch on the partially open window. It was probably a recently bereaved mother, and may have been watching the window for some time. Needless to say, sad though it was, repairs were immediately undertaken to prevent such a recurrence. Perhaps the family had a peg or two of this to recover their nerves!

—————————— MAKES: ENOUGH FOR 4 ——————————

| | |
|---|---|
| **juice of 6 freshly squeezed limes** | **200ml (7 fl oz) rum** |
| | **750ml (1½ pints) fizzy lemonade** |
| **500g (1lb 2 oz) crushed ice** | **750ml (1½ pints) ginger beer** |

1   Mix the lime juice, crushed ice, and the rum and distribute it equally among four tall tumblers.
2   Add some ice cubes, then pour in the lemonade and ginger beer in equal measures.
3   Drink it while it is fizzing.

# SHERRY COBBLER

Here's another knockout, after which I doubt that anyone would be sober enough to enjoy dinner. Little wonder they called it a cobbler! Or do I mean clobberer? I am quoting the drinking instructions here verbatim from the *Indian Cookery Book*: '*Take the preparation through a reed, quill or common straw.*'

    Incidentally, on the next page of the book there are a couple of interesting recipes for the morning after too much of such a 'preparation'. Called '*Emetic Draught*' let me again quote verbatim from the book: '*This is commonly employed for unloading the stomach on the accession of fevers, and in ordinary cases* [after "preparations"?]. *Mix one grain of emetic tartar, 15 grains of powder of ipecacuanha, and an ounce and a half of water.'* Another recipe tells you to: *'Mix a scruple of subcarbonate of ammonia, half a drachm of ipecacuanha, two drachms of cayenne powder and three ounces of peppermint water. In case of poisoning, this is said to be more certain and effectual in arousing the action of the stomach than the preceding draught.'*

MAKES: ENOUGH FOR 4 TO 6

350ml (12 fl oz) sherry, dry or sweet to taste
100ml (3½ fl oz) rum
100ml (3½ fl oz) maraschino

crushed ice
half an orange, finely sliced
maraschino cherries
mint leaves

1 In a cocktail shaker, mix the sherry, rum and maraschino together.
2 Distribute the crushed ice equally into cocktail glasses. Pour in the alcoholic mixture, garnish with the orange slices, cherries and mint, and consume it as described above.

# FRESH LIME JUICE
## *Nimbu Pani*

Limes (nimbu) grow prolifically in India. (Lemons are rare.) One of the best uses for limes is the most refreshing drink you'll find in India. It comes in various combinations and versions – natural, sweetened or salted, with sparkling or still water.

PER DRINK

2 or 3 limes
2 or 3 ice cubes

1 Squeeze the limes and crush the ice.
2 For nimbu pani, add still water to the lime juice and ice in the glass.
3 For nimbu soda, add sparkling water to the lime juice.
4 For nimbu namkeen, add salt to either version above.
5 For nimbu meethi, add sugar to either version.

# CHAPTER SIX
# SOUPS

THERE IS NO DOUBT that the Raj dinner was an occasion of magnificence, and it could consist of as many as six courses, as the next chapters show. This is very much in line with the dining habits of upper-class Victorian and Edwardian England, but it is quite inconceivable to us diet-conscious diners of the 21st century to know where they put the endless procession of rich, high-calorie food that was served to them throughout the day, especially in India where the temperatures were regularly in the forties centigrade and the humidity 80–90 per cent.

But eat they did, and no more so than at dinner with a high degree of pomp and circumstance. At home, when they weren't entertaining, the families would rarely have more than three courses, one of which was usually a soup.

The irascible Flora Annie Steel says: '*In India the bohajee (head cook) invariably makes soup of beef bones. Now you can no more make all soups from one thing than you can make all kinds of puddings. Where guests come unexpectedly, a tin of Bovril or extract of beef should always be within reach. With its aid any soup for two can be made for four.*' Bovril Mrs Steel, Bovril? This is the woman whose book, may I remind you, was *the* best seller for 20 years a century ago!

Wyvern tells us: '*An idea prevails amongst numbers of Indian people that a soup to be good and strong must be dark coloured.*' No stock cubes for him: '*Its liquor should be as clear as sherry . . . but, if you desire a darker tint (which the gods forfend) you must achieve your object by making a caramel of sugar.*' He goes on to explain '*that soup in India must be made in one day. We cannot fall back on the never-empty stock pot of the English kitchen in the [hot] climate of the plains of India.*'

This resulted in delicious soups and broths, of which, using 21st-century techniques and even a stock cube or two, this selection is representative.

# BRIGHT ONION SOUP

The Raj version of this dish used veal to create the base stock. You could use a meat stock, but this version is vegetarian all the way. Do not omit the sherry, though. My grandmother's book poetically talks of 'silvery white onions'. Actually any colour onions will be fine, since we are about to caramelise them to a gorgeous brown colour. Put another way, this is when the starch and bitterness in the onion turns to sugar. That's what makes this soup so tasty.

SERVES: 4

4 tablespoons ghee or
  sunflower oil
500g (1lb 2 oz) onions, cut
  into fine strips
750ml (1½ pints) water
1 teaspoon coarsely ground
  black pepper

3 or 4 bay leaves
1 fresh red chilli, shredded
  (optional)
150ml (5 fl oz) sweet sherry
salt to taste

GARNISH

**some croutons**

1  Heat the ghee in the wok, and add the onions. Stir-fry until they start to sizzle, then lower the heat to maintain the sizzle, but to prevent burning.
2  Fry until the onions become a dark, golden brown colour, with not too much blackening, stirring from time to time. It will take between 15 and 20 minutes, but it is essential to the soup's flavour that the onions are caramelised.
3  Transfer the cooked onions to a 3 litre (5¼ pint) saucepan, adding the water, pepper, bay leaves, optional chilli, sherry and salt.
4  Simmer for about 10 to 15 minutes and serve with croutons.

FACING PAGE  DINNER DISHES: Crab in Shell (page 129), Potato Ribbons (page 158), Chicken Chilli Fry (page 142), Celery and Fennel in Cream (page 156).
FACING NEXT PAGE   CURRIES: Top: Spicy Rice (page 161) with Portuguese Pork Vindaloo Curry (page 52), Dal Curry (page 58), Malay Prawn Curry (page 51).

# DELICIOUS CURRY SOUP

The title is exactly as described in the *Indian Cookery Book*, and who am I to disagree?

My grandmother's method was to *'prepare a strong beef soup, slice some onions, cut up into 16 or 18 pieces a full size curry chicken, take some curry condiments, melt two chittacks ghee, fry and add a spoonful of tamarind, the stones separated from the stocks'*. Here it is, simplified for 21st-century living, but I promise you it's just as delicious.

### SERVES: 4

- 2 tablespoons ghee
- 2 or 3 cloves garlic, finely chopped
- 250g (8 oz) onions, finely chopped
- 1 or 2 fresh red chillies, shredded
- 750ml (1½ pints) chicken stock
- 200g (7 oz) shredded skinless chicken breast
- 1 tablespoon tomato purée
- 1 beef stock cube (optional)
- 2 tablespoons tamarind purée
- 12 to 15 fresh or dried curry leaves
- salt to taste

### SPICES

- 2 teaspoons whole white poppy seeds
- 2 teaspoons roasted and ground coriander seeds
- ½ teaspoon turmeric
- ½ teaspoon roasted and ground cummin seeds
- ½ teaspoon ground ginger
- ½ teaspoon chilli powder

### GARNISH

some snipped chives

1  Heat the ghee in the wok. Add the garlic, onions, and chillies and stir-fry for about 5 minutes.
2  Transfer to a 3 litre (5¼ pint) saucepan, and add the stock. When it is simmering, add the chicken and tomato purée, and crumble in the optional beef cube and the tamarind.
3  Back in the wok, heat the second lot of ghee, add the spices, and a splash or two of water, and stir-fry for a couple of minutes. Add it to the simmering saucepan, swilling out the wok with soup as required.
4  Simmer for about 10 minutes, then add the curry leaves and salt to taste. Garnish and serve as it is, or it is fine served with rice.

# BRIDAL SOUP OR SOUP ELEGANCE

This is described as *'an elegant soup, beautifully transparent, and the colour of light champagne'*. To achieve this the *bobajee* (cook) had to create a veal stock from a calf's head. In addition the soup's trademark was: *'slice the tongue fine, and cut out all manner of devices, such as diamonds, squares, circles, hearts, stars etc.'* No doubt Thumbi enjoyed this bit of designer artistry. The recipe goes on: *'If fancy macaroni be procurable, a tablespoon may be boiled tender then added.'* We'll avoid the former gruesome task by using the bright onion soup, from page 114. Since all manner of fancy pasta is readily procurable, we'll certainly use that. (No need to preboil). As to *'devices'*, my suggestion, if you want it, is that you use sliced ham, adding it very near the end. It strikes me that, with all its bits and pieces, apart from its alcohol content, this is a soup for the nursery, rather than the bridal suite! Still, one thing leads to another, I suppose.

---

SERVES: 4

1 **full batch of bright onion soup (see page 114)**

2 or 3 **tablespoons pasta alphabets, wheels, stars, etc.**

2 or 3 **slices cooked ham, prepared as described above (optional)**

**a glass or two of white wine, to taste**

**some fresh chopped basil leaves**

**salt to taste**

---

1  Cook the bright onion soup to completion, then strain off the solids, and discard them. Return the consommé to the saucepan, and bring it back to the simmer.
2  Add the pasta and simmer until it is *al dente*.
3  Add the optional designer ham, the white wine and the basil. Salt to taste. Simmer for just a few moments more, then serve.

# COCK A LEEKIE SOUP

Originally, this was a Scottish soup using chicken (literally a cock) with leeks. Traditionally it was thickened with barley and additional flavour came from prunes.

In this Raj version, savoured in cold hill stations, and flavoured with garlic and spices, it is the chilli which gives it added heat on a cold night. Barley is still used, and so are the prunes (optional). Dried prunes were another of those status symbols in the Raj. They were one of those prestigious dry provisions, purchased from the Europe stores.

SERVES: 4

2 tablespoons butter
300g (10 oz) white parts of leeks, chopped
1 or 2 cloves garlic, thinly sliced
1 or 2 fresh green chillies, chopped
200g (7 oz) skinless chicken breast cut into small strips

1 litre (1¾ pints) clear chicken stock (or chicken stock cube(s) with same amount of water)
60g (2 oz) whole barley
10 dried prunes, chopped (optional)
salt to taste

SPICES

4 or 5 bay leaves
1 or 2 cinnamon sticks
6 to 8 green cardamoms

GARNISH

basil leaves, chopped

1   Heat the butter in the wok, and stir-fry the spices for about 30 seconds. Add the leeks, garlic, and chillies, and continue stir-frying for about 5 minutes.
2   Add the chicken breast strips, and when they turn white transfer to a 3 litre (5¼ pint) saucepan.
3   Immediately add the stock and bring to a rolling simmer. Add the barley and the optional prunes, and simmer for about 20 minutes. Salt to taste then garnish and serve.

# SOUP ROYAL

This was another of those Raj soups requiring a huge operation in the kitchen. First the inevitable veal stock was made. This was a daily task. Remember, they had no fridges, nor stock cubes, nor ready made chilled stocks at the supermarket. In fact they had no supermarkets either. They didn't need them, since labour was cheap, and the *bobajee* didn't seem to mind all the hard work. Next, a vegetable stew was created with carrots, peas, potatoes, turnip, onion, gram dal and the pulp of an orange. The instructions in the *Indian Cookery Book* then read: '*When* [the vegetables are] *perfectly dissolved, turn them out into a colander, and allow all the water to drain away.*' That seems to me to be throwing out the baby, so we'll keep the delicious water please. It goes on: '*Turn the contents of the colander into a sieve, and pass the vegetables through it, rejecting all such as will not pass.*' Enter the electric blender at this point to achieve '*a consistency of a good potato soup*' i.e. it's thick and nourishing, and a good winter soup. Incidentally, to this the Raj added meat balls, and hard-boiled eggs, and it became a family meal in its own right. You can add both, either or neither of those, but don't forget the port please!

—————————————— SERVES: 4 ——————————————

4 tablespoons vegetable oil
2 or 3 cloves garlic, sliced
150g (5½ oz) onion, sliced
1 fresh red chilli, chopped
750ml (1½ pints) meat or
  vegetable stock or water
4 or 5 bay leaves
1 teaspoon green
  cardamom seeds

2 or 3 carrots, peeled and chopped
85g (3 oz) peas
2 or 3 potatoes, peeled and
  chopped
some turnip, peeled and chopped
25g (1 oz) gram dal
the pulp of an orange
150ml (5 fl oz) port
salt to taste

1   Heat the oil in the wok. Add the garlic, the onion, and the red chilli, and stir-fry for about 5 minutes.

2   Transfer it to a 3 litre (5¼ pint) saucepan, adding the stock or water, bay leaves and cardamom seeds and when it comes to the simmer, add the carrots, peas, potatoes, turnip and the gram dal.

3   Simmer for about 30 minutes, or until the contents are soft. Check the dal and potatoes particularly, and add a little water, in the unlikely event it needs it.

4   Add the orange pulp, then blend it to a purée.

5   Return it to the saucepan. Add the port, and salt to taste. Serve when it is hot enough.

# ROYAL VELVET CHICKEN SOUP

They had such lovely names for things in those days. The velvetiness comes from the milk-based roux use in the making of the soup, and the garnish of thick cream.

In the times of the Raj, the *gai* wallah (milk woman) came twice a day to the bungalow with her five milking buffaloes. The wise memsahib, like my grandmother, had a ritual, where she would sit and supervise the entire process. It would begin with the buffaloes' udders being washed. Next the *chattie* (container) was upturned to prove it had no water in it. The whole milking process was then closely watched to ensure no water was being added.

One day the kids dared my late uncle Jim to ride one of these normally sedate beasts, rodeo style. Naturally, they chose the most assertive-looking one. Jim got ready in good time. He climbed onto the front gate, and as the chosen buffalo passed into the drive, he leapt on to it. The startled animal, who had probably never been so abused in her life, took fright, and careered off round the compound, bucking bronco style, with Jim hanging on for dear life. Of course he fell off and hurt himself, and the *gai* wallah needed considerable mollifying, including a compensation payment, and a lifetime guarantee that such a thing would never happen again. Jim was sent to bed to nurse his wounds. No doubt he missed his supper, which might have included this recipe!

---

SERVES: 4

---

4 tablespoons cornflour
300ml (½ pint) milk
4 tablespoons butter

600ml (1 pint) chicken stock
3 egg yolks
100ml (3½ fl oz) sweet sherry

salt, pepper and chilli to taste

---

GARNISH

---

**some curls of cream**
**some parsley or any fresh herbs, chopped**

---

1  Put the cornflour into a small mixing bowl, then add the milk bit by bit, first making a thick paste, then gradually thinning it down until it is a thin paste. The aim is to get it lump-free.

2  Heat the butter in a non-stick saucepan, then add some of the paste. Stir continuously until it thickens a little, then add some more paste.

Do this until all the paste is used up, then continue to stir until it will not thicken further.

3    Add the stock little by little, in the same careful fashion, until it is well combined. Add the egg, whisking it into the soup, which by now should be thick but not too thick, like velvet in fact. Add salt, pepper, and chilli to taste. Garnish and serve.

# SPICY TOMATO SOUP

Tomatoes were discovered in the new world in the early 1500s, along with chillies. Within a few years, chillies had taken the Orient by storm. It is impossible to conceive Indian cookery without them. Most of the recipes in the *Indian Cookery Book* require them, yet not one Indian recipe asks for tomato. The fact is that tomato, being a distant relative of the highly toxic deadly nightshade family, was regarded with suspicion in northern Europe. And even today in India, they play no part in classic curry cooking. That modernist Wyvern said of tomatoes: '*They form a most valuable portion of our vegetable produce.*' Even Mrs Steel said: '*They can be cooked a hundred different ways. They thrive splendidly.*'

All vegetables grow well in the Indian sun. Tomatoes become particularly tasty, sweet yet tart, and sometimes quite large. I find Canary Island tomatoes taste the best over here, but a small trick which enhances flavour is to use a little tomato purée. This is added to the fresh tomatoes, which themselves are puréed, along with a spicing of Worcester sauce and chilli powder. The optional cream mellows the sharp tastes into a soup of distinction.

SERVES: 4

| | |
|---|---|
| 450g (1lb) fresh tomatoes | 1 teaspoon Worcester sauce |
| 1 red pepper | chilli powder to taste |
| 300ml (½ pint) water | salt to taste |
| 1 tablespoon tomato purée | 150ml (¼ pint) single cream |
| 2 teaspoons sugar | sprigs of parsley, chopped |

1    Coarsely chop the tomatoes and the red pepper and put them with the water into a saucepan and simmer for half an hour.

2    Purée this mixture in the blender or by hand through a sieve.

3    Return the purée to the saucepan, rinsing out the blender jug with water as required.

4    Add the manufactured tomato purée, the sugar, Worcester sauce, chilli powder and salt. Mix well and bring back to the simmer.

5    Serve into a tureen or serving bowls. Curl a little cream around the surface and sprinkle the parsley over this as a garnish.

# PISH-PASH

We met the ayah on page 64.

When she was fifteen, instead of being the young memsahib, and much to her annoyance, Mum found herself being surrogate ayah to her younger sister, Edith. It wasn't that Edith didn't have one. Her ayah was off sick most of the time, and when she did put in an appearance, she professed to have serious toothache or a gum disorder, or something. Whatever it was she had, it resulted in her sitting on the verandah and groaning all day long, and covering her face with her sari. She was unable to do anything, and why my soft old grandmother didn't sack her, no one knew. Perhaps the ayah needed some pish-pash.

*Hobson Jobson* says of this dish: '*It is apparently a factitious Anglo-Indian word, applied to a slop of rice-soup with small pieces of meat in it, much used in the Anglo-Indian nursery. It could have derived from the Persian word, "pashidan", meaning slivered or broken in pieces.*' Not so much of the slop, please gentlemen, this is a super soup, and that's facticious! It was, of course, a great way to use up spare rice. In fact here we're using left-over kedgeree.

———————————— SERVES: 4 ————————————

250g (9 oz) cooked kedgeree (see page 71)

750ml chicken or fish stock
salt, pepper and chilli to taste

1    Put the kedgeree and the stock into a 3 litre (5¼ pint) saucepan, and bring to the simmer.

2    Add salt, pepper and chilli to taste, and serve.

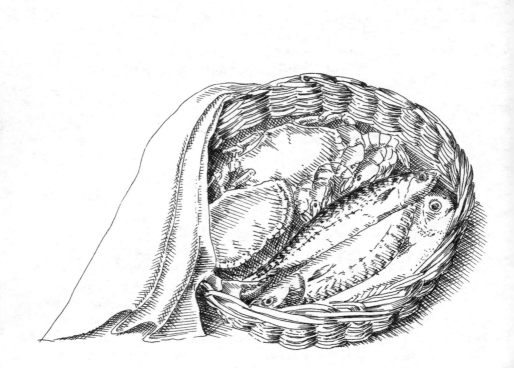

# CHAPTER SEVEN

# FISH AND SHELLFISH

M Y FAMILY WERE not big fish eaters and Raj cookbooks do not feature a great many fish recipes. I suppose that was typical of most Raj families. Fish often appeared as the second course (of six) at the formal occasion, but infrequently at home. This was a pity because there are some very good recipes indeed, and they all make excellent, nutritious main course dishes in this healthy age.

There are literally hundreds of fresh and seawater fish and crustacean species available in India. Mrs Beeton said: *'Fish in the mountain streams are both plentiful and excellent in quality, but those found in the rivers of the plains are lightly esteemed. The murrel, which somewhat resembles the English pike or carp, provides a palatable dish. The native cook either fills them with stuffing, and either bakes or stews them over a low fire. The sea affords an abundant supply. The seer is not unlike the salmon, and is usually dressed in the same way. The pomlet [sic] resembles turbot or brill, the hilsa is almost identical with our mackerel, while the Calcutta becktie, in size and appearance, is similar to cod.'*

And all the major cities, where our family was posted, had and still have large fish markets, with plenty of ice, whose produce was, and is, freshly caught that day and has to be cooked and eaten on the same day.

This is the very best way to eat fish in any case – if only it were possible for most of us today. Nevertheless, we have an impressive array of fresh fish available, backed up by even bigger choice of frozen items including, increasingly, items from India such as tiger prawns, pomfret and the other fish mentioned above, which add greatly to the authenticity of some of these recipes.

# FISH MOOLOO

This is a delicate fish dish cooked in coconut milk. Even the Europe stores didn't have coconut milk in tins like we do now. The *bobajee* had to create it, like everything else he did, the hard way, by splitting coconuts, scraping out the flesh and soaking it in water, before pressing it through a sieve. Coconuts have many uses in India, apart from their flesh. The nuts are used as containers, and their hair used to make ropes and coir matting. Even the trees are useful. They exude a sap which, when fermented, becomes a highly intoxicating liqueur called arrak or toddy.

When they were kids in Mhow, Frank, Jim and Bill were not interested in alcohol. A far more interesting pastime was to try to break the toddy *chatties*, pottery urns, placed high up the coconut palm trees to catch the dripping liquid. The men who did this were called toddy wallahs (nearest translation 'brewer') and part of their skill was scaling up the tall palm trees to attend to their *chatties*. One day, the *ghari* wallah (bullock cart driver) saw the boys throwing stones, and the mystery of how the *chatties* got broken was solved. He informed the toddy wallahs. Next time the boys passed in the bullock *ghari*, a group of toddy wallahs, complete with their fearsome machetes, sprang out of the bushes, and pretended to arrest the, by then, terrified schoolboys.

SERVES: 4

4 tablespoons sunflower or mustard blend oil

4 to 6 cloves garlic, finely chopped

150g (5½ oz) onion, thinly sliced

4 or more fresh green chillies, shredded

200ml (7 fl oz) tinned coconut milk

4 pieces flat white filleted fish, about 225g (8 oz) each

2 tablespoons vinegar

salt and pepper to taste

GARNISH

some fresh coriander leaves
some lime wedges

1   Heat the oil in a large flat frying pan. Add the garlic, onion and chillies and stir-fry for about 5 minutes.

2   Add the coconut milk, and when simmering on a low heat, add the fish pieces, and simmer gently for about 10 to 12 minutes, turning once, halfway through the cooking. During this time, the coconut milk will reduce, so compensate for this by adding water, little by little, to keep things reasonably fluid.

3   Sprinkle on the vinegar, and salt and pepper to taste.

4   Garnish and serve with vegetables or rice.

## TAMARIND FISH

In the summer months at their boarding school in Jubalpore, the girls slept al fresco in the tennis courts under mosquito nets. Whenever it rained they had to roll up the bedding and scamper indoors to their dormitory. The normal schoolday began with a five o'clock breakfast, followed by classes between 6 am and midday. Following lunch they spent all afternoon lying on their beds, while the punkah (fan) women pulled the punkah ropes all the time to keep the kids cool. My mother remembers her schools were keen on the kids having fish for dinner. And why not? *Select a really good fresh hilsa fish, full size, with roes,* urges the *Indian Cookery Book.* Hilsa is an Indian fish, not unlike mackerel, which is available in the west, fresh or frozen. Thumbi would have called it '*heel fiss*'.

SERVES: 4

700g (1lb 9 oz) filleted hilsa or mackerel
2 tablespoons butter
2 tablespoons olive oil
2 teaspoons roasted coriander seeds, crushed
4 cloves garlic, chopped
1 tablespoon shredded ginger

225g (8 oz) onion, finely sliced
1 teaspoon chilli powder
300ml (½ pint) fish stock or water
2 tablespoons tamarind purée
1 to 2 tablespoons chopped fresh coriander leaves
salt to taste

---

GARNISH

**some shredded red chilli
some fresh whole coriander leaves**

---

1 Wash and cut the fish into 2.5 cm (1 inch) cubes.
2 Heat the butter and the oil in the wok. Add the coriander seeds and stir-fry for about 20 seconds. Add the garlic, ginger, onion and chilli powder, and continue stir-frying for about 5 more minutes.
3 Add the fish stock or water and the tamarind purée, and when it is simmering, add the fish cubes.
4 Simmer for about 12 to 15 minutes, or until the fish is cooked. Add the coriander, and salt to taste. Garnish and serve.

# PRAWN PELLOW

*'Pellows or Pooloos are purely Hindustanee dishes,'* says the *Indian Cookery Book.* *'There are several kinds, but some of them are so entirely of an Asiatic character and taste, that no European will ever be persuaded to partake of them. It is therefore considered useless to offer instructions how to prepare such as the ukhnee pellow, in which are introduced cream, milk, butterfat, garlic and lime juice; or the sweet pellow in which almonds and raisins are introduced in addition to sugar.'*

Haven't things changed in the century since those unprophetic words were written? Indeed, my family would have been happy with any dish cooked entirely of an Asiatic character back in 1902! And so say all of us. Meanwhile, we'll make do with this. Incidentally, please do not think I'm criticising that fabulous book. I just adore it, as I hope, by now, you do too. To prove it, stage 5 is written verbatim. I couldn't improve upon it in any case.

SERVES: 4

350g (12 oz) cooked king
  prawns
2 tablespoons ghee
1 clove garlic, finely
  chopped

1 fresh red chilli, chopped
2 tablespoons vegetable oil
350g (12 oz) cooked rice (see
  page 159)

SPICES

6 to 8 cloves
4 or 5 green cardamoms

6 small pieces cassia bark
½ teaspoon peppercorns

1 or 2 blades mace

GARNISH

2 hard-boiled eggs, halved
some chopped bacon, fried
  crisply

some onion tarka (see page 57)
some fresh herb leaves of your
  choice

1  Remove the veins from the backs of the king prawns. Then wash and
   dry them.
2  Heat the ghee in the large wok. Add the garlic and chilli and stir-fry
   for about 30 seconds. Add the spices, and continue to stir-fry for a
   further 30 seconds.
3  Add the rice and stir occasionally until it is hot right through.
4  In a frying pan, heat the oil, and add the prawns. When they are more
   or less hot, add the egg halves and bacon, and carefully stir-fry till hot.
5  Dish up the pellow, strew over it the fried onions (tarka) and garnish
   with the prawns, and two hardboiled eggs, cut in halves, or some other
   device (herbs) and with half a dozen bits of finely sliced and fried
   bacon, to suit the taste of those who like the latter.

# TIGER PRAWN CUTLET

During the family's time in Naini Tal in about 1926, a huge scare about tigers broke out. A savage man-eater was carrying away young girls from the outlying villages. The governor called in Jim Corbett, author and tiger expert, to dispose of the menace. Meanwhile everyone, British and Indians, was at panic stations. No one was allowed out alone. Mum got badly bitten by a neighbour's dog, and was hospitalised, which increased anxiety. Finally Corbett shot the tiger. Sadly it turned out to be an OAP with rotten teeth. Presumably it was too arthritic to catch normal prey, and humans were an easy option.

This is a fine dish in which you can use large king prawns, but best for the job are enormous Bengali or Thai tiger or jumbo prawns. Called tigers because of the gorgeous stripes down their backs, they grow up to 30cm (12 inches) in length, and up to 110g (4oz) in weight.

---

SERVES: 4

---

4 raw jumbo prawns, each about 110g (4 oz)
2 egg yolks
some fresh herbs, such as French marjoram, or hyssop (blue or white)

1 teaspoon garam masala (see page 39)
½ teaspoon pepper
½ teaspoon salt
some cornflour
4 tablespoons ghee

--- SAUCE ---

4 tablespoons sun-dried tomato purée
6 tablespoons tomato ketchup

1 tablespoon chilli powder
some drops of Tabasco sauce
some olive oil

--- GARNISH ---

**a deep-fried fresh herb**

---

1   Shell and wash the prawns, removing the heads, but retaining the tails.
2   Remove the veins by cutting them away from the backs, then carefully, and with a sharp knife, cut each prawn in half.
3   Now gently beat each half flat with a rolling pin or meat mallet.
4   Rub them over with the egg yolk.
5   Very finely chop the herbs, and mix them with the garam masala,

pepper, salt and cornflour. Then dredge the prawns with this floury mixture.

5   Heat the ghee in a large flat frying pan. Fry the prawns on a modest heat, for about 6 minutes. Turn them and continue frying for at least 4 more minutes, or until they are cooked right through.

6   During stage 5, mix the sauce ingredients together, using the olive oil to achieve the required consistency.

7   Garnish with a deep-fried fresh herb, and serve the prawns piping hot, the sauce cold.

# CRABS IN SHELL

Even though this recipe is in my grandmother's cookbook, crab was never on our family menu. In all their postings, they never were near the sea, apart from a brief time when my grandfather's last posting took him to Bombay in 1930. And in the days of the Raj you needed to be by the sea to get crabs on the menu. You also needed a *bobajee* (cook) who knew how to dress a crab. Not all did, but not all the Raj military bases were inland. Bombay, Calcutta and Madras were always the biggest military strongholds, and they are all coastal cities. We are very fortunate these days. Wherever we live, we can get fresh crab, and it's so much better than frozen. Get your fishmonger to give you the meat, coral (roe) and shells ready to use. Pity the family never tasted this. They don't know what they missed!

SERVES: 4

250g (9 oz) fresh white crab meat

250g (9 oz) fresh brown crab meat

1 teaspoon very finely shredded ginger

juice of 2 limes

1 teaspoon green peppercorns in brine

1 teaspoon mushroom ketchup, if available (see page 164)

salt to taste

4 crab shells

some olive oil

60g (2 oz) fresh crab coral (roe)

4 anchovy fillets

1   Mix the white and brown crab meat together with the ginger, lime juice, peppercorns, mushroom ketchup and salt to taste.
2   Wash and dry the crab shells, and brush them with olive oil.
3   Fill the crab shells with the crab meat (not the coral). Depending on shell size it should all fit.
4   Top them off with the coral (roe) and anchovy fillets.
5   Put the filled shells into the oven, preheated to 190°C/375°F/Gas 5.
7   Bake for about 5 to 8 minutes, and serve hot or cold, as a starter or part of a main course.

# FISH IN BATTER

Coolies were porters, or carriers of goods. When the family were posted, they went by bullock *ghari* (cart) and trains. Their goods and chattels were lugged by the coolies to and from stations, and loaded onto freight wagons. When the family went to hill stations, they travelled on narrow gauge trains that wound and spiralled up thousands of feet of hills as they ascended. The scenery was out of this world. Some folk in those days preferred to go the whole way by dandy (a man-powered rickshaw). The coolies needed to be very strong for such work.

My mother's best experience of the amazing powers of the coolies was in Quetta, now part of Pakistan. There the coolies were Pathans (a rather fierce, large war-like tribe, who originally caused problems to the Raj through terrorism, but later became staunch and reliable allies). Their distinctive features were blue-grey eyes, and exceptional resilience. The family upright piano needed carrying. A Pathan coolie tied a rope to the piano, then tied it around his head, while his friends lifted it onto his back, then he single-handedly carried it for some half hour or so to the new bungalow. Perhaps they got their strength from delicious nutritious fish dishes like this one.

4 skinned fillets of any
white fish, about 110g to
150g (4 to 5 oz) each
110g (4 oz) gram flour (besan)
1 egg
1 tablespoon lemon juice
1 tablespoon chopped fresh
coriander leaves

2 teaspoons garam masala (see
page 39)
2 teaspoons dried fenugreek
leaves
1 teaspoon salt
½ teaspoon chilli powder
½ teaspoon lovage seeds (ajwain)

1   Wash and dry the fish.
2   Mix the remaining ingredients for the batter with just sufficient water to achieve a thickish paste which will drop sluggishly off the spoon. Let it stand for at least 10 minutes, during which time the mixture will absorb the moisture.
3   Meanwhile heat the deep-fryer to 190°C (chip-frying temperature) which is below smoking point, and will cause a sliver of batter to splutter a bit, then float more or less at once.
4   Inspect the mixture. There must be no 'powder' left. It must be well mixed.
5   Coat the fish with batter.
6   Carefully lower one piece of fish into the oil. Place the others in, allowing about 20 seconds between each to maintain oil temperature.
7   Deep-fry for 10 to 12 minutes, turning each piece a few times. Remove from the oil. Drain well on kitchen paper, and serve with vegetables or a curry.

# POMFRET POTATO PIE

Another coolie story concerned the young Alec, aged about three or four, who took it upon himself to explore the territory around the Kasauli, the hill station to which the family had just been posted, without informing my grandmother, because she would have refused permission for one so young. She soon noticed he was missing, and after a thorough search of house and garden, and getting increasingly panicky, she called the MPs because she presumed Alec had been kidnapped. A search party was about to set out when, enter Alec, carried aloft in a dandy rickshaw by two coolies, who naturally expected payment for the job. In the way of things, Granny was at first highly relieved, then embarrassed about the fuss she had caused everyone, then absolutely furious, and she gave young Alec a severe wigging. It seems he had become very tired. Then he came across the rickshaw. '*Take me home*,' he commanded in Urdu. And they did, though neither he nor they knew where home was! The search party thought it all a huge joke, and no doubt lived off the story for months. They could live off this self-sufficient dish too.

SERVES: 4

2 tablespoons sunflower or light oil
2 or 3 cloves garlic, chopped
150g (5½ oz) onion, chopped
1 or 2 fresh red chillies, shredded
300g (10½ oz) prawns in brine
300g (10½ oz) pomfret or cod, filleted
1 teaspoon garam masala (see page 39)
10 to 12 young spinach leaves, washed and de-stalked
2 or 3 tablespoons olive oil
4 tablespoons chopped parsley
6 tablespoons chopped rocket
2 eggs
½ teaspoon chilli powder
½ teaspoon salt
½ teaspoon crushed black pepper
2 or 3 tablespoons clotted cream
400g (14 oz) mashed potato
1 tablespoon butter

---

SPICES

**2 teaspoons coriander**
**1 teaspoon cummin**
**½ teaspoon turmeric**

---

1   Heat the sunflower oil in the wok. Add the spices and a splash of water and stir-fry for about a minute. Add the garlic, onion and chillies, and continue to stir-fry for about 5 minutes. If it gets a little dry, add some of the prawn brine.
2   Now add the prawns, then add the pomfret or cod, again using some of the brine to keep things mobile. After about 5 minutes stir-frying, mix in the garam masala and take it off the heat.
3   Preheat the oven to 190°C/375°F/Gas 5.
3   Soften the spinach leaves in the microwave or by a light blanching.
4   Brush a pie dish with olive oil. Spread it with the spinach leaves. Sprinkle on the parsley and rocket, then add the par-cooked curried prawn/fish.
5   Beat the egg, adding the chilli, salt and pepper, and mix it and the cream into the mashed potato.
6   Spread the potato over the fish. Make squirly patterns with your fork, and plop on the butter.
7   Put the dish into the oven, and bake for about 30 minutes, until the topping goes golden. Serve hot with peas or beans, or cold with salad.

# SALMON STEAK

Some luxuries were purchased from the Europe stores in tins, jars or bottles. Favourites were jams and marmalades, which came in huge IXL brand tins. Tinned fruit was another luxury, and although there were abundant exotic fresh fruits all around, which everyone adored, they were considered second best to tinned fruit. Although there was fresh fish readily available in the bazaars, there was never salmon. Without doubt our family's greatest luxury was tinned salmon, with tinned sardine a close second. Though the *musolchi* (kitchen assistant) made a thickened condensed milk by stirring a simmering pan of fresh milk for hours until it reduced, another great tinned favourite was sweetened condensed milk. In around 1915, my uncle Bill took on a schoolboy dare (for a massive 5 rupees – in those days equivalent to the cost of a dressing table or two dining chairs!) to consume a tin of sardines, mixed with a tin of sweetened condensed milk. These were not cheap, of course, but supplied by his parents in the tuck box. He succeeded, of course, and needless to say was violently sick, but he considered it worth it to receive a year's pocket money in one fell swoop.

We are lucky in that we have plenty of gorgeous fresh or frozen salmon, or you could try Indian seer, if you can get it. In this recipe, with a lightly spiced mayonnaise sauce, you'll never find a better way of enjoying it.

SERVES: 4

4 salmon or becktie steaks, each about 250g (9 oz) unfilleted
6 tablespoons mayonnaise
6 tablespoons Greek-style natural yoghurt

2 or 3 chopped anchovy fillets
100g (3½ oz) prawns in brine, chopped
some drops Tabasco sauce
some chopped fresh herbs of your choice

salt and pepper to taste

GARNISH

some thin slices of lime
the black pepper mill
chilli powder

1   Wash and dry the salmon steaks, then place them in a hot steamer or into a large frying pan of simmering water. Cook for about 15 minutes, or until the flesh is cooked right through.
2   Meanwhile mix the mayonnaise, yoghurt, anchovy fillets, prawns and Tabasco together. Add the herbs and salt and pepper to taste. Keep in the fridge until ready.

3   To serve, place each hot salmon steak on a serving plate, and tidily put the dressing on and around it. Place the lime slices on top, and give it a twist of black pepper and a whisper of chilli powder. Serve at once, with minted peas.

# CRAB AND FISH SCALLOPS

The punkah wallah was the person who pulled the fan. Keeping cool was a nightmare to the Raj. Punkahs (fans) were huge square contraptions attached to the ceiling, and hinged at the top. A rope was tied to the punkah and was usually routed outside the room. The punkah wallah's job was to pull the rope whenever required. This was day and night, and a large bungalow could have six or more punkahs, and twelve punkah wallas working in shifts. With a little ingenuity, the rope could be pulled by looping it over the big toe, thus the punkah wallahs could perform their job very comfortably in the prone position.

These are decorative in their scallop shells, but they are rich, so a little goes a long way!

SERVES: 4

2 tablespoons clotted
  cream
225g (8 oz) cod steak
100g (4 oz) white crab meat
100g (4 oz) brown crab
  meat
3 or 4 tinned anchovy
  fillets, finely chopped
6 to 8 pitted green olives,
  chopped

juice of 2 limes
2 or 3 tablespoons Madeira
1 teaspoon Worcester sauce
some drops of Tabasco sauce
1 tablespoon clear honey
½ teaspoon salt
1 teaspoon green peppercorns in
  brine, crushed
4 scallop shells
some olive oil

4 tablespoons breadcrumbs

1   Mash the cream, cod steak, white and brown crab meats, the tinned anchovy fillets and the olives together. Add the lime juice, Madeira, Worcester and Tabasco sauces, the honey, salt, and the peppercorns. Mix well and set aside in the fridge.

2   Preheat the oven to 190°C/375°F/Gas 5.

3   Brush the shells with the olive oil, then fill them with the mixture. You should have some left over. Use in spare shell(s) or freeze.

4   Coat the toppings with the breadcrumbs, and bake the shells in the oven for about 10 minutes. Can be served hot or cold, as a starter or part of the main course.

# ROLLED FISH

Traditionally, pomfret was used as the fish in this recipe, but any flat fillet of white fish will be perfect. A small sausage of minced prawn, spice and flavourings was laid onto the fish, which was rolled around it and then steamed. I find baking works just as well if you do not have a steamer. To serve them, the Raj cooks used to allow them to cool, then cover with aspic jelly. I prefer them hot, garnished with melted butter and fresh coriander.

SERVES: 4

4 skinned fillets of any white fish, about 110g to 150g (4 oz to 5 oz) each
110g (4 oz) shelled shrimps or prawns
2 or 3 anchovy fillets (canned or bottled)
60g (2 oz) onion, finely chopped

1 clove garlic, peeled and finely chopped
1 fresh green chilli, finely chopped
1 tablespoon butter
1 tablespoon breadcrumbs
1 egg yolk
4 lemon wedges
sprigs of parsley

1   Prepare the fish by checking to see that there are no bones or skin, and giving them a quick cold water rinse and dry.

2   Put the prawns and anchovy fillets through a mincer.

3   Place the onion, garlic and chilli in a pan in which the butter is heated. Stir-fry for 5 minutes then add the prawn/anchovy mixture.

4   Finally add the breadcrumbs and egg yolk. Mix well and stir-fry for 5 more minutes.

5   Remove from the heat and, when cool enough, make four sausage shapes with the mixture.

6   Place one sausage on a fillet. Roll the fillet around the sausage mixture and place it upside down (to prevent it from opening up) on an oven tray. Repeat with the other fillets.

7   Cover the tray with foil and place it in the oven preheated to 180°C/350°F/Gas 4, or put the fillet in a fish steamer. Cook for 15 to 20 minutes.

8   Serve hot, garnished with a lemon wedge and some chopped parsley.

# CHAPTER EIGHT
# MEAT AND POULTRY

A T THE TIME OF the Raj meat eating was not only fashionable, it was considered a dietary necessity. A wide choice of meat was available, including beef, veal, mutton, lamb, pork, venison and other game. It was by no means good, though. Wyvern said of it: '*We find John Bull in India as fond of his beef and mutton as he was when a humble cottager in Britain . . . sorrowfully . . . a vast quantity of wretched meat is sold in the Indian market.*' Mrs Beeton said: '*Meat being eaten so soon after it is killed in India is not good. Goat is anything but pleasant to English tastes. The beef is coarse, sinewey and tasteless, the mutton decidedly inferior. Fortunately Indian cooks are so clever in disguising its insipidity.*'

Most Indian cooks were Hindus, who revered the cow, but they had to learn to ignore their feelings when cooking for the Raj. Moslem cooks, although in the minority, were more likely to be encountered in the north. To them the pig was disgusting and unclean, but they too had to come to grips with European customs. The happy solution was to use Goan cooks. Being Christian, they had no problems with any meat. Our family had a Goan cook for one of their postings. I have heard in very rare circumstances of Raj families having Chinese cooks. An interesting option resulting, I'm sure, in some wonderful variations of Raj food.

On the really formal dining occasion, meat or poultry would be divided into two courses. The entrée followed the fish (second) course and consisted of 'made' dishes such as pies and pastries, stews and boiled meats. This course was followed by the roast joint of the day.

Roasting was a technique which had to be mastered by the Indian cooks. It was not a traditional Indian cooking method. Apart from the clay tandoor ovens of the north of India, which work on a different principle,

India does not use conventional ovens. In modern times they have appeared in middle-class Indian homes, but at the time of the Raj, the oven was a rather crude rectangular clay construction fired by charcoal, wood or dung cakes. Nonetheless, once mastered the cook's roasts were excellent, indistinguishable from a traditional British roast.

In this chapter I have concentrated on recipes which show off Raj-style Anglo-Indian cooking in its best light, including one roast dish (goose). Judging by the particularly heavy wear and tear in this section of my grandmother's cookbook, they were the main family favourites.

# BEEF OLIVES

Take some beaten lean steak, roll it around a tasty stuffing, and bake to cook. That's a beef olive. Although they have faded from view today, beef olives have been around in Britain at least since mediaeval times. A recipe appears in the *Harleian Manuscripts*, cookery books from AD 1439, using parsley, onion, marrow, egg yolk, ginger, and saffron.

Hannah Glasse's recipe in her 1747 cookery book (see page 164) uses veal forcemeat (see page 42) and nutmeg.

My grandmother's recipe, typical of the Raj, uses an onion and bread stuffing, with bacon, ginger, garlic, fresh mint and coriander leaves.

Taking a liberty, I've combined what I think to be the best attributes of each recipe. Incidentally, I have no idea why they are called 'olives'!

SERVES: 4

4 lean beef, lamb or veal steaks, each weighing about 175g (6 oz)
4 tablespoons butter
4 bay leaves
4 cloves garlic, sliced
3cm (½ inch) cube ginger, shredded
6 to 8 spring onions, bulbs and leaves, chopped
2 egg yolks
6 slices crustless white bread
30 saffron strands
4 slices streaky bacon, cooked to crispy
½ teaspoon grated nutmeg
½ teaspoon salt
1 tablespoon chopped fresh mint
2 tablespoons chopped fresh coriander leaves

1 Beat the steaks with a meat mallet until they are about 1 cm (⅓ inch) thick.

2 Heat the butter in the wok. Add the bay leaves, garlic, ginger, and onion and stir-fry for about 5 minutes, or longer to soften the onions fully.

3 Let it cool then add the egg yolk, white bread, saffron, bacon, nutmeg, salt, and leaves. Mix well, using a little water as needed to achieve a mouldable stuffing.

4 Divide it into four equal parts. Roll each steak gently but firmly around one part of stuffing. Tie off with string.

5 Put the 'olives' onto a foil-lined oven tray. Cover the tray with foil, and put them into the oven preheated to 190°C/375°F/Gas 5.

6 Bake for about 30 minutes, or until the meat is as tender as you like it. Incorporate any spare juices into a gravy, and serve with potatoes and other vegetables.

## BEEF CHILLI FRY

The younger children were growing up as my mother became a senior at school. They too became borders in different schools all over India. At one time, when the family was posted to Kasauli, Alec was at the nearby Lawrence Military School at Sanawar, the very same school where my great grandmother Alice Beatson had been sent as an orphan, after the Lucknow Mutiny in 1857. In the summer of 1924 she came from Agra to stay with the family for a long visit. It was to be the last time the family saw her. She went home before the long winter began, and died later that year in Agra. She was a large, gentle woman, yet she was elegant in her own way. She quietly took her daily exercise by walking up and down the verandah. She walked in a stately manner, upright and never stooped. Then she'd sit down and the kids would join her on the verandah whilst she told tales of old India. The kids loved her.

My grandmother told me that she had learned this dish from her. It is a sort of spicy cross between a plain stew and a curry. It is of course really tasty, and as for the chillies, you can add as many as you like, but do add some, or its title is meaningless!

SERVES: 4

700g (1lb 9 oz) steak
2 tablespoons vegetable oil
2 tablespoons butter
2 large onions
4 to 6 cloves garlic,
  chopped

5cm (2 inch) cube ginger, finely
  shredded
4 to 8 (or more) fresh red or green
  chillies, shredded
2 meat stock cubes
150ml (¼ pint) water

salt to taste

1   Trim the steak of any unwanted matter, then cut into 4cm (1¾ inch) cubes.
2   Heat the oil in the wok. Fry the meat until it is sealed, stirring frequently, then put it into a lidded casserole dish of 2.25 to 2.75 litre (4 to 5 pint) capacity.
3   Heat the butter in the wok. Stir-fry the onions, garlic, ginger and chillies for at least 10 minutes. We want to get the onions well browned.
4   Add the stir-fry to the casserole, with the stock cube and water. Mix in well, put the lid on, and put the dish into the oven, preheated to 190°C/375°F/Gas 5, and cook for up to an hour, or until the meat is as tender as you wish it.
5   Inspect every 20 minutes, adding enough water to keep things mobile, although it should be fairly dry.
6   Salt to taste and serve with Dal Frezee (see below) and Indian bread.

CHICKEN CHILLI FRY:

*This recipe works well with chicken. Stir-fry strips of skinless chicken breast with the above ingredients, following the Country Captain recipe method on page 147.*

DAL FREZEE:

*An accompaniment which goes particularly well with Chilli Fry is Dal Frezee (or dal fry). Simply fry the seeds of 4 cardamoms, 12 peppercorns, and ½ teaspoon turmeric in butter, then combine 2 parts cooked plain rice with 1 part cooked red lentils, salt to taste and serve.*

# SIMLA STROGANOFF OR CREAMY VEAL STIR-FRY SIMLA

This was a popular dish with my family when they served in the hill station of Simla. In one of her few up-beat remarks, Flora Annie Steel says: *'Simla is a large place, very expensive, very gay, very pretty. Educational advantages are good. No one should go to Simla who has not a bag of rupees and many pretty frocks.'* I do not believe my grandfather was a transvestite, so he had no need for frocks, but when the family were posted to Simla in 1925, he had many pretty army uniforms, being by then a senior officer. And you can be sure the females in the family, including my mother, wheedled bags of rupees out of my soft grandpa, so that they could avail themselves of many a pretty frock. Not surprisingly, the family liked Simla. And they liked this dish. They called it Simla Stroganoff, after the fashionable Russian dish of the same name, which it resembled.

SERVES: 4

| | |
|---|---|
| 675g (1½lb) lean veal | 2 bay leaves |
| 3 tablespoons butter | 150ml (5 fl oz) white wine |
| 1 teaspoon ground white pepper | 250g (9 oz) button mushrooms, peeled and chopped |
| ½ teaspoon paprika | 4 tablespoons natural yoghurt |
| ½ teaspoon chilli powder | 150g (5½ oz) crème fraîche |
| 150g (5½ oz) onions, finely sliced | ½ teaspoon yellow mustard powder |
| 2 cloves garlic, chopped | salt to taste |

GARNISH

**a dusting of paprika**
**some sprigs of parsley**

1   Cut the veal into thin strips. Heat the butter in the wok. Add the veal strips, and stir in the pepper, paprika and chilli powder. Stir-fry for about 3 to 4 minutes.
2   Add the onions, garlic, bay leaves, and white wine and continue stir-frying for a further 3 to 4 minutes.
3   Add the mushrooms, yoghurt, crème fraîche, and mustard. Let this become hot, stir-frying for a final couple of minutes, but it must not boil.
4   Salt to taste, garnish and serve with plain rice.

## STUFFED LAMB HEARTS

Offal was popular in the days of the Raj when nothing was wasted. The *Indian Cookery Book* is full of instructions for the daily process of boiling udders, calves' heads, bones and tongues to create stock. Rather more palatable to our more squeamish tastes is this recipe for stuffed lamb hearts.

---

SERVES: 4

**4 lamb hearts**
**stuffing to fill the hearts (see page 140)**

---

1   Cut open the tops of the hearts, and carefully cut away any unwanted matter, then wash and dry them.
2   Fill them with stuffing made as in the recipe on page 140. Wrap them in kitchen foil. Place them on an oven tray, and into the oven, preheated to 190°C/ 375°F/gas 5, and bake for about 30 to 35 minutes.
3   Inspect to ensure they are cooked right through. Serve with vegetables or spicy rice.

## SUMMER HILL PORK CHOPS

When my grandfather was promoted in 1927, the family moved to Summer Hill, which was one railway station away from Simla. This was the first house where the family had electricity. It hardly made any difference to their lives, as the trimming of the wicks and the filling of the oil, and even the lighting of the lamps, were not their affair. It was done by the bearers.

The new baby, the baba, in 1925 was Arthur. Edith, up till then the missy baba, was toddling, Alec and Edwin, both chota sahibs, were a lively seven and four respectively. My mother was seventeen. And since she and the kids went to bed early they couldn't care less about electricity. Besides, there were no electrical appliances to run. Who needed them anyway, with so many servants? And there was still no radio, TV, or phone then. A new-fangled device, the wind-up gramophone did put in an appearance in some homes, but it too required no electricity. The Summer Hill house had another first for the family used to living in bungalows. It had two floors. Alec marked this phenomenon by leaning so far out of his upstairs bedroom window to talk to a school pal, that he fell out. As luck would have it, he got entangled with the window catch, and he was left hanging and shrieking until he was rescued.

This was a recipe they enjoyed. Wild boar were prevalent in the hills around Simla, and make a great substitute for ordinary pork, and note the peg of alcohol!

SERVES: 4

**8 pork chops, each about 125g to 140g (4½ to 5 oz)**

MARINADE

4 tablespoons olive oil
4 tablespoons milk
2 or 3 cloves garlic, very finely chopped
1 teaspoon garam masala (see page 39)

some drops Tabasco sauce
some drops Worcester sauce
2 or 3 tablespoons apricot brandy
salt to taste

1. Pare unwanted fat off the chops.
2. Mix the marinade ingredients together in a non-metallic mixing bowl.
3. Put the chops into the marinade, ensuring each one is well coated, then cover the bowl with stretch film, and put it into the fridge for 24 hours.
4. To cook, preheat the grill to medium heat. Line the grill pan with kitchen foil. Put the chops onto the pan rack, which you then place in the midway position under the grill.
5. Grill for about 6 to 8 minutes, then turn the chops over, pour over any spare marinade, and cook for a further 6 to 8 minutes. The chops should be well cooked by then. Serve with rice and/or salads, and chutneys and pickles.

# QUETTA DUCK AND LOVE APPLES

Virtually the last posting my grandfather received in 1929 was to Quetta, now in Pakistan. It was an outlandish flat sandy desert kind of place with hills all around it, hot in summer and bitterly cold in winter. Being a very senior officer, Grandpa could organise things which were rare even for the members of the Raj. On one occasion, he organised a picnic from Quetta to a place miles away called Chaman. It was on the Afghan border, and infested with marauding tribesmen. To get into this dangerous and barren place, Grandpa fixed it so that they could be transported on a little open flat four-wheeled railway truck. It was propelled by a very strong Indian railway man who, standing upright, pulled a lever back and forth without a break for the couple of hours it took in each direction.

The only physical features that told where the border was, were occasional whitewashed bollards. The railway line simply went on into Afghanistan. There was no border check point. On the horizon were several Afghan forts, but they were well out of gunshot range. It would have been easy to step into forbidden Afghan territory, just a few steps away, but Mum was too scared to take the step. It was a single railway track, so if a train had wanted to pass it couldn't have. But no trains, indeed no people, were evident as far as the eye could see in all directions. The family had the place totally to themselves all day.

Love apples were the mid-Victorian name for tomatoes, but I've added calvados and real apples to this recipe. Wild duck are prolific in India. We can obtain duck at the game butcher. An alternative is 'magret de canard'. This is a French term, meaning the lean portion (of a fat duck) and refers to duck breasts, filleted, with skin and fat still attached, which you or your poulterer must pare away. The resultant meat, though expensive, is equally good for this recipe.

SERVES: 4

675g (1lb 8 oz) magret de canard
3 tablespoons olive oil
2 or 3 cloves of garlic, sliced
150g (5½ oz) onion, thinly sliced
1 or 2 fresh green chillies, shredded
6 to 8 cherry tomatoes, halved

300ml (½ pint) white wine
2 tablespoons cranberry jelly
1 teaspoon green peppercorns in brine
2 teaspoons brown sugar
50ml (2 fl oz) calvados
2 tablespoons chopped fresh herbs
salt to taste
some small sweet apples to garnish

1   Cut the duck into strips about 5 cm (2 inches) by 1 cm (⅓ inch).
2   Heat the oil in the wok. Add the garlic, onion and chillies and stir-fry for about 5 minutes.
3   Add the duck pieces, and stir-fry these into the mixture for 3 or 4 minutes.

4   Add the tomatoes, white wine, cranberry jelly, peppercorns, and brown sugar, and until the duck is tender, about another 5 minutes.
5   Add the calvados, herbs and salt to taste. Simmer just a while longer, then thinly slice the apples and garnish with them.

# CHICKEN COUNTRY CAPTAIN

The name 'country captain' originated in Bengal. In Raj days, small coastal vessels, called 'country ships' out of Calcutta, plied the coasts of India carrying freight. The skipper was called the 'country captain'. The word 'country' in this context was of course derogatory, meaning 'Indian native'. Somehow it also became the name of a popular Raj dish. The *Indian Cookery Book* says: '*The country captain is usually made of chicken, and occasionally of kid and veal. Cold meats and curries are also sometimes converted into this dish.*'

It is a perfect example of the combination of British and Indian cooking styles. My recipe here is a stir-fried chicken dish, saved from blandness by the light spicing of onion, garlic and cummin seed and coloured golden by the use of turmeric. Heat lovers can add chopped fresh green chillies. It should be quite dryish, but have sufficient sauce to serve it on its own with rice.

––––––––––––– SERVES: 4 –––––––––––––

700g (1lb 9 oz) chicken breast, weighed after boning and skinning
4 cloves garlic
5cm (2 inch) piece fresh ginger
1 large (225g/8 oz) onion
2 green chillies
4 tablespoons clarified butter (ghee)

2 teaspoons white cummin seeds
½ teaspoon turmeric
2 teaspoons curry masala (see page 37)
½ red pepper
½ green pepper
2 fresh tomatoes
2 tablespoons fresh coriander leaves
salt to taste

1 lemon

FACING PREVIOUS PAGE   CURRIES: Top: Hussanee Curry (page 48) with Plain Rice (page 159), Tick Keeah (page 45) with Potato Burta (page 57).
FACING PAGE   CHRISTMAS: Mulligatawny Soup (page 188), Spicy Cranberry Jelly (page 193), Turkey Jhal Frezee (page 191), Pease Pudding Tarka (page 189).

1 Prepare the chicken by removing the skin, bones and unwanted matter, then cut it into bite-size pieces.

2 Finely chop the garlic, ginger, onion and chillies.

3 Heat the butter, preferably in a wok, and stir-fry the cummin seeds for 1 minute.

4 Add the garlic and ginger, and stir-fry for a further minute.

5 Add the onion and chillies and continue to stir-fry for 5 more minutes.

6 Now add the turmeric and curry powder and mix well, followed by the chicken pieces. Stir-fry for about 10 minutes, turning the pieces over from time to time.

8 Meanwhile, chop the peppers, tomato and coriander leaves and add these into the strir-fry after 10 minutes.

9 The dish should be fairly dry, but not sticking, so add a little water if needed.

10 Simmer for a further 5 to 10 minutes, salt to taste and serve with a squeeze of lemon juice.

# GOOSE DUMPODE THE INDIAN WAY

*Hobson Jobson* says: '*Dumpode or dumpoke, deriving from the Persian word "dampukht" for "air-cooked" i.e. baked, a dish as used in the emperor Akbar's kitchen, is the Anglo-Indian name given to a baked dish, consisting usually of a duck, boned and stuffed.*' It could also be goose. Flora Annie Steel sniffily tells us: '*There is not a good breed of geese in India, but some birds might be imported which could be free of the wild, rank taste of the ordinary Indian goose.*' The rather more positive Wyvern denounced: '*The mixture which tradition has handed down to the Anglo-Indian kitchen for the stuffing of ducks and geese is disagreeable owing to its flavour of violent onion, crude sage, and slices of half boiled potato, mixed together lumpily and lubricated with some chopped fat. Let me speedily tell you,*' he goes on, '*that potato has no place whatever in this stuffing, and the crude taste you dislike so much, is from the sage being chopped raw.*'

The *Indian Cookery Book* has no problem with goose or its stuffing. This recipe, goose dumpode the Indian way, is taken more or less straight from the book. It was a family treat from time to time, served in the traditional Anglo-Indian way, as the book says: '*with turnips, parsnips, carrots, onions and potatoes and some hot West Indian pickle*'.

———— SERVES: 4 TO 6 ————

## 3.5 to 4 kg (8 to 9lb) goose

———— MARINADE ————

2 teaspoons yellow
  mustard powder
4 tablespoons olive oil

1 teaspoon salt
1 teaspoon garam masala (see
  page 39)

———— STUFFING ————

450g (1lb) minced chicken
110g (4 oz) beef suet
10 rashers bacon, chopped
the goose liver, chopped
1 tablespoon thyme
1 tablespoon marjoram
1 teaspoon ground black
  pepper

1 teaspoon chilli powder
6 slices white bread, finely
  chopped
½ teaspoon salt
4 anchovy fillets, chopped
12 oysters, fresh or tinned
  (optional)
some truffles (optional)

———— GRAVY ————

the goose bones
the giblets
250ml (9 fl oz) white wine
100ml (3½ fl oz) brandy

½ teaspoon white pepper
2 tablespoons fresh coriander
  leaves
4 bay leaves

salt to taste

1  Bone the goose, a difficult task, but worth the effort. Take care not to pierce the flesh and skin. Wash it inside and out, and dry it thoroughly.
2  Mix together the mustard, olive oil, salt, and garam masala. Then, wearing protective plastic gloves, rub it thoroughly into the goose's inside.
3  Mix the stuffing ingredients together and put into the goose, moulding the boneless carcass around the stuffing. Weigh it to calculate your cooking time. Depending on the original goose size, it will still weigh, with stuffing, about the same as it was before boning. If it is around 3.5 kg (8lb) it will need about 2½ hours. If it is nearer 4kg (9lb) it will take about 3 hours, and so on.

4 Cover the goose with kitchen foil, and put it onto an oven pan and into the oven, preheated to 190°C/375°F/Gas 5.

5 Roast for the time stated. Inspect a couple of times. For the last half hour, remove the foil. To check that the goose is cooked, poke a deep area of flesh with a thin skewer. If the liquid which runs out is not clear, roast for longer. When clear liquid runs out, it is cooked.

6 Leave to rest for about 10 minutes before carving. It will relax the flesh.

7 During the roasting, make gravy by simmering the bones, giblets and the other ingredients for about 45 minutes, during which time it will reduce and thicken. Discard the solids, and serve in a gravy boat with the goose.

# SPICED RISSOLES

This was the Raj version of the Hindoostanee Kawab (see page 45). My mother's handwritten notes in the cookbook say we can omit the egg for a 'cheap version', and use a large slice of bread as a thickener instead. This was probably a reference to the egg shortage in Britain during the Second World War. It would not have affected them in India, nor us now.

SERVES: 4

| | |
|---|---|
| 450g (1lb) lean mince | 1 to 3 fresh green chillies, chopped |
| 150g (5½ oz) very finely chopped onion | ½ teaspoon salt |
| 2 or 3 cloves garlic, finely chopped | 1 egg |
| | flour for dusting |
| | 4 to 6 tablespoons ghee or oil |

1 Mix the mince with the onion, garlic, chillies, salt and egg to achieve a mouldable texture.

2 Shape it into burgers and dust with flour.

3 Heat the ghee or oil in the large frying pan. Fry the rissoles for about 4 to 5 minutes each side for medium rare, or as required for rarer or well-cooked rissoles.

4 Serve hot with vegetables, or cold in crusty bread rolls with salad and pickles.

# POTATO MINCE RISSOLES

These were one of my favourites as a child. Called *'patice'* (patties) or *'cutless'* (cutlets) by the *bobajees*, they must have been popular in the Raj, but apart from the breakfast variant given on page 66, I have not come across a recipe for them in the various old Raj cookbooks. They are mashed potato rissoles, at the centre of which is buried a filling of cooked spicy mince (keema curry). They are then breadcrumbed and fried. Serve hot with peas and brown sauce, or cold as a sandwich filler.

———————————————— MAKES: 8 RISSOLES ————————————————

8 tablespoons cooked
  keema curry (see page 42)
450g (1lb) salted mashed
  potato

2 egg yolks
1 cupful breadcrumbs
6 tablespoons vegetable or corn
  oil

1  Mould the cooked keema into 8 equal-size balls.

2  Take a ball of salted mashed potato, about 6.5cm (2½ inches). Flatten it to a disc shape. Make a depression in the top side. Insert the meat ball. Press the potato over it.

3  Glaze it with the egg yolk, then dab it in the breadcrumbs to cover generously. Repeat with the other rissoles.

4  Heat the oil in the large frying pan. Fry the rissoles until golden, about 3 or 4 minutes each side.

5  Serve hot or cold.

## CHAPTER NINE
# VEGETABLES

OLD HABITS DIE HARD, and if the British and the Anglo-Indian community adored meat, they conversely were none too keen on the accompanying vegetables. The reason for this was probably because many cooks were taught to over-cook all vegetables. In the *Indian Cookery Book*, we are told to boil broccoli for half an hour, whilst cabbage and cucumber get a full hour, and of carrots it says: *'Put them on in boiling water, with some salt in it, and boil them from two to three hours. Very young carrots will require one hour.'*

Little wonder they were unpopular. They must have tasted of little, had the texture of glue and had all their nutrients stewed out of them.

Even salads did not escape vandalisation. Lettuce, exhorts the cookbook, must be: *'washed in water containing a tablespoon of boracic powder to clean the lettuce of deleterious germs'*. The same paragraph recommends that boracic powder be: *'sprinkled about in the haunts of cockroaches. It effectively gets rid of them.'* And in an army cooking manual of the period we are told that borax and boracic acid should be added to mess tea to: *'quell the rampant (sexual) urges so prevalent in the young unmarried other ranks'*. Another method for cleaning vegetables was to use permanganate of potash. This colours the water a delightful purple, fine if you enjoy purple lettuce, radish or cucumber.

I make no apology to the Raj for omitting such additives, nor for re-working these otherwise delightful vegetable recipes, so that the results are crisp, tasty and full of goodness.

# BUBBLE AND SQUEAK

This is so simple, and yet it is so tasty. It was one of the Raj's favourite vegetable dishes, as a way to use up yesterday's left-over vegetables. The Raj version uses spices which make the dish doubly delicious. The *bobajees*, however, were none too keen about cooking left-overs. Centuries of conditioning meant that food in India was cooked fresh for every meal. It was too hot for food to be kept safely for another meal. Scraps were always given to the sweepers. They had to be trained in all the strange ways of the Raj, of which this was the strangest.

The *Indian Cookery Book* suggests that cold meat is combined with ready-boiled vegetables and spices, and enough stock to cover: '*Simmer until the stock is reduced to half, it will then be ready. Serve it up bubbling and squeaking.*'

My version here uses vegetables and spices but omits the meat and shortens the cooking to a quick stir-fry. Sadly this seems to omit the sound effects, but I assure you it tastes just as good.

SERVES: 4 AS AN ACCOMPANIMENT

330g (12 oz) total weight, using 3 or more of the following (weighed after preparation): cauliflower, turnip, cabbage, carrot, or brussel sprouts
2 tablespoons ghee or vegetable oil

1 large (225g/8 oz) onion, finely chopped
1 clove garlic, finely chopped
5cm (2 inch) piece of ginger, finely chopped
½ teaspoon ground cummin
½ teaspoon chilli powder (optional)
225g (8 oz) mashed potato

1   Prepare the vegetables that you choose to use by washing them and removing unwanted matter.
2   Wash again and cut them into bite-size pieces, then cook them in boiling water until crisp but cooked (average 8 minutes).
3   Heat the wok with the ghee and stir-fry the onion, garlic, and ginger for 5 minutes.
4   Add the cooked and still warm vegetables, the ground cummin, optional chilli powder and mashed potato. Mix well and salt to taste.
5   Serve hot.

# CHILLI STEWED MUSHROOM

Talking of left-overs, as I was in the previous recipe, my grandmother always told the kids to leave some food on their plates for 'Mr Manners'. My mother, aged seven, thought she knew all the friends, neighbours, trades people, and servants who came to the bungalow, but no amount of interrogation ever seemed to yield the identity of Mr Manners. It took her some years to realise that these scraps were actually being eaten by the *methars* (sweepers/cleaners). They were 'untouchables', or beneath caste. It meant that they were not allowed to eat with the other servants, nor be given any food by them, nor live in the compound. They relied on the scraps.

Yet their job was indispensable, the more so because cleaning was beneath the other servants. The memsahib was therefore saddled with checking to see they did their job and with the responsibility of their well-being. My grandmother personally saw to it that her *methars* got their expected scraps of food at every mealtime. Not all of the memsahibs agreed. The abominable Flora Annie Steele wrote: '*The fear of trespassing on time-honoured bad habits, and the sweeper's perquisites, should not prevent you from giving your poultry what is the very best thing for them, viz, the constant variety afforded by, what is called in India, the "sweeper's tin". It will be better to give the methar an extra 8 annas a month.*'

My grandmother always gave her *methars* the choice of scraps of food or extra pay. Her *methars* always elected to go for the food. In return no bungalow was cleaner than hers.

SERVES: 4

450g (1lb) mushrooms, any type
1 tablespoon butter
3 or 4 anchovy fillets, chopped
2 cloves, crushed
some freshly grated nutmeg

pinch of ground mace
½ teaspoon whole peppercorns, crushed
1 to 4 fresh red chillies, finely chopped
1 teaspoon Worcester sauce
1 tablespoon brandy (optional)
salt to taste

1   Wash the mushrooms, peel, and chop them.
2   Put the mushrooms together with the other ingredients into a hot pan, and stir as required until the liquids seep into the mushrooms. When they are hot, serve at once.

# CELERY AND FENNEL IN CREAM

Boarding schools had their ups and downs for the kids of the Raj. The boys' dormitory at their school in Jubalpore back in 1915, was next to the head's apartment. The beak's wife used to hang her cream and milk in *chatties* (earthenware containers) in the shade on her balcony, to keep it cool. Since it was within reasonable reach of my uncles Bill, Jim and Frank, a challenge was born. It was soon solved by means of a long thin bamboo reed, which could be twisted into the *chattie*, while the perpetrators remained unseen. A deep suck set up a siphon, and soon much of the milk was transferred to the boys' tummies. Although neither the head nor his wife ever interrogated the occupants of the dorm about the incident, after a few days the *chatties* were transferred to the other end of the balcony, well out of reach of reeds and small boys. This creamy recipe uses neither.

SERVES: 4

1 bunch celery
1 bulb fennel
2 tablespoons butter
1 teaspoon celery seeds
1 teaspoon fennel seeds
150ml (¼ pint) milk

1 teaspoon green peppercorns in brine
200ml (7 fl oz) double (heavy) cream
4 tablespoons yoghurt
salt to taste

GARNISH

snipped chives
paprika

1  Clean the celery and the fennel, and chop it into bite-size pieces. Blanch it to soften it.
2  Heat the butter, and stir-fry the seeds for 30 seconds. Add the milk and as soon as it starts to warm, add the peppercorns and the celery and fennel.
3  When this becomes warm, not hot, add the cream and the yoghurt, stir until it is eating temperature, then salt to taste and serve at once, garnished attractively.

# ROAST ONION SURPRISE

When the kids travelled to school, it was necessary to send a bearer with them. Sending the bearer in the first class section was expensive, though his return journey would be a third class fare. On one occasion the bearer who, unusually, had transferred with the family when they were posted from one hill station to another (Naini Tal to Simla) had not been home to see his own family for some years. He asked for a month's holiday. Since Frank's schooling was at a critical exam stage, he alone remained as a boarder at St Joseph's college in Naini Tal. The obvious solution was for the bearer to travel with Frank at the end of the school holidays. As Frank was on his own, and he wouldn't need waiting on, it was decided to save money by sending the bearer third class. At least he would be on the same train if he were needed. All went well to begin with, until the first stop. Then there was a terrible commotion on the platform outside Frank's compartment. It was the bearer. Once away from parental control, he had decided it was beneath his dignity not to be with his *chota sahib*, and he was telling the world about it in loud terms. Frank was embarrassed, of course, and rather than let the scene continue at each stop, of which there were dozens, he quietly paid the difference in the fare from his pocket money, and the bearer took his 'rightful' place in his compartment.

My grandfather later reimbursed Frank, and the bearer, a very loyal servant, proudly reappeared in Simla after his month's leave. Nothing was said, but Grandpa learnt a lesson.

Here's a super hill station recipe and a remarkable way to cook and enjoy onions. For extra economy, they can be baked when the oven is already being used to bake some other savoury dish. And the surprise is a garlic inserted in the base.

---

SERVES: 4

---

**4 large pink onions, unpeeled**
**4 large cloves garlic, peeled**
**salt, pepper and chilli powder**

---

1   Chop off the 'hairy' base of the onions, in a manner which will make the onions stable when they stand on this base.
2   Using a potato parer or small sharp knife, gouge out a hole at the centre of the base, where the pithy bit is located.
3   Insert a garlic clove into each hole.

4   On an oiled oven tray, stand the onions up on their base, so that the garlic cloves cannot fall out.

5   Put the tray into the oven preheated to 190°C/375°F/Gas 5, and bake for about 20 to 30 minutes. Dust with salt, pepper and chilli powder and serve hot.

# POTATO RIBBONS

My mother finally left home to begin training as a nurse in Bombay. But being a home person, as all the kids were, she'd be on the train home to see her parents, no matter where they were, every time she had leave. On one occasion, she went from Bombay to Quetta, always a long and strenuous journey. A particularly savage monsoon was racing before her, sweeping away many bridges. There were many unexpected train changes, and then the toing and froing started. A journey which should have taken just eighteen hours took four days. Mum was so confused she had no idea where she was, and just for once she didn't have a bearer.

Then the train came out of the monsoon, and into the Thor Hyderabad desert. Instead of lashing rain, it was sand everywhere. It was on the bunks, on her skin, creeping under her clothing to make her body itch, in her hair and in her mouth. For the first time, even the dining room lost its thrill. The thought of eating more sand was just too awful. Then there was the fear that her pocket money would run out, so much was being handed to the coolies for moving her luggage each time she had to change train. This little recipe, a kind of potato crisp, was a family favourite, and no doubt was one of the attractions of home.

SERVES: 4

**2 large potatoes**
**oil for deep-frying**
**salt and garam masala (see page 39)**

1   Wash the potatoes, but do not peel them.

2   Using a potato peeler or small sharp knife, cut them into thin strips round and round, keeping the width, about 2cm (¾ inch), as equal as possible. Each strip should preferably be at least 20cm (8 inches) in length.

3   Put the strips a few at a time into the deep-fryer, whose oil temperature is 190°C (chip-frying) temperature. Fry briefly until pale and golden.

4   As you bring them out of the oil, rest them on kitchen paper for a few minutes, during which time they will dry off and crisp up. Dust with salt and garam masala, and serve hot.

5   If they have not gone crisp, a second brief deep-fry, or a short spell in the oven, will do the trick.

## PLAIN BOILED RICE

Use basmati rice, boiled in ample water. Follow this recipe accurately and you'll have fragrant, fluffy dry rice.

SERVES: 4 (MAKES 4 PORTIONS)

**300g (10 oz) basmati rice
2 litres (3 pints) water**

1   Pick through the rice to remove grit and impurities.

2   Boil the water in a 3 litre (6 pint) pan. It is not necessary to salt it.

3   While the water is heating up, rinse the rice briskly with fresh cold water until most of the starch is washed out.

4   Run boiling water from the kettle through the rice at the final rinse. This minimises the temperature reduction when you put the rice into the pan's boiling water.

5   When the water is boiling properly, put the rice into the pan. Start timing. It takes just 8 to 10 minutes from the start to cook. Stir until the rice is circulating. Put the lid on the pan until the water comes back to the boil, then remove the lid. Stir frequently.

6   After about 6 minutes, taste a few grains. As soon as the centre is no longer brittle but still has a good *al dente* bite to it, strain off the water. The rice should seem slightly undercooked.

7   Shake off all the excess water, then place the strainer onto a dry tea towel which will help remove the last of the water.

8   After a minute or so place the rice in a warmed serving dish. You can

serve it now or, preferably, put it into a very low oven or warming drawer for at least 30 minutes and at most 90 minutes. As it dries, the grains will separate and become fluffy.

9  Just before serving, fluff up the rice with a fork to aerate it and release the steam.

# COOKING RICE BY ABSORPTION

Cooking rice in a pre-measured ratio of water which is all absorbed into the rice is undoubtedly the best way to do it. Provided that you use basmati rice, the finished grains are longer, thinner and much more fragrant and flavourful than they are after boiling.

The method is easy, but many cookbooks make it sound far too complicated. Instructions invariably state that you must use a tightly lidded pot and precise water quantity and heat levels, and never lift the lid during the boiling process etc. etc. However, I lift the lid, I might stir the rice, and I've even cooked rice by absorption without a lid. Also, if I've erred on the side of too little water, I've added a bit during 'the boil'. (Too much water is an unresolvable problem, however.) It's all naughty, rule-breaking stuff, but it still seems to work.

It's useful to know that 300g (10 oz) is 2 tea cups of dry rice, and 600ml (20 fl oz) is about 1⅓ volume of water to 1 of rice. This one to two numerical ratio is easy to remember, but do step up or step down the quantities as required in proportion. For small appetites, for instance, use 225g (8 oz) rice: 450ml (16 fl oz) water to serve four people. For large appetites use 350g (12 oz) rice: 700ml (24 fl oz) water.

Cooking rice does need some practice, but after a few goes at this you'll do it without thinking. Here is my foolproof method.

———————— SERVES: 4 (MAKES 4 PORTIONS) ————————

**300g basmati rice**
**600ml water**

1   Soak the rice in water to cover for about 15 minutes.

2   Rinse it until the water runs more or less clear, then drain.

3   Bring the measured water to the boil in a saucepan (as heavy as possible, and with a lid) or casserole dish with a capacity at least twice the volume of the drained rice.

4   As soon as the water is boiling, add the rice and stir in well.

5   As soon as it starts bubbling, put the lid on the pan and reduce the heat to under half. Leave well alone for 5 minutes.

6   Inspect. Has the liquid on top been absorbed? If not, replace the lid and leave for 2 minutes. If and when it has, stir the rice well, ensuring that it is not sticking to the bottom. Now taste. It should not be brittle in the middle. If it is, add a little more water and return to the heat.

7   Place the saucepan or casserole into a warming drawer or oven preheated to its lowest setting. This should be no lower than 80°C/175°F and no higher than 100°C/210°F/Gas 1. You can serve the rice at once, but the longer you leave it, the more separate the grains will be. Thirty minutes is fine, but it will be quite safe and happy left for up to 90 minutes.

# SPICY RICE

Plain rice is delicious accompanying certain dishes, but spicy rice, usually called pullao rice is delicious, too, with its tasty flavours and fragrant spices.

SERVES: 4

1 batch cooked basmati rice (either of the 2 previous recipes)
2 tablespoons ghee
½ teaspoon yellow food colouring powder (optional)
2 tablespoons coconut milk powder
1 tablespoon ground almond
salt to taste
20 to 30 saffron strands (optional)
2 tablespoons milk (optional)
pinch red food colouring powder (optional)

────────── WHOLE SPICES ──────────

2 whole green cardamoms,          2 whole cloves
  crushed                             5cm (2 inch) cassia bark
                  ½ teaspoon fennel seeds

1    Prepare and cook the rice by boiling or by absorption.
2    Heat the ghee in a large frying pan or wok. Add the whole spices and cook for about 30 seconds on medium heat.
3    Add about three-quarters of the rice, the optional colouring, coconut and almond, and salt to taste.
4    If you want to use saffron, warm it in 2 tablespoons of warm milk, let it stand for 10 minutes, and add to the rice in stage 3.
5    Either allow the rice to cool and reheat later (it will keep very happily for a full day in the fridge) or serve at once. Just before serving mix in the remaining quarter of prewarmed white rice. You'll get a nice yellow/white mixture.
6    If you want red/yellow/white, mix red food colouring powder (a pinch) with some white rice previously put aside. Allow it to stand for a few minutes then mix it in with the white and yellow rice.

# MACARONI PIE

Wyvern describes macaroni as the best known of '*the numerous varieties of the Italian paste* [sic] *family*'. He warns: '*Remember it is a much handled comestible, and that washing in water is not enough.*'

Various pastas were available at the turn of the 19th century at the Europe stores, but the *Indian Cookery Book* gives a recipe for making its own dough, using eggs, and flour ('*English or American preferable to country*') and no water. '*Roll it out to a sheet the thickness of an eight anna piece, then cut it into small squares, diamonds, or circles, or into any shape or design you please. If pipe macaroni be required, cut the sheet into ribbons of the required width, put longways over glass pipes, and draw the pipes out as the pastry hardens.*'

Mrs Steel, who as we have seen finds nothing correct about anything in India, pronounced: '*Macaroni is almost invariably ruined in India by being dressed with eggs.*'

We are fortunate that we can buy ready made fresh or dry macaroni, so we can dispense with eight anna pieces and glass tubes. It is perfectly clean already, and as for dressing with eggs!

SERVES: 4

250g (8 oz) dried macaroni
2 tablespoons cornflour
300ml (½ pint) milk
2 tablespoons butter
2 tablespoons olive oil
2 or 3 fresh red chillies, shredded
several sprigs parsley, chopped

1 teaspoon garam masala (see page 39)
1 teaspoon salt
175g to 225g (6 to 8 oz) Cheddar cheese, grated
some vegetable oil
2 or 3 celery sticks cut into long strips
6 or 8 thin slices of tomato

GARNISH

**some snipped chives
some hard-boiled quail eggs, sliced**

1  Boil the macaroni until it is *al dente*. Drain and set aside.
1  Meanwhile, put the cornflour into a jug or bowl, and use just enough milk to make a creamy lump-free paste. Work in the remaining milk, keeping it lump-free.
2  Heat the butter and olive oil in a non-stick pan. Add some of the milk paste, and stir until it starts to thicken. Once it does, slowly trickle in the remaining milk paste, stirring all the time, until it will thicken no more. It should be lump-free, but don't worry if it is a bit lumpy. Mix in the chillies, parsley, garam masala, salt and the cheese.
3  Oil an oven dish, line its base with the celery strips. Put the preferably still hot macaroni in next. Pour over the cheesy mixture. Top off with the tomato slices.
4  Put the dish into the oven, preheated to 190°C/375°F/Gas 5.
5  Bake for about 20 to 30 minutes, until the top looks golden with brown heat patches. Garnish (include a dressing of eggs!) and serve.

# AN OLDE KETCHUP AND AN OLDE CURREY

Hannah Glasse wrote her cookery book *The Art of Cookery Made Eafy* [sic] in 1747. She was as highly regarded as was Mrs Beeton, more than a century later, and our own Delia Smith today. Her book was reprinted in 1983 by Prospect Books. This is one of her recipes for '*Captains of Ships*' specifically to take to the '*Indies*'. At the time of its writing, the building of the Suez Canal was over a century ahead. The journey until then was around Africa's Cape of Good Hope and it took four months. Not long after Ms Glasse's book was published, on one of these ships to the Indies, would have been my ancestor with the name of Lawrence. No doubt he would have known this ketchup well (not to mention '*ftrong beer*', '*ftale*' or not!) and he could have probably told us what a '*race*' weighed. Here's the recipe, virtually unaltered, except I have changed the 'f's for 's's. With some experimentation you could make this ketchup yourfelf!

By the way, the word 'ketchup' is derived from the ancient Chinese words *koe*, pickle in brine, and *tsiap*, sauce, which in Malaysia became *katsup*.

FOR CAPTAINS OF SHIPS: TO MAKE KETCHUP TO KEEP TWENTY YEARS
'*Take a gallon of strong stale beer, one pound anchovies, a pound of shallots, peeled, ½ ounce of mace, ¼ ounce pepper, 3 or 4 large races ginger, 2 quarts of large mushroom flaps, rubbed to pieces. Cover, and let simmer till it is half wasted, then strain it through a flannel. Bottle when cold. You may carry it to the Indies. The stronger the beer, the better the ketchup will be.*'

Incidentally, Hannah Glasse's 1747 recipe for curry is of interest too. I quote again, this time keeping the 'f's in place.

TO MAKE A CURREY (SIC) THE INDIAN WAY
'*Take 2 fowls or rabbits, cut them into fmall pieces, and 3 or 4 fmall onions, peeled and cut very fmall, 30 peppercorns, and a large fpoonful of rice. Brown fome coriander feeds over the fire in a clear shovel, and beat them to a powder. Take a teafpoonful of falt and mix all well together with the meat. Put all together into a faucepan or ftew pan, with a pint of water. Let it ftew foftly till the meat is enough, then put in a piece*

*of fresh butter, about the fize of a walnut, shake it well together, and when it is fmooth and of a fine thicknef, difh it up, and fend it to the table. If the fauce be too thick, add a little more water, and more falt if it wants it. You are to observe that the fauce muft be pretty thick.'* Fffew!

# CHAPTER TEN

# PUDDINGS AND DESSERTS

M OST OF MY grandmother's handwritten notes in her *Indian Cookery Book* are recipes for puddings and desserts. This was partly due to the fact that both my great grandparents were interested in patisserie and confectionery, to the extent that they intended to open a bakery in Agra in 1909 specifically to serve the memsahibs. No doubt the shop would have done well. There was a huge contingent of British military there, who were looking forward to using the shop, but Alexander's premature death led to the venture closing after the shop had been fully equipped, and before it had baked a single cake.

Recipes such as the ones in this chapter certainly appeared at the Raj family dinner table, normally as their third course. At the grander dinner occasion, the pudding course was called the 'entremets', the course after the entrée, and it could, depending on the scale of the banquet, be the fourth or fifth course. Puddings were always hot dishes.

The endless banquets of the early days of the Raj were the highlights of the social evening. They could stretch for hours and it seems the longer they lasted, and the more courses they served, the better they were considered to be. It seems inconceivable that after the entremets pudding, any more could happen, but two more courses were often served as a 'surprise'. First came the savoury course (see page 177), which was a very light 'refresher' and would be of tiny quantity. At last came the final course. Technically, this course was called the dessert, literally meaning the course at the end of the dinner, the word coming from the French, *desservir*, to clear the table. Like the savoury course, it too was a 'refresher' and a mere morsel. It could consist of a selection of fruit or it could be a lightly made-up dish, such as sorbet or ice-cream, but it would always be cold. Today, its descendant is the sweetmeat served with coffee, but in those days coffee, although it was native to India, was not served at the dinner table. The memsahibs would withdraw (to the drawing room) for coffee and gossip. The sahibs would stay at the table to swig the port, smoke cigars and gossip.

Any of these light sweets can be served as the pudding course for normal family meals, as they were by the Raj household, or they make excellent little snacks at any time.

# CHOCOLATE CUSTARD

Of all the puddings my grandmother made, this was my absolute favourite. Her cookery book describes the start of the operation thus: '*Rasp three ounces of fine Spanish chocolate, which has the vanilla flavour. Make a paste of it with the smallest quantity of water.*'

Use 'bitter' chocolate, which contains at least 70% cocoa solids. Custard powder, an invention not around at the time the *Indian Cookery Book* was written, contains vanilla, though I like to add a little extra vanilla, which you can do if you wish. Chocolate custard is always served hot, and it has the texture of thickish custard. Thinning it down with tinned evaporated milk was one Raj luxury this recipe must have.

--------------------- SERVES: 4 ---------------------

140g (5 oz) 'bitter' chocolate (see above)
600ml (1 pint) milk
2 tablespoons custard powder

2 tablespoons sugar, or more to taste
a few drops of vanilla essence
a pinch or two of salt

1  Select a heatproof glass bowl which fits comfortably over a saucepan. Cut or break the chocolate into small squares, and put them into the bowl. Bring some water to the simmer in the saucepan. Put the bowl

onto the pan, ensuring the bottom does not touch the water. The chocolate will melt fast, helped by stirring.

2 Using just enough of the milk (a couple of spoonfuls), make a paste with the custard powder in a large jug.

3 Bring the milk to the simmer in a 3 litre (6 pint) non-stick saucepan. Little by little, pour it into the jug of custard paste, stirring all the time.

4 Pour it back into the saucepan, adding the melted chocolate, the sugar, vanilla and the salt.

5 Stir continuously until it will thicken no further. Serve hot, with a jug of evaporated milk.

# LEMON CUSTARD

Like the previous recipe, although it is made differently, this one is also the consistency of runny custard. It is a beautiful translucent lemon colour, and has an amazing taste combination of acid tartness and sweetness. When my grandmother made it she always served it with a little jug of canned evaporated milk, a Raj luxury, and this added a creamy, luxurious element to the dish.

SERVES: 4

110g (4 oz) butter
juice of 4 lemons
a pinch or two of salt
1 large cup granulated
  sugar

1 heaped teaspoon cornflour
1 tablespoon water
1 beaten egg

1 Heat the butter, lemon juice, salt and the sugar in a saucepan on a low heat, stirring until it dissolves.

2 Make a paste of the cornflour and water. Add it with the beaten egg into the pan. Stir continuously until it thickens.

3 When it will thicken no more, serve hot on its own, or with cream or evaporated milk.

# BANANA FRITTERS

These are scrumptious served hot with ice-cream. We can easily purchase high quality ice-cream these days, but as there were no freezers in those days, they had to make their own. The cook purchased blocks of ice from the bazaars. In Moghul days blocks of ice were carried from the Himalayas to wherever the Moghuls were at court, by runners. In the days of the Raj giant blocks of ice came by sea from Canada. Initially the ice was there merely to keep a crop of apples fresh. But it was quickly found that the ice had more value than the apples. By keeping the blocks huge, they were able to reach inland cities like Agra. By then the blocks were smaller, and very expensive, but they were a necessary luxury. Anyway, the cook purchased blocks of ice, which he broke up into a special wooden ice-cream pail, along with some saltpetre, which retarded the melting rate of the ice. Into this was placed the cream mixture in its own container, with its lid in place. Then it was the really monotonous chore of turning the handle. This was a job the kids took in turns, though there was always an unfortunate servant, a *mati* (kitchen helper), waiting in the wings. Of course, the motivation for the kids was the end product – delicious homemade ice-cream.

SERVES: 4

4 large, very ripe bananas
3 heaped tablespoons
  custard powder
2 heaped tablespoons
  cornflour
3 heaped tablespoons
  coconut milk powder
1 large egg

1 teaspoon ground green
  cardamom
½ teaspoon caraway seed
pinch of salt
1 tablespoon caster sugar
milk as required
4 tablespoons butter ghee
icing sugar for dusting
lemon wedges to serve

1   Mash the bananas with the custard powder, cornflour, coconut milk powder, egg, cardamom, caraway, salt and caster sugar to make a thick batter which will drop off the spoon, adding milk to reach the right consistency.

2   Leave the mixture to stand for 20 minutes.

3   Heat the ghee in a large frying pan. Dollop 2 tablespoons of batter into the pan. Fry the fritter for a couple of minutes.

4   Turn it over and fry the other side for a further couple of minutes,
    until it is crisp. To keep its shape you might have to prod the edges
    with a spatula.

5   Repeat with the remaining mixture. Dust with icing sugar and serve
    hot with lemon wedges.

## PINK BRANDY PANCAKES

The *Indian Cookery Book* tells us that pink pancakes '*are very rarely seen at the
English table, though they form a very pleasing variety*'. It then tells us to '*boil a
beetroot and pound it to a pulp in a marble mortar, and strain through muslin*'. Best
of all, it says to '*add a wineglass full of brandy to the batter*'. I certainly approve
of the latter, although we can save ourselves a lot of effort by using red
food colouring to achieve the pink colour. The book concludes this recipe
by requiring you to '*garnish with green candied sweetmeats*'. The kids enjoyed
spending their few pice pocket money in the bazaar on sweeties. One pice
bought a lot of 'thousands and ones'. Some green ones might have found
their way onto the pink pancakes.

SERVES: 4

110g (4 oz) plain white flour
50g (1¾ oz) vegetable oil
2 eggs, beaten
250ml (9 fl oz) milk,
    warmed
1 tablespoon sugar

3 or 4 drops vanilla essence
some drops of pink colouring
50ml (2 fl oz) brandy
some ghee for frying
icing sugar for dusting
lime wedges

1   Sift the flour into a bowl and mix in the oil, eggs, warm milk, sugar and
    vanilla, colouring and brandy. Mix well and leave to stand for about 10
    minutes. The batter should be of pouring consistency.

2   In a very hot omelette or griddle pan, heat a little ghee. Pour in enough
    batter which, when swirled around the pan, makes a thin panacke.

3   Cook to set, then turn over and briefly cook the other side. Turn it out
    and repeat with the others. Sprinkle with sugar and serve with lime
    wedges.

# FRUIT SALAD

This recipe was written in my grandmother's handwriting, on one of the blank pages on her *Indian Cookery Book*, I'll guess when she had just married in 1902. The handwriting is still young and sprightly. Collecting recipes was something the memsahibs liked to do. On a page nearby in the same handwriting is a recipe for *'Mrs Notley's Mango Pickle'*. Maybe this idea was from Mrs Notley too. It is really simple.

I particularly like her final instruction: *'Top with Bird's custard.'* Evidently custard powder made its appearance at the Europe stores at around the end of the 19th century. Brand names were everything then, as they still are. So are logos, and the chicken logo on the Bird's tin was a source of amusement for Raj kids. Like so many of the brands available then at the Europe stores, Bird's is still around, logo and all, and is still going strong.

SERVES: 4

| | |
|---|---|
| 8 guavas | 2 tablespoons sugar |
| 4 bananas | juice of 2 limes |
| pinch of salt | 75ml (3 fl oz) rum |

1  Cut up the guavas. Slice the bananas. Put them into a bowl. Sprinkle on the other ingredients.
2  Cover the bowl and let it rest in the fridge for 2 hours or so.
3  Serve cold, but top with hot custard.

# MANGO FOOL

Fools are simple to make, fresh fruit being cooked, then pressed through the sieve. They are delicious to eat, and are always served chilled. They were very popular in Victorian times, and they were good candidates for the Raj, where the sieve seemed to make a regular appearance. We can avoid the chore of sieving, by using tinned fruit and the blender. Here I'm using mango, but equally good fruits are apple, gooseberry, rhubarb, indeed, anything you like. The dish is quite rich, so I've kept the portions relatively small.

SERVES: 4

400g (14 oz) tinned mango slices in syrup
½ teaspoon ground cinnamon

3 or 4 tablespoons icing sugar (optional)
300ml (½ pint) whipping cream

1 Put the mango slices and the syrup, the cinnamon and sugar into the blender and make a smooth purée.
2 In a large mixing bowl, whip the cream so that it is at least double the volume you started with.
3 Now, using the technique of cutting and folding, add in the mango purée. The technique retains air, and keeps the fool light.
4 Cover the bowl and chill in the fridge for an hour or two, then serve.

# SPICE PICE APPLE SLICE PIE

Try saying that when you've had a *burrah* peg! I don't know exactly who christened this dish with that name, but it was a dish my grandmother often turned out in early autumn, when the house was awash with windfall apples. Apples grew prolifically in the hill stations, where they liked the cool climate. And windfalls were equally prolific in the homes there in autumn. One highlight of Quetta was a fruit garden called Galbrey Spinney, where admission was free, and you could eat all the fruit you liked when you were inside (at least that's what the kids said) but you had to pay for any you carried out. Of course the kids paid nothing upon their exit, but my grandmother was always suspicious about why they wouldn't eat their lunch. This pie was a favourite. A pice was a coin, as we saw on page 72. There were 64 to the rupee, but what it was really saying was that this pie cost virtually nothing to make. And it's simple to make, too. It has no top pastry crust, only a bottom lining of shortcrust pasty, which makes it a tart, really.

SERVES: 4

500g (1lb 2 oz) shortcrust pastry

some melted butter

3 or 4 medium-size firm cooking apples

demerara sugar

2 tablespoons butter (not melted)

1   If possible, use a circular pie dish, of about 25cm (10 inch) diameter.
2   Roll out the pastry so that there will be enough to line the pie dish generously.
3   Brush the pie dish with some of the melted butter. Then gently press the pastry into the dish, and up the sides. Cut off any surplus pastry with a knife.
4   Halve the apples, then cut away the core and pith. Now slice the apples into thin slices. Arrange the slices very decoratively, so that they overlap each other, and follow the round shape of the dish. Work in circles from the centre, outwards, so there are 4 or 5 circles.
5   Liberally coat the apples with the sugar, and randomly place the butter on top in small blobs.
6   Put the pie into the oven, preheated to 180°C/350°F/Gas 4.
7   Bake for about an hour. Serve hot or cold with cream and/or custard.

# FUDGE

Fudge got its name from the fact that it was invented in error in nineteenth-century Victorian Britain when a sweet maker got his recipe for toffee wrong and it came out soft instead of hard. This version was one of my absolute treats as a young child. It can be made with or without the chocolate.

MAKES: ABOUT 350G (12OZ) FUDGE

3 tablespoons cocoa
 (optional)
75ml (3 fl oz) milk
400g (14 oz) icing sugar
1 tablespoon salted butter

125ml (4 fl oz) water
pinch salt
1 teaspoon vanilla essence
400g (14 oz) tinned sweetened
 condensed milk

1   Mix the optional cocoa with a little milk to make a paste, then bit by
    bit add the remaining milk until it is all mixed. This is to prevent
    lumps forming.
2   Add the sugar, butter, water and salt, pour into a non-stick saucepan,
    and stir it to the boil.
3   Simmer for about 15 minutes, stirring as it bubbles to keep the mixture
    a smooth consistency.
4   Add the vanilla essence and the condensed milk, stirring all the while
    and regulating the heat, as it can easily burn. After a few minutes, the
    bubbles will lightly pop.
5   Pour into a flat tray with a shallow edge.
6   Before it sets, score lines across the fudge which will enable you to
    break or cut it into squares later.
7   Serve when cold. It will keep for weeks in an airtight jar or tin.

NOTE: *Without the chocolate paste, it is vanilla flavoured. Other flavourings
can be added, such as coconut, walnuts, ground almond, and red, green or yellow
colourings can also be considered.*

# CHAPTER ELEVEN
# SAVOURIES

ONE OF THE TRADITIONS of the Victorian banquet in Britain and the Raj was the fifth (sometimes sixth) course, the savoury, which followed the pudding. The idea was sound. A tiny, strongly flavoured but mouth-watering morsel of food was intended to refresh the palate and to assist with the digestion of the considerable amount of food that had preceded it. It was also intended, presumably, to prepare the way for the considerable amount of alcohol, in the form of port, Madeira and brandy, which inevitably followed. In fact, as we saw on page 167, more food could still follow in the form of the dessert!

The savoury course has all but died out these days, apart from its close relative, the cheese board. In France this is consumed before the pudding or dessert, to preserve the palate for dry red wine, but in Britain it is taken after.

If the savoury recipes have gone anywhere, they have become canapés with the aperitif, or as the main food feature at the cocktail party, a role which suits them admirably. They can, of course, be increased in portion size to become starters.

But just for a change, try them in their traditional role at your next dinner party. The idea will draw comment and, hopefully, approval. Some are served hot, some cold.

Serve them with a dry Madeira, by Blandys, or vintage port by Warres, both of which were old faithfuls of the Raj dinner table, and continue to this day to be the best examples of their kind.

# RUSSIAN EGGS

These savouries are really sweet, by which I mean not sweet to taste, but sweet to look at. The reason is that although hen's eggs are fine for the job, a dozen quail eggs are far prettier and more delicate. And since delicacy is the object, I'd use quail eggs every time. They are stuffed with caviar, and topped with a fresh green herb leaf. Incidentally, tinned caviar was one of those supreme luxuries from the Europe stores, contrarily especially valued since caviar came from Russia, and relationships with that country were none too good throughout the duration of the Raj.

SERVES: 4

| | |
|---|---|
| 12 **quail eggs** | **Tabasco sauce** |
| 4 to 6 **teaspoons of caviar** | **fresh shreds of basil or other herb** |

1   Prick the blunt ends with a pin to prevent the eggs cracking during the boiling. Hard-boil the quail eggs. It takes 4 minutes exactly providing you place the eggs into already boiling water. Shell them and allow them to cool.
2   Try to locate the yolk, which won't be dead centre. Carefully, with a really sharp knife or razor, halve the eggs longways. Also, if necessary, cut a wee bit off the bottom to make them stable when standing up. Very carefully take out the yolk. Keep these and the spare white bits for another job (see Turkish Toasts below).
3   Now put enough caviar into the hole to fill it generously. Pop a dash of Tabasco on, and top it with a little bit of the herb.

# TURKISH TOASTS

Before you ask, I have no idea why this recipe is called Turkish toasts. All I know is that it is a great way to use up the spare egg from the previous Russian Eggs recipe. Talking of eggs, well feathers anyway, Reggie Craven's family, whom we met on page 106, lived across the road in the telegraph office, since Reggie's dad was the boss. Like our family, they kept a typically varied Raj collection of quails, chickens, ducks and geese, with a servant all their own, the *murghi wallah* (poultry keeper). One day the kids were on a feather collecting mission, an expedition not without danger, since the rules required the feathers to be plucked from live birds, not just picked up off the ground, and preferably they should come from birds which were not from your own compound. Naturally, as with so many such missions, it went wrong. The pen fence was designed to keep poultry in, and not to support children's body weights. It collapsed, with squawking poultry running and flapping in all directions. The geese, by then more than indignant, gave chase with much honking and snapping.

------------------------------ SERVES: 4 ------------------------------

2 or 3 tablespoons finely chopped prawns in brine
2 tablespoons butter
1 tablespoon finely chopped parsley
1 teaspoon curry masala mix (see page 37)

½ teaspoon chilli powder
2 tinned anchovy fillets, finely chopped
some left-over cooked egg yolk and white (see page 178)
some digestive or water biscuits

------------------------------ GARNISH ------------------------------

**Some sprigs of parsley**

1   Mix the ingredients into a coarse paste, using a little of the oil from the anchovy tin as needed.
2   Tidily place a dollop of the mixture into the centre of a digestive or water biscuit.
3   Garnish with a sprig of parsley and serve cold.

# CHEESE CRAB

Flora Annie Steel warned that butter should be kept out of the hands of the *khitmugar* (head butler). He should: '*generally be discouraged from making it the medium for a display of his powers in plastic art; it is doubtless gratifying to observe such yearnings after beauty, even in butter, but it is suggestive of too much handling to be pleasant.*'

The ghee wallah supplied butter, though being made from buffalo milk, it was different in taste from regular butter. This could be bought at a price from the Europe stores in tins, the most expensive of which was by Crosse and Blackwell. He also supplied ghee, which was sometimes called 'kitchen butter'. Even the normally content Wyvern described this as a *'terrible preparation . . . which looks like the compound used for greasing the wheels of railway carriages'*. Not everyone agreed. If the ghee wallah came at the same time as the *roti* wallah (bread man) the kids used to take a fat slice of hot crusty bread, and put hot ghee onto it, then sprinkle it with sugar. They thought that a big treat.

There's a bit of butter, no ghee but not too much 'plastic art' in this recipe.

MAKES: 8 SAVOURIES

- 25g (1 oz) **Cheddar cheese**
- 1 **anchovy fillet**
- 2 **tablespoons white crab meat**
- ½ **teaspoon made English mustard**
- 1 **teaspoon vinegar, any type**
- ½ **teaspoon chilli powder**
- 1 **hard-boiled egg yolk**
- 1 **teaspoon butter**
- salt **to taste**
- freshly milled black pepper to **taste**
- 2 **slices white or brown bread**

1 Grate the cheese, and mince or purée the anchovy. Add these to all the other ingredients except the bread, mixing them into a thick paste.
2 Thinly slice two pieces of bread. Using a round pastry cutter of about 5cm (2 inches) diameter, cut each slice into 4 discs. Toast on both sides.
3 Spread the paste on generously. Just before serving, pop them under the grill so that you can serve them sizzling.

# SARDINE TOASTS

The *moochi* (shoemaker) was an occasional visitor to the Raj bungalow. He measured everyone's feet, then on his next visit would produce perfect handmade shoes, their style copied exactly from English originals. The *dirzi* (tailor) worked the same magic with clothes. He would sit lotus position on the verandah and do minute invisible repairs. My grandmother was a thoroughly modern memsahib, however. She was in possession of a most cherished new-fangled possession. It was a hand operated Singer sewing machine, the envy of many of her memsahib friends, and something she had brought back from England on her one visit there. This was one savoury the memsahibs adored.

SERVES: 4

3 or 4 tinned sardines in olive oil
4 to 6 black olives, pitted and finely chopped

6 capers, finely chopped
1 (or more) fresh red chilli, finely chopped
1 teaspoon vinegar, any type

salt and pepper to taste

1    Ensure the bones are removed from the sardines, then mash them with their oil with the back of a fork.
2    Add the other ingredients. Spread on thinly sliced fingers of crust-free, buttered white or brown bread, or on hot or cold toast.

# ANCHOVY TOASTS

One servant Raj families often shared was the *chokidar* (night watchman). In Mhow my family shared one with their neighbours, the Austins, and the bachelor sergeants who lived next door. A rumour which circulated amongst all Raj families was that all *chokidars* always slept on the job. That the rumour had also reached the ears of the *chokidars* was evident. It was part of their job description, it would seem, to dispel that rumour, at least from time to time during the night. Periodically, the *chokidar* would walk round the outside of the bungalows, pointedly coughing and spitting, spluttering and wheezing, and noisily banging and scraping his *lathi* (fat stick) on the ground. This was clearly a demonstration designed to prevent sleep rather than the presence of burglars. No doubt having woken all the households, the *chokidar* would resume his own sleep until his next interruption. Or maybe he would eat. He brought his own meal with him in 'tiffin carriers'. One recipe he would not have tried was the simple but effective anchovy toasts.

SERVES: 4

6 to 8 (about 50g) tinned anchovy fillets
2 teaspoons olive oil

½ teaspoon English mustard powder
1 teaspoon vinegar, any type
some dashes of Tabasco sauce

1  Finely chop the anchovy fillets, or run them through the food processor, adding the other ingredients, to create a spreadable consistency.
2  Spread on thinly sliced fingers of crust-free, buttered white or brown bread, or on hot toast.

# DEVILLED BISCUITS

Other visiting servants included the *dhobi wallah* (laundry woman) who came on a bullock cart daily, to collect today's laundry and return the previous day's washing, fully starched and ironed. The *dahi wallah* (yoghurt man) used to turn up and, like many of the other traders who visited, he'd squat on the verandah to display and sell his yoghurt to the memsahib from two *chatties* (containers) suspended from a pole which he carried on his back.

The *mali* (gardener) lived out. In the really hot weather, the family would lower special blinds which encircled the verandah, and the mali would douse them with water from a pot. It helped cool the bungalow a little.

This is a crafty recipe. It uses up slightly stale cream cracker biscuits. Best are small dainty ones, and of course, they do not have to be stale to start with. A virtually instant 'sauce' is spread on the biscuits, and they are oven baked or put under the grill.

CHOTA CHEESE CREAMS

SERVES: 4

| | |
|---|---|
| 3 or 4 tablespoons butter | ½ teaspoon ground white pepper |
| ½ teaspoon chilli powder | ½ teaspoon curry masala mix (see |
| ½ teaspoon English | page 37) |
| mustard powder | ⅓ teaspoon salt |

Some lemon wedges

1 Mix the butter with the powders until it is creamy.
2 Spread it onto the biscuits. Place them into a hot oven or under a hot grill for 2 or 3 minutes. Serve piping hot, with a wedge of lemon.

# CHOTA CHEESE CREAMS

The *bhisti* (water carrier) was a regular visitor. He had a goatskin tightly stitched into a container shape to make it waterproof. His mission was to collect drinking water from a source, filling his skin to capacity. Then, slinging his heavy burden on his back, he'd carry it, sometimes for miles, to be purchased by households who had no water. When the family were in military quarters, they had piped water laid on, so the service wasn't always needed.

A special commemorative book, *The Queen's Empire*, published to commemorate Victoria's Golden Jubilee in 1897, says: '*The trade of the bhisti is an ancient and honourable one. Although British rule is gradually covering India with a vast system of irrigation works, for the most part water is still carried by means of a primitive appliance . . . a water-tight skin called "mussock". Easy to carry when empty, and easily adjusted when full, it has held its own since Abraham.*'

These savourites are an ice-cold offering. *Chota* means small, so make them as tiny as you wish. Remember, the smaller they are, the more dainty they seem. The tidiest presentation requires you to pipe them out of a piping bag with a fluted nozzle. It's a bit of an effort, so only bother with the bag when the occasion is important. Otherwise, just put tidy blobs onto greaseproof paper and freeze.

SERVES: 4

4 tablespoons butter
6 tablespoons cottage
cheese
2 tablespoons very finely
grated Cheddar cheese

1 finely shredded fresh red chilli
1 teaspoon very finely shredded
fresh coriander leaves
⅓ teaspoon salt.

TO SERVE

some tiny lettuce leaf 'cups'
some lime wedges

1 Melt the butter, then in the same pot, off the heat, mix the other ingredients together.
2 Preferably, while still warm, pipe or place a little bit of mixture onto greaseproof paper on a tray. When all the blobs are done, put the tray into the freezer. Serve straight from the freezer in a tiny lettuce cup with a wedge of lime.

# DIABOLITINS OF CHEESE

It was not uncommon for the more important and personal servants of Raj military personnel to form so strong an attachment to their family, and vice-versa, that they would move a long way from home when the inevitable postings came. The bearer was one such, as was the *khitmygar* (butler). Thumbi, the family's favourite cook, became so valued that not only he, but his family too, stayed with our family from 1902 to 1923, moving from Mhow to Agra and back again. Jim, Frank and my mother would, from time to time, pay a sneaky visit to the *barwachi khana* (cookhouse) especially at about 6pm, when they knew Thumbi and his wife Luchmi and their kids were having their evening meal. All of them would sit lotus position on the kitchen floor, eating really authentic, delicious curries with their fingers. If my grandmother knew about it, she turned a blind eye, probably because, like the kids, she preferred the real thing, and she took the trouble to learn the art from Thumbi.

From time to time it was natural to allow unattached special servants to go home, expenses paid, to visit their families. One story which circulated concerned a friend's servant, who requested leave twice in the period of just over one year. The first visit home was because his grandfather was dying. On the second occasion, his compelling reason was that his wife was expecting. *'But,'* said the sahib, *'you haven't been home for a year. How come your wife is only now due to have a baby?'* *'Sahib,'* said the servant, *'God is good, and my brother is there!'*

No doubt Thumbi would have regarded both that story and this recipe as having something to do with sorcery. In fact it has more to do with saucery – Tabasco and Worcester, that is!

SERVES: 4

1 tablespoon cornflour
some milk
2 teaspoons butter
some dashes of Tabasco
  sauce

some dashes of Worcester sauce
2 or 3 tablespoons finely grated
  Cheddar cheese
1 egg
salt and pepper to taste

TOPPING

some anchovy paste
chilli powder

1  Mix the cornflour with enough milk to make a creamy, lump-free paste.
2  Heat the butter in a non-stick pan. Stir in the flour paste adding dribbles of milk until it will not thicken any more.
3  Mix the other ingredients in well.
4  Transfer the mixture in suitable-size dollops to a pattie tin, which you then place into the oven, preheated to 190°C/375°F/Gas 5.
5  Bake for about 10 minutes. Top with a smearing of the anchovy paste, and a dusting of chilli powder. Served hot is better than cold, but either way is acceptable.

## CHAPTER TWELVE

# THE RAJ CHRISTMAS

Most indians are Hindus or Moslems. Neither religion recognises Christmas as a religious festival. A few Indians are Christian. The family once had a cook from Goa, the beautiful coastal state in south western India, ruled throughout the time of the Raj by the Portuguese. Goans are Christians and Christmas is of great importance to them. But all Indians love a festival, and Christmas is still universally recognised as a holiday in India to this day.

Christmas was a big festival in the India of the Raj. It was celebrated from Christmas Eve until Twelfth Night, and the memsahibs attempted to come up with a different festive menu for each of the twelve days. Our family were more often than not posted to hill stations which, being thousands of feet above sea level, were lovely and cool during the summers, but pretty darned cold in the winter. It did not snow there though, so the prospect of a white Christmas had to wait until Blighty!

In the times of the Raj it was as big a day to the *bobajee* (the cook) as it was to the family. He was up at the crack of dawn, preparing dishes he only did once a year. The roasting of the fowl in his simple oven was the most crucial job. Turkeys were available and goose equally common on the great day. Boxing Day often produced spicy left-overs, and ham and spicy pease pudding always turned up somewhere. In warmer postings there were many Christmas picnics, and cold food was, of course, the rule. My grandmother was an expert cake maker, and her plum pudding and mince pies were eagerly awaited. But of all her Christmas recipes it is her

Christmas cake which had the most impact on those who were lucky enough to try it. It includes the usual cake mixture, but she did some magic things with walnuts, carrots, treacle and port. I urge you to try it next Christmas, if you're sure you can wait until then!

# CHRISTMAS SOUP

This is mulligatawny soup in another guise. And you would not expect me to omit this, perhaps the most famous of dishes to come out of the Raj. It is the perfect example of the type of modification that took place to Anglicise a truly authentic age-old Indian recipe. One Mr E. Hoole, a missionary in Madras in 1820, wrote about 'mulugu tanni' in his personal narratives, that it was '*in a brazen pot, a hot vegetable soup made chiefly from pepper and capsicums (chillies)*'. In *Hobson Jobson*, we are told that '*the name of this well known soup is simply a corruption of the Tamil "milagu-tannir", meaning "pepper-water", showing the correctness of the popular belief which ascribes the origin of this excellent article to Madras*'.

The *Indian Cookery Book* agrees about Madras, but by now the Raj cooks had got hold of this dish and changed it from a fiery hot consommé to a thick meat-based pottage, largely designed to use up the left-overs. '*In many families,*' it says of mulligatawny, '*the remains of cold meats, if not required for other purposes, are made into Madras mulligatawny. In ninety-nine cases out of a hundred, consumers cannot tell the meat is not fresh.*'

Wyvern wrote: '*It is a meal in itself.*'

But here in this version is my compromise. Meat is omitted, and it is a thin soup, spicy, but not fire-water. If you do have meat or poultry left-overs, add them in. Serve it hot or cold on Christmas or any other day.

SERVES: 4

1 litre (1¾ pints) vegetable or meat stock
2 tablespoons blended mustard or sunflower oil
2 teaspoons curry masala mix (see page 37)
2 or 3 cloves garlic, finely chopped
110g (4 oz) onion, finely chopped
1 or 2 fresh red chillies, shredded
1 tablespoon dry basmati rice
1 tablespoon polished split red lentils (massoor dal)
2 tablespoons tamarind purée
2 tablespoons chopped fresh coriander leaves
some fresh or dry curry leaves, if available
salt to taste

1 Bring the stock to the simmer in a 3 litre (5¼ pint) saucepan.
2 Meanwhile, heat the oil in the wok and stir-fry the masala for 30 seconds. Add the garlic, onion and chillies and stir-fry for a further 3 or 4 minutes.
3 Add the fried items, the rice and the lentils to the simmering stock, stirring at first to ensure that nothing sticks to the bottom of the pan.
4 Simmer for some 10 minutes, then add the tamarind purée and the leaves.
5 Give the soup a final 3 or 4 minutes simmering, then salt to taste. Serve hot or cold.

# PEASE PUDDING TARKA

Pease pudding is as traditional an English dish as one can find. It uses red lentils, which when cooked go yellow, and traditionally accompanies a roast or boiled ham. Here, as in the Raj, it is cooked with small chunks of ham, and a light spicing. It is a greatly nutritious dish in its own right eaten just with plain rice. Alternatively, try it to accompany the Christmas roast, or for example, with the goose dumpode recipe on page 148. Or if you don't fancy that, enjoy it on Boxing Day. Incidentally, The *Indian Cookery Book* had specific instructions about obtaining a good texture purée for dal: '*When thoroughly boiled, churn the dal by twirling it in a wooden instrument called a ghootnee.*' I have no idea what a 'ghootnee' looks like, I'm afraid, but you can achieve a good result with the electric whisk.

SERVES: 4

200g (7 oz) red massoor lentils, split and polished
3 tablespoons ghee
2 cloves garlic, finely chopped
150g (5½ oz) onion, chopped
2 fresh green chillies, shredded

1 teaspoon garam masala (see page 39)
1 teaspoon yellow mustard powder
100g (3½ oz) cooked ham, chopped into small pieces
salt to taste

1   Pick through the lentils to remove any grit or impurities. Rinse them several times, then drain, and immerse them in water for about 1 hour.
2   To cook, drain and rinse, then measure an amount of water twice the volume of the drained lentils into a 2.25 litre (4 pint) saucepan. Bring to the boil.
3   Put in the lentils and simmer for about 30 minutes, stirring from time to time. By then the texture should be pourable, not too thick nor too thin. Apply the electric whisk here, if you wish to purée the lentils (see above).
4   During stage 3, heat the ghee in the wok. Add the garlic, onion and chillies, and stir-fry on a lowish heat for about 15 minutes, stirring from time to time.
5   Add the fried mixture to the lentils at the end of stage 3, plus the garam masala, mustard and the ham.
6   Allow this to become hot, stirring frequently. Salt to taste, and serve.

# TURKEY JHAL FREZEE

A huge roast turkey or goose was often the Christmas treat in our family. Even a large family found it a filling dish, and there were invariably left-overs for Boxing Day. The memsahib and *bobajee* (who was by now exhausted from his Christmas efforts) banked on it. This stir-fry ('jhal' means pungently hot, and 'frezee' means fried) was a standard way of cooking left-overs.

You can use left-overs, but here I am using fresh turkey or chicken breast. It is delightful served with spicy rice, or if you do have it at Christmastime, try it with some of the other dishes in this chapter. Incidentally, in the Bengal Hills, a Buddhist tribe called the Mogs can still be found. In Raj days, many Mogs became *bobajees*. Jhal frezee or jalfri was, and is, a Bengali/Bangladeshi speciality, and it was the Mogs who taught the memsahibs this delicious way to cook the left-overs. The thing about this recipe is that it is really quick to do, under 15 minutes, in fact.

SERVES: 4

700g (1lb 9 oz) turkey or chicken breast, weighed after skinning and boning
3 tablespoons ghee or oil
2 teaspoons white cummin seeds
1 tablespoon curry masala mix (see page 37)
3 or 4 cloves garlic, finely chopped
2.5cm (1 inch) cube ginger, shredded
2 or 3 fresh green chillies, shredded

4 or 5 spring onions, bulbs and leaves, chopped
3 tablespoons red bell pepper, chopped
6 to 8 cherry tomatoes, quartered
2 or 3 tablespoons coconut milk powder
2 teaspoons garam masala (see page 39)
2 tablespoons chopped fresh coriander leaves
salt to taste

GARNISH

**some chopped fresh mint leaves**

1   Cut the meat into bite-size pieces.
2   Heat the ghee or oil in the large wok. Add the seeds and stir-fry for a

few seconds. Add the curry masala, and a few splashes of water, and continue stirring for about 30 seconds more. Add the garlic, ginger, chillies, and spring onions, and stir-fry for about 3 or 4 minutes, continuing to add splashes of water.

3   Add the red bell pepper, and the meat, and stir until the meat is evenly coloured and sizzling. Then add the tomatoes and gently sizzle for about 8 minutes, adding sufficient water to keep things mobile.

4   Now add the coconut milk powder, garam masala, fresh coriander leaves and salt to taste. After a couple more minutes frying, it should be ready. Check that the meat is cooked right through by cutting one piece in half and ensuring that it is white right through. Then garnish and serve.

# SPICY CHESTNUTS

Tinned chestnuts were available at the time of the Raj. We can go one better and get them fresh or vacuum packed all year round.

---

SERVES: 4

350g (12 oz) cooked, peeled chestnuts
1 tablespoon sunflower or olive oil
1 tablespoon very finely chopped ginger

1 tablespoon dark muscovado sugar or molasses
1 teaspoon garam masala (see page 39)
Tabasco sauce
salt to taste

---

1   Halve the chestnuts. Heat the oil in the wok. Add the ginger and stir-fry for about 30 seconds.

2   Add the chestnuts, sugar or molasses, garam masala, a few drops of Tabasco sauce and some splashes of water. Stir all this around carefully, and when it is all hot and sizzling, salt to taste, and serve.

## SPICY CRANBERRY JELLY

Thus is such a simple and effective way to enhance bottled cranberry. You simply decant the jelly into a pan with some sweet and aromatic spices and apply heat. Then simply cool, re-bottle, and leave it for as long as you like in the cupboard to absorb those aromatics. And at Christmas time . . . wow! They were clever, those memsahibs. By the way, if your jar size is different from mine, proceed with the recipe anyway, adjusting the spices *pro rata*.

—————————————— MAKES: AN AMPLE PORTION ——————————————

I **teaspoon roasted and crushed coriander seeds**
**6 to 8 cloves, crushed**
**5cm (2 inch piece) cassia bark**

**6 to 8 green cardamoms, crushed**
**300g (10½ oz) bottled cranberry jelly**

1   Heat a non-stick saucepan, and dry-fry the spices for about 30 seconds.
2   Decant the jelly into the pan, and let it melt. As soon as it does, take the pan off the heat.
3   When it is cool enough, re-bottle it in the same jar. Cap it and leave it alone for a few weeks, by which time it will be ready to enjoy.

## GRANNY'S CHRISTMAS CAKE

Even though it meant a lot of work, my grandmother enjoyed the Raj Christmas. It was a bizarre affair in India. She herself had never been in England at that time, nor had she ever seen snow. It was in some postings insufferably hot, yet no effort was spared to make it as much like 'home' as it could be. Many memsahibs bought their Christmas cake and Christmas puddings in tins from the Europe stores. Not so my grandmother. She adored making her own, and with her total command of Hindi, she inspired her *bobajee* to help her. Even though the oven was primitive, their results were the talk of the station, and many of the less confident memsahibs were sure to call round while cakes were being baked to ask for a recipe or perhaps just a little help. She taught many a double-barrelled name the art of cake making. The kids wanted to help too. Licking out the tasty cake mixture from the bowl was yet another treat straight from heaven. It was, indeed, a treat she used to give to me when, years later, she lived with us in Ealing. So any excuse to lurk nearby was dreamed up. On one occasion in 1913 in Mhow, Bill, aged just ten, catching a whiff of cake cooking asked what he could do to help. Granny said, 'Turn the cake,' meaning twist it round in the oven, so that it would cook evenly. Bill took it to mean turn it over. He duly inverted the gooey mixture which at once ran all over the oven, and 'bang' went their Christmas cake that year!

The *Indian Cookery Book* cleverly interspaced blank pages between text pages (why don't we do that?) and these are crammed full of my grandmother's handwritten notes, the ink fading now, the hand young and energetic in some, and more reserved and tighter in others as she grew older and, presumably, more tired with all those mouths to feed. Her notes obviously went on throughout her lifetime, because a few pages show a hand which is by now quite wobbly with old age. Maybe such recipes were written in those halcyon days when Granny lived at our house and cooked for me.

One thing she never once defaulted on for over 50 years, as far as I can tell, was the Christmas cake. That recipe written in her own hand, I know not when, simply says '*Xmas Cake (My Way)*'. And there was no better way. Try it and see. It has some surprises, like gravy browning and carrots, but it sure does work.

———————— MAKES: A FULL SIZE CAKE ————————

250g (9 oz) butter
⅔ teaspoon gravy
 browning
225g (8 oz) golden syrup or
 treacle
2 tablespoons brandy
280g (10 oz) plain white
 flour
1 tablespoon semolina
175g (6 oz) golden sultanas

175g (6 oz) raisins
175g (6 oz) shredded, then
 chopped carrot
175g (6 oz) walnut halves
60g (2 oz) candy peel
½ teaspoon ground allspice
4 eggs
½ teaspoon salt
3 tablespoons rum
2 tablespoons port

1   Mix the butter, gravy browning, syrup and brandy together in a large cake-mixing bowl until it is well creamed.

2   Add a quarter each of the flour, semolina, sultanas, raisins, carrot, walnuts, candy peel, allspice, and one egg. Work it well into the previously creamed mixture.

3   Repeat this procedure three more times until all these ingredients are mixed in.

4   Now add the salt, rum and port and give everything a final brisk mix.

5   Transfer the mixture to a large cake tin, about 20cm (8 inches) in diameter, lined with greaseproof paper.

6   Bake in the oven at 150°C/300°F/Gas 2, for 3 hours. Inspect in the third hour to check that it is not burning. (It shouldn't be.) Then give it a final 30 minutes at 140°C/275°F/Gas 1.

7   After a day or two, the cake must now be liberally covered in marzipan, but before that keep on seeping it with brandy or port to keep it moist. Finally, it needs icing and decorating with Christmassy items.

# POSTSCRIPT

## THE JOURNEY HOME

THE TIME HAD finally come. My grandfather had served nearly forty years in the Indian Army. He had done well. He'd survived disease, got to love India, learned her languages, found a wife, and he'd bred and educated nine healthy children. He'd started as a private, the lowliest of the low, the 'BOR', or British Other Rank, and ended as a senior officer. His retirement papers landed on his desk one summer's day in 1930, causing him to reflect.

Commissions from the ranks were very unusual indeed in the Raj. For the last few months he had been holding down someone else's job. His immediate boss, a full colonel, had been caught accepting bribes and was being court-martialled. Grandpa was the only officer qualified to take over. He was promoted to 'acting' colonel and he took command of all matters concerning army pay in northern India. He got a better and bigger bungalow and the pay to match, but the crafty old army did not make him a full substantive colonel because his retirement was imminent and, if they had done so, they would have had to increase his pension.

In fact, his health was beginning to fail. He had bad sciatica and was himself being retired early. He smiled ruefully as he wondered, if he had served his full term of another few years, whether he would have made a general – after all, it was the next step up, and his overall boss was a brigadier in charge of the pay corps of all India, himself due to retire shortly. Still, it was not to be.

Grandpa enjoyed being an officer, but if he was truthful, the rank he enjoyed most was that of sergeant major. For a brief few years he had held the status of colour sergeant, the most senior non-commissioned rank. This brought a great deal of power, reasonable pay and minimal expenses. Even a junior commissioned officer had to shell out for mess bills, special uniforms, extra servants and so on. But my grandfather was ambitious. He enjoyed challenges, and when the opportunity of a commission came, he took it.

All that was history now. He wondered what the new life in England would bring.

A replacement officer eventually arrived, a Sandhurst trained whipper-snapper, already a full colonel, fifteen years Grandpa's junior, on his first Indian posting. The hand-over was completed and Grandpa, a major once more, moved to Bombay with the younger members of the family, including my mother, to await orders to join a ship bound for England.

In a few weeks the orders arrived. The vessel was a troopship, HMS *Somerset*. All their belongings were packed, then on a bright hot sunny September morning the family set off for Bombay's Ballard Pier for embarkation. A train of army orderlies and bearers carried cases and belongings into the hull of the ship amid much shouting and hassling. Then, with three blasts on the ship's siren, HMS *Somerset* cast off.

Tears came into all the family's eyes and huge lumps in their throats as they stood on deck and watched India slide away over the horizon. All of them except Grandpa had lived all their lives there, and he had been only fourteen when he arrived in India. It was a massive wrench. They went down to their cabins and howled for hours.

At dinner, he described the difference between their luxury officers' cabins on this vessel and his journey out, in a hammock in the stinking munitions store. He was sure he'd made a mistake signing up for Indian service, and his first few months there did nothing to change his mind. He got dhobi itch (prickly heat), the tormenting itchy rash which covered the sufferer from head to toe, and he generally hated the food, the lifestyle, the heat, the place, being a BOR, in fact everything and everybody.

But that was forty years ago. The family had a choice to make. Whether to stay in India for a comfortable retirement or whether to return to England. Even in 1930 it was obvious the Raj was not going to last. They chose the latter.

When HMS *Somerset* finally docked at Portsmouth, it was a typical grey damp rainy cold autumn day. There were no teams of smiling, noisy servants to do the chores. Suddenly life became third class. Home was a tiny Portsmouth terraced house with a minuscule garden. It was cold, dull and uninspiring. It was a huge let-down. The family knew that things would never be the same, and they frequently longed for India and the Raj.

My grandmother missed her cooks, but she stoically became the full-time cook, learning to recreate the family favourites from her *Indian Cookery Book*. Eventually she mastered it all, despite being nearly blind, and despite considerable difficulty in getting spices in Portsmouth.

India may have ceased to be a part of their remaining lives, and England never really replaced it for them. But through the pages of her *Indian Cookery Book*, Granny was always able to recreate the taste of the Raj.

## APPENDIX
# THE CURRY CLUB

**P**AT CHAPMAN always had a deep-rooted interest in spicy food, curry in particular, and over the years he built up a huge pool of information which he felt could be usefully passed on to others. He conceived the idea of forming an organization for this purpose.

Since it was founded in January, 1982, The Curry Club has built up a membership of several thousands. We have a marchioness, some lords and ladies, knights a-plenty, a captain of industry or two, generals, admirals and air marshals (not to mention a sprinkling of ex-colonels), and we have celebrities – actresses, politicians, rock stars and sportsmen. We have an airline, a former Royal Navy warship, and a hotel chain.

We have fifteen members whose name is Curry or Curries, twenty called Rice and several with the name Spice or Spicier, Cook, Fry, Frier or Fryer and one Boiling. We have a Puri (a restaurant owner) a Paratha and a Nan and a good many Mills and Millers, one Dal and a Lentil, an Oiler, a Gee (but no Ghee), and a Butter but no Marji (several Marjories though, and a Marjoram and a Minty). We also have several Longs and Shorts, Thins and Broads, one Fatt and one Wide, and a Chilley and a Coole.

We have members on every continent including a good number of Asian members, but by and large the membership is a typical cross-section of the Great British Public, ranging in age from teenage to dotage, and in occupation from refuse collectors to receivers, high street traders to high court judges, tax inspectors to taxi drivers. There are students and pensioners, millionaires and unemployed . . . thousands of people who have just one thing in common – a love of curry and spicy foods.

Members receive a bright and colourful quarterly magazine, which has regular features on curry and the curry lands. It includes news items, recipes, reports on restaurants, picture features, and contributions from members and professionals alike. The information is largely concerned with curry, but by popular demand it now includes regular input on other exotic and spicy cuisines such as those of Thailand, the spicy Americas, the Middle East and China. We produce a wide selection of publications, including the books listed on page ii.

Obtaining some of the ingredients required for curry cooking can be difficult, but The Curry Club makes it easy, with a comprehensive range of products, including spice mixes, chutneys, pickles, papadoms, sauces and curry pastes. These are available from major food stores and specialist delicatessens up and down the country. If they are not stocked near you, there is the Club's well-established and efficient mail-order service. Hundreds of items are stocked, including spices, pickles, pastes, dry foods, tinned foods, gift items, publications and specialist kitchen and tableware.

On the social side, the Club holds residential weekend cookery courses and gourmet nights at selected restaurants. Top of the list is our regular Curry Club gourmet trip to India and other spicy countries. We take a small group of curry enthusiasts to the chosen country and tour the incredible sights, in between sampling the delicious food of each region.

If you would like more information about The Curry Club, write (enclosing a stamped addressed envelope, please) to: The Curry Club, PO Box 7, Haslemere, Surrey, GU27 1EP.

# GLOSSARY ONE

## RAJ SERVANTS AND TERMS

### SERVANTS

*abdar* wine waiter or head servant
   at the Club
*amar* man servant
*ayah* lady's maid/nanny
bearer general servant
*bhangi* sweeper
*bhisti* water man
*barwachi* cook
*bobajee* cook
*buddli* temporary servant
*chaprassi* office servant/messenger
*chokidar* night watchman
*coolie* porter/carrier of goods
*dewan* gate keeper
*dhobi* laundry man/woman
*dhye* wet nurse

*dirzi* tailor
*gai* wallah cow/milk person
*hookabardar* smoking pipe
   attendant
*khansamah* butler/head waiter
*khitmygar* ditto
*mali* gardener
*methar* sweeper
*murghi* wallah poultry keeper
*musolchi* kitchen helper
*nappi* barber
*ountwallah* camelman
*punkah wallah* fan puller
*syce* groom/coachman
*toddy wallah* brewer (of arrack)
untouchable see *methar/bhangi*

### GENERAL

Anglo-Indian person of Indian and
   British blood (see half-caste)
*arrack* very strong alcoholic spirit
   (or toddy) from coconut or
   cashew palms

*baba* baby or young child
*barwachi khana* kitchen
*burra* big
*burra peg* large drink (three finger
   measure)

*burra* memsahib  very important female

*burra* sahib  very important man

*chiko*  child

*chittack*  an Indian cooking weight of 2 oz (see page 70)

*chokra*  inexperienced young sahib or native boy

*chota*  small

*chota* peg  small drink (two finger measure)

*chota sahib*  son of the sahib

chutney Mary  Indian woman with European ways – derogatory

country bred  British person educated in India – derogatory

country born  British person born in India – derogatory

*dastur*  financial bonus or tip

dhobi itch  prickly heat

Europe stores  shops stocking European tinned and other provisions (see pages 76 and 133)

go-down  outside building/ storeroom

griffin  army newcomer

half-caste  see Anglo-Indian – derogatory

memsahib  important female/ wife of the boss

*mofusil*  up country

*missy baba*  daughter of sahib

*qui-hai*  (Keehai) literally meaning 'is anyone there?' it was the word for calling a servant. It was usually the first Hindi word new arrivals fresh from England learned. It was also a term used to refer to a well-seasoned 'old hand' who had been in India for years (see page 98)

sahib  important male/boss

sepoy  native other rank soldier

*subadhur*  Indian army officer

toddy  see arrack

# GLOSSARY TWO

## FOOD WORDS

The purpose of this glossary is to explain certain key ingredients – mostly spices – used in this book and where necessary give them a translation (in italics) to enable the reader to obtain them from Asian stores. See also the Appendix on page 201.

| | |
|---|---|
| ajwain | see lovage seed. |
| allspice | Native to the West Indies. Related to the clove family, the seed resembles small black dried peas. Called allspice because its aroma seems to combine those of clove, cinnamon, ginger, nutmeg and pepper. |
| asafoetida | *hing* A rather smelly spice extracted from the gum of a tree. Its odour disappears when cooked. |
| bay leaf | Aromatic and very English. Used whole but not eaten. |
| besan | see gram flour. |
| cardamom | *elaichi* Green, white and (larger) brown/black varieties available. All are pods containing aromatic black seeds, the latter being more astringent. |
| cassia | *dalchini cassia* A sweetly fragranced spice. The corkey brown outer bark of a tree, related to cinnamon (see below), which is often misnamed (see below). Comes in pieces or quills. Less fragrant than cinnamon, but stands up to more robust cooking. |
| chilli | *hare mirch* or *lal mirch* The world's most popular and hottest spice. Available fresh green, yellow or red and at various heat levels. The raj used the long thin cayenne |

(Indian) variety (about 8/10 on the heat scale). Also available dried or powdered (both only red).

clove    *lavang* Dark brown, 'nail-shaped' spice (from the Latin *clavus* meaning nail). The rounded head of the clove is an unopened flower bud.

coconut    *narial* The flesh of the world's largest nut produces thick cream or milk (available in cans or dried powder).

coriander    *dhania* India's most prolifically used spice; either whole or ground, it has a sweetish flavour.
*hare dhania* Its leaves are an important herb, though its foetid flavour (*coris*, the Greek word from which the word coriander is derived, means bed bug) is an acquired taste.

cummin    *jeera* Called white cummin or cumin, the seed and powder is in fact greeny-brown. It is also an important Indian savoury flavouring.

curry    The only word in this glossary to have no direct translation into any of the subcontinent's 15 or so languages. The word was coined by the British in India centuries ago. Possible contenders for the origin of the word are: *karahi* or *karai* (Hindi), a wok-like frying pan used all over India to prepare masalas (spice mixtures); *kurhi*, a soup-like dish made with spices, gram flour dumplings and buttermilk; *kari*, a spicy Tamil sauce; *turkuri*, a seasoned sauce or stew; *kari phulia*, *neem* or curry leaves; *kudhi* or *kadhi*, a yoghurt soup; or *koresh*, an aromatic Iranian stew.

curry leaves    *neem patia* or *kari phulia* Small leaves, available dried and occasionally fresh, which give a distinctive fragrance to southern Indian dishes.

dalchini    see cassia and cinnamon.

dhania    see coriander.

elaichi    see cardamom.

fenugreek    *methi* A very savoury spice, bitter if over-used, popular in northern Indian dishes.

garam masala    a mixture of aromatic spices, see page 39.

garlic    *lasan* The pungent but all-important bulb used fresh for flavouring. A powdered form is occasionally used.

ghee    clarified butter or margarine.

ginger    *sont* A rhizome used fresh or powdered.

garam flour    *besan* Flour made from gram dal (chana). Used in pakoras.

| | |
|---|---|
| hare dhani | see coriander leaf. |
| hare mirch | see green chilli. |
| hing | see asafoetida. |
| jaifal | see nutmeg. |
| javitri | see mace. |
| jeera | see cummin. |
| kalonji | see wild onion seeds. |
| lal mirch | see red chilli. |
| lavang | see clove. |
| lemon grass | The fibrous stem of a very aromatic and fragrant oriental grass. Available fresh, bottled or dried and used in Malay curry. |
| lavang | see clove. |
| lovage | *ajwain* A slightly bitter round seed. |
| mace | *javitri* The other part, or tendril, of the nutmeg. |
| masala | a mixture of spices. |
| methi | see fenugreek. |
| mirch | see chilli and pepper. |
| mustard | *rai* Small seed which becomes sweet when cooked. Use brown/black ones, not yellow, for Indian cooking. Yellow powder – the famous stuff which Colemans are world famous for. |
| narial | see coconut. |
| neem | see curry leaves. |
| nutmeg | *jaifal* The much loved hard round, pale brown spice ball. |
| pepper | *mirch* India's 'King of Spice', enjoyed black or white, whole or ground. |
| rai | see mustard seeds. |
| rosewater | *ruh gulab* A clear essence extracted from rose petals to give fragrance to sweets and rice. |
| saffron | *zafron* The world's most expensive spice – the stigma of a crocus variety. Used to give a delicate golden colour and aroma to rice dishes and certain curries. |
| sesame seeds | *til* Small, flat, round, pale cream seeds. |
| til | see sesame. |
| zafron | see saffron. |

# INDEX